Desperately Seeking Sisterhood

Desperately Seeking Sisterhood: Still Challenging and Building

Edited by

Magdalene Ang-Lygate, Chris Corrin and Millsom S. Henry

Taylor & Francis
Publishers since 1798

UK Taylor & Francis Ltd, 1 Gunpowder Square, London EC4A 3DE

USA Taylor & Francis Inc., 1900 Frost Road, Suite 101, Bristol, PA 19007

First published 1997

A Catalogue Record for this book is available from the British Library

ISBN 0 7484 0409 0
ISBN 0 7484 0410 4 (pbk)

Library of Congress Cataloging-in-Publication Data are available on request

The WSNA (UK) 1995 Annual Conference logo, used on the front cover design of this book, was designed by Scottish artist **Jan Sutherland** who described it as a symbol representing women's sisterhood. The spiral which begins 'just before midnight' captures a sense of beginning and yet each turn of the spiral brings us to a familiar but different place. Based on an ancient Celtic motif, the thirteen moons are intricately interlocked. They symbolize the beauty and magic of women working together in spite of their different perspectives and seasons in life. Special thanks to Jan for her permission to use the logo for the cover of this book.

Typeset in 10/12 pt Times
by Best-set Typesetter Ltd., Hong Kong

Printed in Great Britain by SRP Ltd, Exeter.

In Memoriam: Joy Gardner
1953–1993

Contents

Contents

viii

Acknowledgements

The authors wish to give thanks to all the contributors, present and silent, for their efforts and patience over the past year. In addition, we would like to thank all the conference staff, our hardworking volunteers, all participants and the University of Stirling for helping to make the *Desperately Seeking Sisterhood Conference* such a success. This book has emerged from the conference papers, plenaries and contributions.

We also wish to thank those at Taylor & Francis who worked to very tight deadlines to enable the publication of this volume, in particular Alison Chapman and Fiona Kinghorn.

Finally, but by no means least, we would like to acknowledge both the challenges and the opportunities raised for us by being part of a collective that attempted to be sisterly in practice as well as in theory.

Introduction

Magdalene Ang-Lygate, Chris Corrin and Millsom S. Henry

This book was engendered by the Eighth Annual Women's Studies Network (UK) Association Conference – *Desperately Seeking Sisterhood: Still Challenging and Building* – which took place in Stirling in June 1995. The Conference was organized to provide a forum where different aspects of feminist scholarship and work could be elaborated, reviewed and explored around notions of 'sisterhood'. As conference organizers, it was also our intention to create a space which would place an equal emphasis on theory, practice and campaigning, where contemporary issues that concerned women could be addressed from the various perspectives held by feminist academics, practitioners and activists. Feedback received from conference participants suggested that those primary objectives had been achieved. When the opportunity materialized to compile a conference volume for publication, it was interesting that as co-editors we each had to work through our own commitments to 'sisterhood' – to continue to work together not only to produce a book for publication but to do it in such a way that lessons in sistering were neither lost nor ignored. Issues of respect – respecting women's words and ways of expression, respecting women's time and commitments – and listening were all aspects of our work together.

Sistering is hard work, much harder than organizing a conference or editing a book because it asks that our more familiar feminist critical stance – an odd combination of arrogance and defensiveness – be tempered with self-awareness and a caring affection. We learn much about ourselves in our working coalitions with other women, in testing the boundaries of our sisterhoods and in attempting to extend them.

Given our collective commitment to feminist praxis and to fostering new ways of feminist thinking, it was not surprising that a book such as this would result. What you will not find here is a defence of the viability of the notion of a single sisterhood, nor a series of neat chapters explaining theories of sisterhood, nor feminist strategies for the next century. Instead, what follows is a diverse collection of ideas about the largely taken-for-granted concept of 'sisterhood', most of which was explored during formal and informal conference sessions. Each of the four parts contains accounts of the powerful impact that women have on, and for, one other. In this sense, sisterhood can never be a theoretical concept for us, as we practise sisterhood in many avenues of our lives and work. Yet the appreciation and celebration of diversity in sisterhood cannot be realized without first acknowledging and analysing the differences that lie between us. Accordingly, at risk of appearing contradictory or incoherent, the contributions in this volume seek to reflect the many voices that are raised as the worlds of sisterhoods collide and coalesce.

The three aspects of campaigning, theory and practice arose from our core belief in feminism as a praxis, building theory from women's experience and using theory to change practice. This may be apparent in the ways in which we practise our politics, in policy-making circles, in the ways we relate to each other and/or in what and how we teach in Women's Studies and elsewhere. The avoidance of a paper-thin sisterhood, as insubstantial as the pages within which it is conceptualized, is a very real challenge for Women's Studies in the years ahead. It is in this belief and insistence that sisterhood is not an option for feminists that we reflect on the key issues of sameness, difference, collaboration, connectedness and ethical considerations around power. These reflections could enable us to recognize and respect different positions and situations, re-search and re-state representations of our theories and practices, challenge power imbalances and prejudices and work in coalitions to generate progressive change for women.

Part I Sistering: Sameness and Difference

This part is full of questions: 'Can we be sisters in the skin?', 'Who are the sisters?', 'Must I call every woman sister?' While sistering involves at the outset a recognition of our 'sameness' – where as women we have commonalities in our skins – there must also be a shared recognition and understanding of our 'differences'. Ailbhe Smyth's eloquent and effervescent opening piece outlines the complex nature of 'sisterhood'. In posing the question 'Can we be sisters in the skin?', Ailbhe expresses her own vision of sistering and sisterhood as one where the hurts of betrayals, confusion, ignorance and indifference have not been allowed to quench her desire that we, as feminists, continue to choose to grow together. This contribution provides an excellent context for the next two chapters. Felly Nkweto Simmonds and Annette Kilcooley offer us their detailed scrutiny of difference in terms of 'race' and gender. Felly focuses on the question 'Who are the sisters?' as she examines the relationship between difference, feminism and friendship. For her, the notion of 'sisterhood' has blurred and dominated the nature of feminism and friendship at both a political and a personal level. This contribution reminds us all that 'sisterhood should evolve through our actions not just words', because some differences between 'sisters' are based on power inequalities and unexplained advantage. Felly argues that sisterhood as a political stance is suspect, unless those sisters who enjoy privileges denied to other sisters are seen to share the responsibility of dismantling such differences. Annette describes a set of circumstances where the relations of power, gender and race have combined to create a series of incidents which have had devastating consequences for Black people and Black women in particular. Annette points out that notions of sisterhood can change dramatically from one site of conflict to another and warns against a feminist solidarity that is unaware of 'racism and signifiers of "race" as complicating variables between white women'. It is clear that we all need to ask difficult questions of ourselves and our 'sisters'.

Part II Re-sistering a Space to Speak

Finding a place to speak, from which to develop our individual and collective voices as sisters, is fraught with difficulties. This is true not just in theory, but in the practice of Women's Studies. Feminists have long questioned the underlying biases that permit the privileging of some voices over others. What counts as knowledge and passes for truth has been identified as a product of power hierarchies. Yet some postmodernist feminists further infer that a plurality of positions denies any possibility of feminist solidarity. In short, while ways of thinking modelled on postmodern intellectualism admit the inevitability of fragmentation, they do not permit the possibility of collective politics. Although many postmodernist ideas have been usefully employed in feminist theory and postmodernism as an intellectual 'fashion' has been strongly established within Women's Studies, important challenges still remain as we seek to reconcile such thinking with actual instances where women have chosen to speak collectively from 'essentialized' positions. Yet, the determined will to choose and to transgress given boundaries for the purposes of identification and solidarity is at the heart of feminist campaigning work. The nature of our affiliations and connections can change in various locations and through different moments and struggles, so this need for a critical location from which to speak remains essential.

In asking 'why it is still necessary to discuss two (or more) catagories of feminism', Diane Richardson's arguments about how radical feminism is (mis)represented and (mis)understood raises a set of important questions. Diane analyses the development of contemporary feminist theory as the 'shape of our political identity and chosen theoretical perspective can interact with how we are positioned as "Other"'. Further questions are raised regarding the ways in which shifts in feminism impact upon women's lives and experiences. Renate Klein and Susan Hawthorne continue this theme with regard to those belonging to dominant groups, having the power to make 'choices'. This chapter focuses on making some links between the fragmentation inherent in postmodern theories and the increasing medicalization and 'technologization of women's Selves'. In Chapter 6, Sharon Tabberer also critiques the rhetoric of 'women's choice' through an examination of the history of the abortion pill RU 486. She argues that women's sexual self-determination is much more than just acceptance or rejection of new reproductive technologies (NRT). In their three-part chapter, Usha Brown, Clara Connolly and Pragna Patel write about how feminist theory and practice can work together leading to coalitions for change. This chapter provides a different set of examples which aim to find a place from which women can speak in a collective voice. Usha Brown highlights the economic and political contexts that have resulted from global shifts in the technology revolution where flexible working patterns and the increased poverty of women combine to challenge and strain the concept of sisterhood. Both Clara Connolly and Pragna Patel analyse some of the ways in which feminists work together across boundaries of differences in order to resist imposed positioning and restate the politics of sisterhood in thought and practice.

Part III   Re-searching Sisterhood

Searching and re-searching for feminist scholars entails viewing social developments from women's perspectives and challenging oppressive constructions. Like a number of previous contributors, notions of 'accountability' and 'responsibility' are paramount. This section addresses these issues not only with respect to how research benefits women, or who gains from feminist research work, but also by considering the relational aspects of working together as feminists within the research process. In writing about her involvement in the Zero Tolerance Campaign, Susan Hart shows how feminist theory and practice can successfully combine to translate feminist research into campaigning. Such campaigns have resulted in publicly funded programmes to raise public awareness about issues of violence against women. Using examples from their own experience, Celia Jenkins, Maggie O'Neill and Ruth Swirsky focus on the collaborative nature of the research process and the difficulties faced by feminists who are employed as researchers. Their chapter examines the ways in which feminist research is being affected and undermined as feminist academics are under increasing pressure to bring in or undertake contract or commissioned research. These are both pleasures and perils for feminists working together. Pamela Cotterill and Gayle Letherby also emphasize the importance of collaborative writing both in terms of women's positions within the academy and in terms of the production of academic knowledge. As student and teacher, disabled and able, Julie Matthews and Cathy Lubelska work through some of the differences that underline their collaborative work on disability issues and on writing up feminist research. Their contribution considers how women's exclusion from the dominant language which mediates ideas has been challenged by feminist scholarship in academia. Yvon Appleby continues this theme of language, ethics, responsibility and the interrelations of power and difference between researcher and researched in her study of lesbian women and education.

Part IV   The Trick is to Keep Sistering

This final section further highlights the different locations from which feminist thinkers are developing critiques of dominant 'malestream' accounts of social and political development. Political difference has been at the centre of debates around the danger or usefulness of reproductive technology to women as outlined earlier in Part II. Robyn Rowland counters and moves further the 'rights based' discourse on technology, by supporting a power analysis and developing a stronger ethical and political basis for her arguments. The notion of 'power' is again in view when Anne Gatensby and Nora Jung outline the imbalances between Eastern Europe and the Western industrialized nations. Bringing together their separate analyses – on Hungarian women's movements and feminist critiques of science and technology – they collaborate to critique the gendered language of technology transfer. Their analysis challenges the inequitable gender and geopolitical relations which underline deteriorating material conditions and economic oppression in Eastern Europe *vis-à-vis* the West.

The final three chapters consider body image and maintenance, age, class and 'race'. Marilyn Poole, Dallas Isaacs and Judy Ann Jones develop a 'sisterhood' theme for older women committed to exercise. For the women in their study, sociability was important in terms of their connections with other women to achieve feelings of self-worth, respect and social power. Even though Britain is a class-divided society, Christine Zmroczek and Pat Mahony argue that class is not addressed within feminism and Women's Studies in terms of difference and power relations between women. This chapter arises from their conversations with working-class women in Britain. Finally, in Quibilah Montsho's piece we are returned to the themes of our physical embodiment and the reality of our skin – how we do bleed when cut. Quibilah reminds us that crying in silence is an isolating and alienating experience, yet as a survivor she gives generous thanks.

As editors we recognize that there are many unaddressed silences in this book. Whether we read this volume as academics, practitioners or campaigners, or as all three, let us remind ourselves that the luxuries of time, energy and resources that feminist debates demand are still outside many women's reach. For example, in the preparation of this book, ill-health and other life circumstances prevented some contributors from completing. Much to our regret our planned section on technology was reduced as we had wanted to explore debates around conceptions of Cyber Sisterhood. Given the interweaving of feminist concerns, it was not problematic to find appropriate locations for the remaining technology contributors.

While the question 'Must I call every woman sister?' is debatable, it is without doubt that the answer to an equally pertinent question 'Am I my sister's keeper?' has to be a resounding 'Yes' every time it is asked. When women are determined to work together in spite of the different priorities and worlds of sisterhoods to which we belong, we can expect to see current notions of sisterhood reformulated and redefined through such practices.

Yet some differences can be fatal. For Joy Gardner, difference was not a theoretical consideration: it was a physical factor in her death. Perhaps this is where many of the crucial considerations in Women's Studies are in danger of being forgotten, undervalued or suppressed. That women die for political reasons within patriarchal, racist, homophobic societies must be a factor worthy of feminist consideration and analysis. The praxis within feminism and Women's Studies is such that if we theorize from Joy Gardner's experience we may well move our practices and campaigns forward in ways that will inform and challenge the social and political relations condoning femicide. The slogan 'Sisterhood is Dead' is an insidious lie. It cheats us into thinking that our present struggles are in vain, when in fact the living spirit of sisterhood is still gathering strength and momentum in women's lives.

It was not in vain that our sisters Joy Gardner, Audre Lorde and Franki Raffles lived and died. Although they were not with us at the Stirling Conference, these women were very much alive in their contribution to the Conference and in the huge influence they have had on key aspects in this book. Who they were, what they symbolized and stood for, continues to inspire and motivate us in overcoming barriers and meeting fresh challenges without fearing that our present struggles will be wasted. The validity and contribution of each of their lives and those of many like them have made it possible for us to be poised towards a more progressive feminist future. In her summing up at the Conference, Pauline Brown, a Black counsellor in Glasgow, observed that although at times sisterhood requires a lot of work – exemplified by the conference – there was controversy, some pain and discomfort, there was also a sense of unity. We *are* our sisters' keepers. We are *still* challenging and building. And so, sisters, the trick is to keep sistering . . .

Part I

Sistering: Sameness and Difference

Chapter 1

Sistering in the Skin

Ailbhe Smyth

In Memoriam: Audre Lorde

Do you ever wonder
what they would think
if they knew what you think at home alone in your head at night
as you try to touch the parts of yourself
you hate you hide
the parts of yourself
lost frozen denied
the anxieties the fears
the betrayals the lies
the failures of courage of energy of voice
the hopes the highs the great expectations
of yourself of your sisters of our aspirations
the shiver in your spine the tingle on your skin
the wildness the madness the private celebrations?

My skin is cold, damp to the touch, tangible sign of distress.

I have wanted it, hoped for it, worked for it, failed it, been let down by it, fought for it, fought over it, fought around it, been contradicted, confronted, bewildered, confused, believed in it, sensed it, touched it.

You do not touch lightly on the livings of sisterhood. How to talk about it without giving your life away? How to find a way into your life that doesn't expose your most tender self? What might they do with the knowledge you give them, if they hear it, if they care, if they know what your self is talking about? How can you say 'it's my whole life I'm talking about, talking to you about?' How can you say your whole life in the time allotted?

Who is *she* to be talking to us to be saying such things to be so free with her intimacies?

Who are *you* so politely silent so discreetly distant from my public emotions?

9

Ailbhe Smyth

We are damned, my sisters,
we who swam at night
on beaches, with the stars
laughing with us
phosphorescence about us
we shrieking with delight
with the coldness of the tide
without shifts or dresses
as innocent as infants.
We are damned, my sisters.
(Nuala Ni Dhomhnaill)

We, my sisters, who are *we*?

Will you condemn me for this 'we', the dilemma and delight of my life? Will I dare you to double-damn me, we who are damned already, you and I, who have chosen damnations beyond their salvations, you and I, who shriek together through our isolation, our separation, you and I, who move and struggle and laugh in the face of their multifaceted condemnations?

Will I be brave beyond my means? Will you know what your bravery means to me?

Will I be able to use those words we set apart for intimacy? Will I turn away from those words, at a moment of truth, because I know the fragility of truth? Because I am afraid it may be broken by unbelief? Because I turn away from conflict and collision? Because I am afraid?

Will you turn away from me, at a moment of my truth, because you do not believe in truth? Because you do not believe my truth? Because you are wary of complicity and collusion? Because you are afraid?

Will we turn away from each other, you and I, because we are not intimate, you and I? Will we turn away from each other for fear of being doubly damned, exposed? Because we fear the pain of skin being stripped clean away? Because we're ashamed of cowardice, of weakness, of guilt revealed? Will we turn away from one another in anger, in wariness, in weariness, in despair, in desperation?

Will we not risk the knowledge of touch?

And will you believe that I know one woman's truth, at a given moment in a particular place, is never, can never be enough even for her? Especially for her alone? That she cannot be alone for alone she is nothing?

I keep coming back to the wanting, the needing, the aching, the reaching for skin. The touching of you and I, in and across and through our separateness.

'We're all sisters under the skin.'

Ah no, that may not be so, who knows? But it's the skin I am reaching for. Its sheen, its warmth, its touch. Can we be sisters in the skin?

I keep coming back to the plain and demanding and beautiful words of intimacy, like truth and strength and passion, understanding, generosity and respect, tenderness, solace and trust. Love over all, unconditional, given without question, received with grace.

I say less and less
paring them down to the bone
those words I have
skinned alive
for fear there will be no space no time no silence
to hear how and where they may fall
coalescing with yours
for fear I will be dead before they do
I say them plainer and plainer
for fear of interference
in a world of indifference
to hearing
to suffering
to the gross obscenity of gross inequalities
'We are suffering' they said
'from compassion fatigue'

These days we all play cool calm and collected.
Our lips could turn blue just shooting the breeze . . . (Emmylou Harris)

No one dies from compassion fatigue.

'O Sisterhood! It's been done to death.'
I hate it when hope is killed stone dead, before it can grow into the fullness of
    its becoming.
'Come back to me, Sisterhood, all is forgiven.'
But can it ever be?

Throwaway apologies
regrets recycled for every
oppression

will not do.
You don't want me to say 'sorry'
sorry for my whiteskin privilege, my able-bodied privilege
for all my positions and powers and postures of privilege
sorry for women men children people
far away throwaway
done to death and to gross destitution.

I have to know the wrongness the vastness of my silence, my ignorance, my
    indifference, and worse.
I have to end it.

I tell myself my four truths
and more
fair and square
no twisting of the knife
I lay them out
up and down and across
look at them long and hard
and set to work
not twisting out of your sight

Stay with me as I do?
Why would you?

Let's get together, Sister,
As you treat me and mine like dirt.
Let's get together Sister,
Now Capital has donned a skirt.

Let's get together
Let's get together,
Let's get together,
SISTER!
(Marsha Prescod)

I couldn't live without the voices
in my head, in my life
my life lines across the lines
that keep some of us alive, within limits
difficult and dangerous
both safe and treacherous
angry, affectionate, arguing
voices
contradicting conflicting consoling

in turns
and twists and turns
they will not go away
part of me, who I am
what I think, what I do
what I believe
those voices of my life from other women's lives
I have always with me
yet I am not mad
damned, but not mad
or my insanity is an ache for humanity.

We have no patterns for relating across our human differences as equals. (Audre Lorde)

I miss her, that sister I never met, whose imagining, thinking, feeling, doing and being have touched me to the quick. You could survive through her forever, and you do. Even as you miss her. That woman had a grip to strong you knew she would never let you go, would hold you in the balm of her understanding, until you reached some part of your own, of your self, to reach out in turn to some part of another, and ever further and on and outwards.

Who is my sister?

blood sister bone sister
gut sister soul sister lust sister
stranger sister lover sister
tender sister
tough sister
power sister poor sister
passion sister
silently shrieking sister
soldier sister struggle sister
here and now sister
over there far away forever sister
drowning sister
keeping head above water sister
singing sister
tired sister
crying sister dying sister
proud sister loud sister
little sister big sister
holding hands and hearts sister
dancing laughing loving sister
red black white and green sister

resisting, revolting, rebelling sister
sweet sister
sister of my dreams
truth sister
'ma soeur ma semblable'
same sister different sister
never indifferent sister
never let her go sister

Who is my sister?

I cannot find her in the abstract where no one lives and struggles and laughs
and loves and dies.

Where is my sister?

To the south, to the north, to the east, to the west.
Before me, behind me, beside me, among me.
She is where she needs to be, where she is free to be, where she has chosen to
    be.
She is where she had *not* chosen to be, where she would *never* choose to be,
    where she is rooted and nailed to the spot.
She is where I least expect her to be where I am with her where I cannot be
    with her.

*The direction that needs to come back into the movement is the coming together
of the separated. (Urvashi Vaid)*

There is no blue-print for a sister, no definition that will hold for you and for
me and for all of us for all time. There is only – but it is everything – the
existence of women connected in wanting to end 'this bitter charade of isolation and anger and pain' (Audre Lorde). A litany of sisters, not infinite,
although none of us knows where it began or when it will end. Legacy for a
future I still believe in. Sisters for all seasons.

'There is a bottom line,' she said, and I agreed. Then it ran and ran through my
head for days and years and I could never keep it still, until I understood that
it must run always in new and open directions or disappear.

*When we get the monsters off our backs, all of us may want to run in very
different directions. (June Jordan)*

I am sisters with that woman, this woman, those women, not because our
provenances are the same, our directions the same, our lives the same, our
struggles the same in all their particular and unequal complexities. They are

14

not. Some of us, in all our four truths and more, have privileges and freedoms denied to most others, but freedoms not shared are oppressions imposed, which keep us apart.

Are freedom, justice, truth and happiness the bottom line, in all directions?

We will continue to speak the truth of our history
the truth of our pain
the truth of our oppression
the truth of our colonization
And through this truth, we will be free.

This is our prayer to you, Sisters.
Listen to it with your soul, Sisters.
(Puanani Burgess, Hawaii)

Listen, just for a moment, to the silence we can make
say what you hear, speak louder, shout yourself hoarse
look, just for an instant, at the space we can make
can we go, even just a little way,
together,
enough to change a piece of the world, yours or mine or ours?
Sister, don't leave me,
don't let me leave you,
don't let me go
don't let me, ever, off the hook.

Ah! *Don't the wars come easy and the peace come hard.* (Buffy Sainte Marie)

'I'm friending with her,' the little girl said, the one I am still learning to mother now she is fully grown, as I am still learning to daughter, to friend, to lover, to sister, as I am still learning to love, without holding back, with all of the parts of my self I am still learning to integrate.

I wasn't born knowing how to do these things.
So there is learning to be done.

Will you sister with me?

We need each other or some of us will die
for different reasons in different places in different ways
as we do, already, damned and dead, every day.
An uncertain number most certainly die because no one gives a damn.

In sister deprivation lies no salvation.

You and I, damned together, have to want still to change the world, because it is wrong, unjust, violent, greedy, cruel.

This world in which we are
not all sisters
is not
the same as the world we want.

THERE IS NO WAY WE WHO WANT TO CHANGE THE
    WORLD CAN DO IT ON OUR OWN
THERE IS NO WAY YOU OR I CAN CHANGE THE WORLD
    FROM WHERE WE STAND ALONE
WE HAVE TO MOVE
WE HAVE TO TALK
WE HAVE TO LISTEN WE HAVE TO HEAR
WE HAVE TO LEARN
WE HAVE TO TRY
TO WORK
TO DO IT TOGETHER SHOULDER TO SHOULDER
SKIN ON SKIN
SISTERING OUR SELVES

Not all of us all the time all together ever, but enough to make a difference, and always 'keeping the rest of womankind in view'. (Shahidah Janjua)

We strip, you and I
to the skin
your cotton, my silks
our differences
habitually
visible
the easy ones
passionately
to be skin on skin
tiny traceries beneath your breasts
where your heart beats in rhythms
my heart does not know
in my elbow crease
the marks you never notice
trying to skin myself alive
the hard ones
we have to talk about

And then know that the talking is never enough but in the skin is a beginning.

my sisters speak of violence
against women
'such and such said ...'
'in a book i read ...'
'this woman told me ...'
'oh, what a terrible story ...'
'the conference gave out papers ...'
'i've spoken to one survivor ...'
'we've got to put up a support group ...'
'we support each other ...'

i sit, a shadow in a corner
puffing my deadly winstons
overwhelmed by theories
i, a living memory
mother of another
i go home, silent.
(Aida F. Santos)

Sistering, no, is not shadowing, policing, censoring, cornering, judging, silencing.

Sistering is an aching, reaching and touching, a making, doing, learning, improvising, in our skins and our truths and our needs in the here and the now.

It must become necessary for all of us to feel that this is our world. And that we are 'here' to stay and that anything that is 'here' is 'ours to take' and to use in our image. And watch that 'our' – make it as big as you can ... (Bernice Johnson Reagon)

And bigger. Not including within, but opening outwards to more and greater freedoms. It must be a world made not only of the common ground, the ground we share, the ground we inhabit together. It must be the world of the differences between us, those we have chosen in freedom, and those imposed through injustice and oppression, to be combated by all. It must be the world of your struggle, the world of my struggle, each seeking to give to the other what she asks for and needs.

To each according to her need, but to the one in gravest need, more, most, must be given, in love, without question or judgement or stinting.

However and by whomsoever damned, pain and pleasure not separate but fused, for an all but elusive moment
Whyever and by whomsoever stripped, knowledge and ignorance, experience and emptiness exposed, in an all but fleeting space,

17

However and wherever and still ever our incandescent phosphorescent incalescences coalesce.

I want to touch them, those beautiful words, not just their sound, not just with my tongue, with my voice. I want their sound and sense and substance integrated in my being and my doing and my believing.

Incandescence: glowing with heat

Phosphorescence: self-luminous

Incalescence: increasing in warmth

Coalescence: the growing together of separate parts

References

BURGESS, PUANANI (1994) 'Hawaii Pono'i', in ZohI de Ishtar, *Daughters of the Pacific*, Melbourne, Spinifex Press.

JANJUA, SHADHIDAH (1995) 'Poem', *Women's News*, Spring, Belfast.

JORDAN, JUNE (1985) 'Report from the Bahamas', in *On Call: Political Essays*, Boston, MA, South End Press, p. 47.

LORDE, AUDRE (1984) *Sister Outsider: Essays and Speeches*, Freedom, CA, The Crossing Press.

NI DHOMHNAILL, NUALA (1986) 'We are damned my sisters', trans. from the Irish by Michael Hartnett, in *Selected Poems*, Dublin, Raven Arts Press.

PRESCOD, MARSHA (1987) 'Womanist blues', in Lauretta Ngcobo (Ed.) *Let It Be Told: Black Women Writers in Britain*, London, Pluto Press.

REAGON, BERNICE JOHNSON (1983) 'Coalition politics: turning the century', in Barbara Smith (Ed.) *Home Girls: A Black Feminist Anthology*, New York, Kitchen Table I Women of Color Press, p. 365.

SANTOS, AIDA F. (1994) 'VAW', *Women in Action*, 2 March, Isis, Manila, Philippines.

VAID, URVASHI (1993) 'Get real about feminism', *Ms Magazine*, **IV**, 2.

Chapter 2

Who are the Sisters? Difference, Feminism and Friendship

Felly Nkweto Simmonds

Sisterhood

Some definitions from *A Feminist Dictionary* (Kramarae and Treichler, 1985).

> More than a word. It is a responsibility. It will become more important than status, colour or money. (Vann, 1970)

> A discovery of shared oppression . . . (Beth Brant, 1983)

> Is a joining threatened by pollution from 'the two "ideals" of feminine fulfilment, namely "unselfconscious inclusion" (tokenism) and feminine self-sacrifice.' (Mary Daly, 1978)

> Cannot be forged by the mere saying of words. It is the outcome of continued growth and change. It is a goal to be reached, a process of becoming. (bell hooks, 1981)

Friendship

A Feminist Dictionary has one definition.

> Is derived from an old English term meaning to love, and . . . is akin to its roots to an Old English word meaning free. The radical friendship of Hags means loving our own freedom, loving/encouraging the freedom of the other, the friend, and therefore *loving freely*. (Mary Daly, 1978) (Kramarae and Treichler, 1985)

Introduction

I have chosen to use only definitions from *A Feminist Dictionary* to introduce this chapter because I want to locate 'sisterhood' and 'friendship' in the historical development of feminism and of feminist theory. *A Feminist*

Dictionary has a particular place in that history. Its epistemological aims included challenging 'traditional lexicographic practice' (p. 1) and presenting a female (feminist) definition of the world by using 'women's *own* words' to create meaning (p. 4). This is what made the dictionary an important text in the theory and practice of feminism. It also succeeded in capturing the mood and spirit of the time and women's ideas about themselves and their world. As a piece of history, it captured some of the concerns of feminism. Sisterhood was such a concern; friendship was not. It is therefore not a coincidence that sisterhood is given more intellectual (and real) space, in the dictionary, than friendship. Sisterhood has been constructed as more important to feminist theory than friendship. In fact sisterhood was constructed as political act, whereas friendship remained in the personal/private. The feminist slogan, 'The Personal is Political', failed to unseat this personal/political dichotomy in its very definitions of sisterhood and friendship.

I want to argue that this difference in how as feminists we have valued sisterhood and friendship has historically created tensions in working out which of these relationships was of value to feminism. To put it simply, sisterhood has overshadowed friendship at a political and personal level. And still we have not adequately looked at what relationship, if any, there is between sisterhood and friendship. I feel that this continues to create tensions in the everyday reality of feminism and feminist theory, and the practice of sisterhood and that of friendship. I want to explore this contradiction by asking: Who are sisters and who are friends? Are all sisters friends?

The Problem of Sisterhood

Sisterhood as a feminist principle has been based on commonality between women. However, historically it failed to recognize the different priorities that women had, even within the broader framework of the women's movement. It failed to contend not only with autonomous groups within the movement, but also with how diverse groups of women could hold together as a larger-scale coalition: The Women's Movement.

Sisterhood as an idea was not enough. What was needed was the negotiation of what sisterhood as a practice could be. For example, how was sisterhood to deal with the tension between demands for autonomy, for example by Black women and by lesbian women, and those of coalition, in the main suggested by white middle-class heterosexual women? This tension, between autonomy and coalition, has been picked up, for example, in Gail Pheterson's definitions of 'solidarity' and 'alliance'.[1] Pheterson defines 'solidarity' as 'knowledge of, respect for, and unity with persons whose identities are in certain essential ways common to one's own', and 'alliance' as 'knowledge of, respect for, and commitment between persons who are in essential ways different but whose interests are in essential ways akin' (Pheterson in Albrecht and Brewer, 1990, p. 36). It was the working out of such tensions within the rapidly fragmenting women's movement that put issues of commonality and difference on the feminist agenda.

One of the most celebrated books on the issue of commonality and difference is Gloria Joseph and Jill Lewis' *Common Differences: Conflicts in Black and White*. In their introduction, the authors argued for 'the importance of Black women and white women connecting their specific understandings of oppression to an understanding of the political totality that thrives on these oppressions' (Joseph and Lewis, 1981, p. 14). Looking back now, it is shocking how little attention was taken of such a stance by many feminist theorists and practitioners and if anything how such a stance was viewed as divisive.

Sisterhood as Powerful and Global[2]

White feminists of the second wave, such as Robin Morgan, used the symbolism of sisterhood, of belonging to womanhood, as a way of articulating an urgent message for constructing a global feminism based on personal and political alliances between women. The idea was powerful and seductive. As Judith Roof has argued:

> *Sisterhood* simultaneously presents the motive for feminist action and reports the exposure of oppression as feminism's happy result . . . However, the unification of different women into a single sororal protagonist pitted against a figurative father . . . tends to complete the erasure of positional differences among women (and all issues relating to position). (Roof in Elam and Wiegman, 1995, pp. 56–7)

Robin Morgan's second book on sisterhood, *Sisterhood is Global*, a 'collection of original articles from seventy countries . . . (which crossed) . . . cultural, racial, class and ideological boundaries as well as geographical borders to provide a powerful and often shocking statement on the status of women throughout the world', was hailed as the definitive work on the international women's movement and was in fact seen in itself as proof of the existence of an international sisterhood and a solution to women's oppression worldwide. It was as if producing a text on the status of women worldwide could minimize the differences in women's experiences of oppression.

Yet out there in the real world, in the year that *Sisterhood is Global* was published (1984), the women's movement was having a crisis of confidence. Sisterhood as a central ideology for feminism was being called into question at personal/political and local/global levels, as a theory and an experience. In the USA for example, Black and white women were questioning sisterhood by centring the notion of *difference*. As Joseph and Lewis state in their introduction:

> This book is a committed attempt to examine the ways in which racial and sexual factors interact in the oppression of women . . . This doesn't mean that we will ignore class and cultural differences that exist among White women, and among Black women . . . Our aim is to open up, through discussion, some of the features of oppression peculiar to Black women in contrast to White women . . . (in a) society where privilege (race, class or sex) means power. (Joseph and Lewis, 1981, pp. 3–4)

In Britain, Black women had embarked on similar projects. Hazel Carby's influential essay 'White women listen! Black feminism and the boundaries of sisterhood', for example argued that:

> In arguing that the most contemporary feminist theory does not begin to adequately account for the experience of Black women we also have to acknowledge that it is not a simple question of their absence, consequently the task is not one of rendering their visibility. On the contrary we will have to argue that the process of accounting for their historical and contemporary position, does in itself, challenge the use of some of the central categories and assumptions of recent mainstream feminist thought. (Carby in Center for Contemporary Cultural Studies, 1982, p. 213)

This challenge was also taken up at the international level in the context of the United Nations Decade for Women, where women of the South – from Asia, Africa and Latin America – challenged the definitions and consequent actions of a global feminism. If anything, the three conferences (Mexico, 1975; Copenhagen, 1980 and Nairobi, 1985) highlighted the need to take account of the difference of experience between women in a world that socially, politically and economically divided them. What then were to be the issues for women across the world?

At the Copenhagen conference, this became *the* question at the centre of all the conference proceedings. The Israeli occupation of Palestine provided the focus. Paragraph 5 of the conference report was a call 'to eliminate imperialism, colonialism, neo-colonialism, Zionism, racism and apartheid'. The Israeli delegation, supported by Australia, Canada, the USA and most of the European countries, not only rejected the language of the paragraph but concluded that the inclusion of Zionism in the paragraph was 'malicious, tendentious and inaccurate'. One of the members of the Canadian delegation argued that 'only a fraction of debating time at the conference had been devoted to the key political questions of concern to women; the restructuring of family responsibilities; equal remuneration for equal value; an equal share of the benefit of economic development and in all decision-making, among other issues'. In the final vote of the draft Programme of Action, Australia,

Canada, Israel and the USA voted against. All the European delegations abstained. The draft, however, was supported by all the delegates from the South and the Eastern Block of Nations.

At an international level, the global sisterhood that Morgan was so sure had arrived was a sham. The international feminist agenda was still being dictated by white women from the North. At a global level, while Western women were seemingly content to grapple with the consequences of gender oppression, Black and Third World women saw the task of feminism as challenging both the epistemological foundations of feminist critique and challenging global structures of oppression, not just for women, but for all oppressed peoples.

Difference, Feminism and Sisterhood

In the rest of the chapter I want to re/examine the feminist notion of sisterhood and what kind of friendship relations develop from the parameter of sisterhood. I want to examine some of the ways in which sisterhood has shaped personal non-sexual relationships between women. My concern here is with personal relationships between women and what I see as the inbuilt contradiction in such relationships. I want to argue that the (mis)uses of the concept of sisterhood has left us suspicious of the intentions and practices of other women – for example, those with whom we don't share experiences – and also vulnerable to those sisters with whom we share commonalities. Here I want to examine the particular relationship of sisterhood between Black women in Britain today and how the sisterhood of sharing the experience of racism can undermine that of friendship.

What we may need to define clearly are our notions of sisterhood and friendship, because we often conflate the two and often have no clues as how (if necessary) we are to separate personal and political solidarities and alliances. If, as feminists, we believe that the personal is political, are we to take it that any act of forming a friendship relationship with another woman is a political act? An act of solidarity? Is it possible for us to have 'just' friendships?

I want to argue that some of us, as feminists, have developed 'pathological' friendship relationships with other women because we have used feminism and the notion of sisterhood as adequate bases for female friendships in themselves and not questioned, for example, the qualities expected of women in most friendships, such as 'altruism, vulnerability and self sacrifice'[3] and how these have an effect on what kind of friendships we make and our expectations of ourselves and others in such friendships. For example we can ask: What kind of friendships are engendered by notions of sisterhood and are all sisters friends?

Who are the Sisters? Friendships between Black Women

When a friend of mine sent me a copy of bell hook's book *Sisters of The Yam: Black Women and Self-recovery*, I was excited by what it might tell me. I even hoped, naïvely, that it might help me clarify this vexed question of who my sisters were. When I read it I was filled with both envy and dismay. First, bell hooks seems to be quite sure who Black women are and that their experience is similar enough to form a solid base for sisterhood. I was struck by the very first sentence of the book after the Audre Lorde quote: **'Healing takes place within us as we speak the truths of our lives.'** But what is the truth of our lives as Black women in Britain?

One of the problems for us as Black women is the fact that although we are quite willing to engage in debates on sisterhood at local and global levels we have failed to have constructive debates between ourselves about *our* differences and how we can unite through this diversity and the commonality of our experiences. The reality is that often Black sisterhood prevents us from speaking the truth about ourselves, in similar ways to how white feminism has, historically and globally, prevented us from speaking the truth about ourselves as women. As Black female academics in Britain, for example, there are few (and far between) forums that take on the tasks identified by Abena Busia in the concluding chapter of *Theorising Black Feminisms: The Visionary Pragmatism of Black Women*:

> as a group of scholars we felt the need to meet to discuss what it meant to be Black feminists in the academic context. We had gathered as community to discuss our commonality as Black women, academics, activists and artists. Yet to do this we also had to discuss our differences, across continents, across states, academies and disciplines. We needed to ask ourselves what it meant to be African–American as opposed to African: what it meant to be Africans in the USA as opposed to Africans at home; what it meant to be African–Americans who had been in Africa and for whom Africa was the field of Study. What had been our various experience? (Busia in James and Busia, 1995, pp. 285–6)

In Britain, such a debate is still to be had. And although attempts have been made at such a debate,[4] it is hard to forge links between Black female academics. We are partly impeded in this task in the contradiction of the hegemonic construction of Blackness as a political category (especially in academia and academic writing) and the reality of racism in Britain which divides not only Black and white, but different 'Black' and 'ethnic' communities. The cultural and political construction of Blackness in Britain is still fraught with contention. At its most basic, the question still remains: What is the basis of this identity? Who, for example, are the 'Black women' we speak of in Black British feminist theory? What is the basis of such a construction?

One of the underlying problems of such constructions is the reality that the dominant definitions of 'Blackness' in Britain have historical roots in the politics of representation, in which Black as a cultural and political identity has continued to define particular groups of people. The basis for such constructions was clearly established in the 1970s and 1980s by the work carried out by Stuart Hall and The Center for Contemporary Cultural Studies at Birmingham University. The earliest definitions worked on the idea of:

> shared culture . . . (reflecting) . . . common historical experiences and shared cultural code which provide us as 'one people', with stable, unchanging and continuous frames of reference and meaning, beneath the shifting divisions and vicissitudes of our actual history . . . This 'oneness', underlying all other, more superficial differences, is the truth, the essence of 'Caribbeaness', of the Black experience. (Hall in Rutherford, 1990, p. 223)

It is this idea of 'one people', adopted in popular understandings of Blackness by those of Caribbean descent in particular, that has been challenged as essentialist[5] by those who do not subscribe to this hegemonic construction of a Black identity. Even Stuart Hall was writing of:

> the end of the innocent notion of the essential Black subject. Here again, the end of the essential Black subject is something which people are increasingly debating, but they may not have fully reckoned with its political consequences. What is at issue here is the recognition of the extraordinary diversity of subject positions, social experiences and cultural identities which compose the category 'Black'; that is, the recognition that 'Black' is essentially a politically and culturally *constructed* category. (Hall in Donald and Rattansi, 1992, p. 254)

My concern here is, as Black women, our sisterhood must rest on our ability to speak about our difference and our different experiences of this constructed category 'Black' and the consequences of living in a white society. As we have insisted on speaking our difference in feminist theory, so we must do in British Black feminism. We should also be aware of the problems that can arise when we use the political label, Black, as an unproblematic starting point for both sisterhood and friendship. The assumption that my 'political' sisters are also my friends is a false starting point. Friendships that are based on such assumptions can, in fact, prevent us from speaking the truths about our lives, especially if this truth is at odds with the truth about our political lives. For example, one of the areas least debated in Black academic debates is precisely what kind of relationships we have with white people (women and men) and indeed with other Black people. As a

Black woman, living up to the feminist ideal of personal as political means censoring personal truths out of our political truths.[6]

When Abena Busia asks 'what is meant to be African in the USA', I too want to ask the question: What does it meant to be African in Britain, when the Black politics continues to overshadow the particularity of being African, as opposed to being of The African Diaspora, which in any case has taken the Atlantic as its centre.[7] The silences around our different histories and experiences as Black women has cost us both personal and political alliances.[8] This has been a painful and lonely experience for many of us. If we could speak our truths, we might be able to heal the hurt we inflict on each other.

Sisterhood and Friendship

I want to suggest that the emphasis placed on solidarities based on sisterhood at a political level has had another negative effect. It has limited the scope of friendships that women develop at a personal level. I want to suggest that we need to separate 'political sisterhood' from 'personal friendships'. That is not to argue that political sisters cannot be friends, but rather that sisterhood alone is not an adequate basis for friendship. One of the reasons is the fact that we haven't negotiated sisterhood itself. Any relationship thus based on sisterhood alone can be questioned. There's also a need to negotiate sisterhood separately from friendship. If we are lucky, the two can be negotiated in tandem. But most of us are not that lucky and find that our so-called 'sisters' cannot be our friends.

We must also, as a matter of fact, be able to deal with the friendships that we make across differences of 'race' and of experiences of womanhood and even Blackness itself. We need to ask what friendship is for and what sisterhood is for. In her book *What Are Friends For?* Marilyn Friedman defines friendship in terms of:

> a relationship that is based on approximate equality . . . and a mutuality of affection, interest and benevolence . . . Friends should be able to respect and take an interest in one another's perspective. (Friedman, 1993, p. 189)

As feminists we have a lot to learn from such a definition. Friendship, like sisterhood, cannot be built solely on what we see as a shared experience (of womanhood, or oppression). How do we in reality translate this sharing of experience? We cannot, for example, ignore the fact that oppressed groups often have to contend with what Pheterson defines as internalized oppression:

internalisation of oppression can consist of 'self-hatred, self-concealment, feelings of inferiority, resignation, isolation, powerlessness' . . . Internalised oppression isolates people from one another, especially from others like themselves, and thereby prevents solidarity. (Pheterson in Albrecht and Brewer, 1990, pp. 35–6)

Internalized oppression can have a profound effect on how we make friendships within oppressed groups. For Black female academics, this can be compounded by our isolation from other Black people (working in the North East, for example) and from each other (in institutions). These factors can make us suspicious of each other and defensive in what we do, leaving us vulnerable and powerless. This is not the kind of environment in which solidarities and alliances can flourish between ourselves and with other women.

Black Women and White Women in Friendships

Because I live in a white society, and because I live in a very white town, most of my women friends are white. What strikes me about all my friendships with white women is what I can legitimately make part of the friendship. This, of course, applies to all friendships, but I feel that there is something quite specific about crossing the 'racial' boundary in friendships that means I have to quite clearly work out the why and how questions of friendship. Why are we friends? And how are we going to maintain this friendship? If this all sounds too controlled, it is. And it is a new experience for me, because like most of us (of my age anyway) I was seduced by feminism and I was seduced by the idea of sisterhood. There were many times when I was desperate for friendships and made what I can only now see as problematic relationships.

One of the things I may not be able to share with many of my white friends are experiences of racism within the relationship itself. The very first time, nearly twenty years ago now, that a white woman (a friend!) said to me, 'I don't see you as Black', she literally left me speechless. Now, as an academic, feminist colleagues can play on our (apparent) commonality of class and profession to cancel out my particular experience of being a Black woman academic and the racism I face every day in my academic environment. This, of course, is quite ironic because I'm also expected to be an 'expert' on teaching issues of 'race' in an abstract and theoretical way.[9] Black women (and Black people in general) at various points have been asked to explain ourselves and our experiences of oppression by those that have a stake in power, those who seemingly don't have to explain their advantage. It is this basic imbalance of power that makes sisterhood suspect as a political stance and almost unworkable at personal levels. We are, indeed, unequal sisters. A friendship of unequals is hardly a choice that we should make, as feminists.

Conclusion

Any future agenda for sisterhood has to take on the notion of 'sistering' as suggested by Ailbhe Smyth in Chapter 1. Sistering must be about translating the idea of sisterhood into practice. It should be about being able to speak the truth about our lives, but also hearing the truth of other women's lives. It should be about respecting personal and group autonomy as well as recognizing the potential for coalition across difference. It should be about our daily contact with other women, in our teaching and in our learning, in our friendships and in our loving. Let sisterhood develop through our actions not just our words. In our sistering we may find friends, personal and political. If we do, the friendships we make as a result of sistering will be altered, for at the heart of such friendships will be a recognition of difference. That in itself will change the idea of sisterhood.

But let me end with Gloria Anzaldua's words: 'One must posses a sense of personhood before one can develop a sense of sisterhood . . . not one sisterhood but many' (Anzaldua in Albrecht and Brewer, 1990, p. 225).

Notes

1 Gail Pheterson, 'Alliances between women: Overcoming internalised oppression and internalised domination', in Albrecht and Brewer (1990).
2 Robin Morgan's two books on sisterhood, *Sisterhood is Powerful* (1970) and its companion volume three *Sisterhood is Global* (1984) were the most influential texts on sisterhood in the second wave.
4 See Sarah Lucia Hoagland in Anne Minas (1992) *Gender Basics: Feminist Perspectives on Women and Men*, Belmont CA, Wadsworth Publishing Company.
5 See Felly Nkweto Simmonds (1990) 'Difference, power and knowledge: Black women in academia', in Hinds *et al. Working Out: New Directions For Women's Studies*, London, The Falmer Press.
6 See, for example, Anthias, F. and Yuval-Davis, N. (1990) 'Contextualising feminism – gender, ethnic and class divisions', in T. Lovell (Ed.) *British Feminist Thought*, Oxford, Basil Blackwell.
7 See, for example, Felly Nkweto Simmonds 'Love in Black and white', in Lynne Pearce and Jackie Stacey (1995) *Romance Revisited*, London, Lawrence & Wishart.
8 See Paul Gilroy (1993) *The Black Atlantic: Modernity and Double Consciousness*, Cambridge MA, Harvard University Press.
9 There are many undocumented painful disintegrations of Black women's groups in Britain which have not become part of the publicly accepted experiences of Black women. At the core of some of them has been the question of 'What is it to be Black?'

10 See Nellie Y. McKay chapter, 'Acknowledging difference: Can women find unity through diversity?' in James and Busia (1995).

References

ALBRECHT, LISA and BREWER, ROSE M. (Eds) (1990) *Bridges of Power: Women's Multicultural Alliances*, Philadelphia, PA, New Society Publishers.

CENTER FOR CONTEMPORARY CULTURAL STUDIES, UNIVERSITY OF BIRMINGHAM (1982) *The Empire Strikes Back*, London, Hutchinson.

DONALD, JAMES and RATTANSI, ALI (Eds) (1992) *'Race', Culture and Difference*, London, Sage/Open University Press.

ELAM, DIANE and WIEGMAN, ROBYN (Eds) (1995) *Feminism Beside Itself*, New York and London, Routledge.

FRIEDMAN, MARILYN (1993) *What Are Friends For? Feminist Perspectives on Personal Relationships*, Ithaca, NY and London, Cornell University Press.

GILROY, PAUL (1993) *The Black Atlantic: Modernity and Double Consciousness*, Cambridge, MA, Harvard University Press.

JAMES, STANLIE and BUSIA, ABENA (Eds) (1995) *Theorising Black Feminisms: The Visionary Pragmatism of Black Women*, New York and London, Routledge.

JOSEPH, GLORIA and LEWIS, JILL (1981) *Common Differences: Conflicts in Black and White*, Boston, MA, South End Press.

KRAMARAE, CHERIS and TREICHLER, PAULA A. (1985) *A Feminist Dictionary*, London, Pandora.

MORGAN, ROBIN (Ed.) (1970) *Sisterhood is Powerful: An Anthology of Writings from the Women's Movement*, New York, Vintage.

MORGAN, ROBIN (Ed.) (1984) *Sisterhood is Global: The International Women's Movement Anthology*, London, Doubleday.

RUTHERFORD, J. (Ed.) (1990) *Identity, Community, Culture and Difference*, London, Lawrence Wishart.

Further Reading

DUBOIS, CAROL and RUIZ, VICKI L. (Eds) (1990) *Unequal Sisters: A Multicultural Reader in US Women's History*, New York and London, Routledge.

HINDS, HILARY, PHOENIX, ANNE and STACEY, JACKIE (Eds) (1992) *Working Out; New Directions for Women's Studies*, London, The Falmer Press.

LOVELL, TERRY (Ed.) (1990) *British Feminist Thought*, Oxford, Blackwell.

MINAS, ANNE (Ed.) (1992) *Gender Basics: Feminist Perspectives on Women and Men*, Belmont, CA, Wadsworth Publishing Company.

PEARCE, LYNNE and STACEY, JACKIE (Eds) (1995) *Romance Revisited*, London, Lawrence Wishart.

Report of The World Conference of The United Nations Decade For Women: Equality, Development and Peace. Copenhagen 14–30 July 1980, (1980) New York, United Nations Publications.

Chapter 3

Sexism, Sisterhood and some Dynamics of Racism: A Case in Point

Annette Kilcooley

Must I call every woman sister? bell hooks (1994)

My idea for this chapter was fused by bell hooks' presence at the Women's Studies Network conference in 1994. In her address, hooks raised a number of complications around cultural imperialism and sisterhood, enmeshed in which was lodged the question: Must I call every woman sister? (hooks, 1994). In respect to hooks' enquiry, this chapter is an attempt to come to terms with certain problematics within the logic of sisterhood, around notions of mutual recognition and political collectivity. Given that the politics of sisterhood can change dramatically from one site of negotiation to the next, the example of a case in point is used to explore a link which appears at one level to bind the business of anti-sexism with racialized representations and/or images of sexuality and, at another level, to show how the notion of sisterhood as an ideological commitment politically fails feminism at moments when sexism is complicated by issues of 'race' and racism. By exploring some dynamics of racism between white women, I will try to show how unacknowledged complications of sisterhood can serve to disrupt feminist politics and women's solidarity against sexism.

That sisterhood can be recognized as a problematic, it has to be said, comes more out of advances in feminist movement than it does from failures in feminism or 'post-feminist parading' (hooks, 1994) and this immediately raises questions for 'women's solidarity' in the political and cultural arena. Through broadcast media support of the anti-feminist backlash, women such as Naomi Woolf or Camille Paglia, in a projection of some kind of neo-feminism, can claim to speak of alternative *feminisms* while trashing feminist politics. Must we call these women sisters? bell hooks referred to Naomi Woolf's politics as the politics of greed, which doesn't threaten cultural imperialism but instead assists it because the underlying ethic in Woolf's position seems to be how to protect and sustain being rich as well as being a woman (hooks, 1994). Indeed the media imagery of shere Hite's retro-femininity raises related questions. In a different way, however, Victoria Gillick's preoccupation is preventing children in state schools from receiving sex education. Gillick is a regular guest on daytime TV audience shows where she presents

31

as something of a moral expert on teenage sexuality. Though it has been said that Gillick 'looks like' a feminist, her angel-in-the-house brand of feminine sentimentality belies the more insidious logic in which her appeal is dressed.

Current Echos

Trying to say something of sisterhood today, and refusing to be coerced by the forces of post-sisterhood cynicism, it's worth bearing in mind that feminism as a political movement remains irrepressible. The WSN (UK) annual conference is always a current echo. Indeed, I would argue from the outset that a sense of sisterhood is essential to any idea of feminist politics that recognizes itself as progressive. I approach it here, however, with a mixture of hesitation and desire, perhaps as Gayatri Spivak has suggested, in the habit of critical intimacy (Spivak, 1993).

As a reference for the political character of feminism, 'sisterhood' has its contemporary relatives in women's studies, feminism and feminist theory. We might also recognize the generative character of feminism, through its critical impact in academic areas such as cultural studies, lesbian and gay studies, gender studies, 'the new men's studies', etc. (Richardson and Robinson, 1994), as well as the impact of feminism on the broader dissemination of critical enquiry in the world at large. I think it is also desirable to think of the effects of sisterhood as broad and narrow cast projections. Broadly, for example, in ideas of universal or global sisterhood, or in terms of 'The Woman Question', which in 1982 (in the book of the same name) was posed that in terms of social power and control women remain less privileged than men (Evans, 1982). Equal rights and privileges with men is indeed a very broad politics. Narrow cast, perhaps, within feminism we can hold the conceptual framework of sisterhood as a problematic – from mutual self-recognition to recognizing complexities. In particular those raised by Black feminist thinkers.

When the politics of the Women's Liberation Movement first gave rise to the project of anti-sexism, the idea of sisterhood became tied to a continuity between women's rights activism, anti-sexist struggles and a critique of the language of sexism. In light of which 'sisterhood' has since become recognizable as a founding expression of women's solidarity in the face of patriarchal oppression. At its broadest, perhaps, challenging women's oppression on the grounds of sex, and in the context of patriarchy, tying sexism to men.

Reading 'sisterhood' historically it is interesting to note that as a political ethic, it comes into being both as a cause and an effect of women's solidarity and movement. Ethico-politically, sisterhood was 'sister inhabited', 'woman powered' and characterized by the pursuit of women-centred values, aims and objectives. The politics of sisterhood emerged through personal experience and *self-recognition* in common with each other. Sisterhood had its material base in 'mutual recognition' though often without recognition of 'race' or class issues. Sisterhood placed personal experience before abstract political theory

– politically based in experience and not in books. Personalized and politicized, masses of women came together in women's CR[1] groups which writers in feminism have since described as if it was 'spontaneous'.[2]

Politicizing Sexuality

Politicizing sexuality has undoubtedly been one of the major achievements of the women's movement. In 1970, Katet Millett identified the political relationship between the sexes as the 'uncharted' territory of sexual politics (Millett, 1977). Though patriarchy is a political institution, it is also, she argued, an ideology which derives its foundations in biological materialism. In addition, because the so-called sexual revolution was aimed at the *structures* of patriarchy, social processes and regulations had virtually remained intact. Millet's exposition of sexism and misogyny in the context of literary criticism was fired, in part, by what she saw as the reactionary influence of Freud and Freudian thought, on dominant power structures. *Sexual Politics*, however, has since become a founding text for feminist theorizing around sex, sexuality and, of course sexism. And although opinions in feminism markedly differ, there is, it seems, no escaping the impact of Freud on the (re-)production of feminist theory and critique.

From almost the beginning, critics within feminism have argued that a model of universal sisterhood casts an uncomplicated opposition between 'women' and 'men', where women in general are both oppressed and united, in claiming equality with men's rights and privileges. Black feminists and others, have raised questions about the universal or general character of a politics that privileges some women's experiences at the expense of others. 'Difference' as Felly Nkweto Simmonds has argued, 'is perceived to be outside and not within feminism and has been more readily accepted in relation to men.' Interests that ostensibly bind have been more readily incorporated than conflicting interests. 'Difference has been deemed divisive' (Simmonds, 1992), 'an impediment to universal sisterhood' (Bhavnani and Coulson, 1985). Kum Kum Bhavnani and Margaret Coulson, too, have questioned the assumption of *commonality* and as a basis for political unity. They argue that in addition to 'difference', feminism has to engage with complexities of power, particularly where white women may be privileged, oppressed or both. For instance, in power dynamics between white women and Black men. When conflicts of interest and difference between women become politically subsumed, it evades what Bhavnani and Coulson have termed 'the challenge of the charge of racism' (Bhavnani and Coulson, 1985).

White Sisters, Black Men

Where issues of 'race' and racism shift political interests, notions of 'common oppression' can erupt into conflicting models of sisterhood and pseudo-white supremacy. Where seemingly straightforward campaigns against violence against women have been complicated by 'race' and racism, Bhavnani and Coulson also identify the issue of power as one of *colonialist* power. That is to say, colonialist power operating through stereotypes and images of black men as a threat to the safety of white women. Though no great feminist, Franz Fanon, in the context of liberation politics and colonialism, analysed the notion of equal rights as one imbued with rights in common with white men. In addition he found that when equal rights' politics is born of an assumption of parity with white men, no threat is posed to the established order of white supremacy and privilege. In Fanon's analysis, the colonial situation produces a dynamic which 'brings about the emergence of a mass of illusions and misunderstandings' (Fanon, 1986). Inequality, he argued, was not only born of material conditions, but also human attitudes towards those conditions.

Policing ...

Black sisters were outraged when white feminists, campaigning around safety for women, marched though areas where Black people lived, demanding safer streets for women and better policing. For which women, they asked – and for whom were they demanding better policing? Certainly not for Cherry Groce who was shot by a police inspector in Brixton in 1985, while police raided her home apparently seeking to arrest her son. When Black people and other local residents staged a protest march to the police station, police reaction to a deputation, in newspaper reports of the incident, was said to be 'insensitive, even flippant and provocative'.[3] It was largely the reaction of the police that to a great extent inflamed the situation and subsequent public protest in the area. Not for Cynthia Jarrett either who died during a police raid of her home in north London in 1985,[4] while police were seeking to arrest her son who didn't even live there. Nor for Joy Gardner, whose death in London in 1993 was precipitated by policing activity at her home. Police officers involved in the circumstances of her death were subsequently tried and acquitted of all connected charges. It has also been upheld that police were acting in the line of duty when Joy Gardner was killed. Different women, Bhavnani and Coulson argued, are differently placed in relation to state power, authority and police protection and feminism cannot ignore that the state deals with different women differently *and* has different policing strategies for Black and white groups. Paul Condon, Commissioner of the Metropolitan Police, has since been acclaimed in the national press[5,6] for his 'new realism on crime and race'. As part of a 'new' policing initiative in London, Commissioner Condon has written to 40 'ethnic community leaders' and Black MPs in London by way of an appeal for 'the black community' to come to the aid of the police. In his letter the Commissioner has stated 'it is a fact that very many of the perpetrators of mugging are very young black (sic) people, who have been excluded from school ... I am sure I do not need to spell out the sensitivity of dealing with this'. Commissioner Condon is not new to 'racially sensitive' issues and, as reported in the *Daily Telegraph*, has a long history of involvement in racially sensitive policing activities around public safety in London. The policing strategy which began in August 1995 is based on a Metropolitan Police survey and targets areas of London, particularly those with a high proportion of Black residents. The strategy rests on targeting 'essentially young Black males' as crime suspects and encouraging 'the public' to come forward and inform the police of suspicion of criminal intent. The police survey from which the statistics arise has not to date been published.

Although body colour is not usually a variable in statistical formula for street robbery in Britain, or surveys on exclusions by The Department for Education,[7] targeting the Black population for policing initiatives and strategies is a more familiar phenomena. What is odd about the press coverage, however, is that it poses the current strategy as a new initiative when it is also a fact that there is nothing new in targeting areas for 'race sensitive' policing and public safety initiatives in specific parts of London. In response to this latest set of initiatives, Professor Jock Young[8] and others have continued to argue that patterns of crime are affected more by class, lifestyle, economic and educational deprivation, than by any other given or racialized variable.

Must we call Victoria Gillick sister?

I would call Victoria Gillick 'the gendered enemy' because the only thing that is remotely sisterly about Gillick is her gender. Consequently it is rather alarming that Gillick's position on sex education has also been misrecognized as looking like a feminist one. Gillick is a woman, talking up the morals of preventing sex education and disallowing contraception to girls under sixteen, in current debates and discussions around teenage pregnancy and parenthood. Gillick's moral mission emerges in the context of sexual politics, though she is clearly unenlightened by feminism in her overt drive to protect children, especially little girls, from sex education and knowledge. In her relentlessly sexist adamance around issues of sex education, Gillick occupies a frontline position within the anti-sex education lobby and on whose behalf she can be heard regularly mixing up anti-sex morality with anti-sexism. Gillick invents inflammatory figures on daytime TV.[9] Gillick doesn't cite her sources. For instance, she recently stated that one in three girls under eleven are heterosexually active in terms of sexual intercourse. In Gillick's rather insidious logic, little girls are sexually permissive *because of* sex education in schools. According to Gillick's anti-stance, it is right and indeed moral that sex education is not a part of a general or public curriculum. Where ignorance prevails, so the logic proceeds, then innocence around matters sexual should prevent and prohibit sexual exploration and activity. Thus for Gillick and co, sex education, rather than an issue for the State schools system, should be a parental prerogative, morally based on the marital reproductive family of

Victorian values. I suggest Gillick is 'the gendered enemy' since her reckoning of sexual intercourse and girls under 11 points more to issues around incest and questions of child sexual abuse than it does to sexual promiscuity as a result of sex education. However, a number of alarming alignments also emerge. In the logic of Gillick's anti-sex position, promiscuity is virtually equalized with girl child rape, where sex with children is figured as (hetero)sexual intercourse. Evidently for Gillick, rape is not a pressing issue for sex education. Nor is the material reality of sexual inexperience in girls under eleven, or adolescents of either sex.

In effect, Gillick's mixed-up message is one of past-age values enshrined in ethico-political closure. Gillick notwithstanding, however, in my own experience, working in a not very sought after urban comprehensive, the direction of sexual development apparently has as much if not more to do with adolescent peer-group ratings than any other given or imposed variables. Indeed, it is sexual *inexperience* that appears to dominate adolescent development in the school environment, evidently without respect to culture, class or gender background. It is therefore hardly surprising that in real terms, adolescents are rarely more sexually adventurous now than in recent generations. However, and quite apart from Gillick's inflammatory figures, sexuality is often a frontline for institutional regulation, as well as disciplinary measures in the education system. In addition, 'gender' has become something of a rallying point for women in education, through issues of anti-sexism and sexual politics.

Gender Trend

In debates within feminism it has also emerged that a politics modelled around universal sisterhood is based on uncritical formulations – not necessarily of woman as feminist, but necessarily woman as gendered subject (Wilkinson and Kitzinger, 1993). It has also been argued within feminism that such a politics fails to recognize the implicitly patriarchal bias in stabilizing questions of 'gender' on a heterosexual platform.

Current scholarship on gender often seems to blur the distinctions between sex, sexism, sexual discrimination and prejudice. But as Monique Wittig and others have argued, sex is a political category and not a biological one; the only place that sex is essential to gender is in the history of the biological sciences (Wittig, 1985). Nonetheless, a critique of gender can point away from biology and bodies, and biological materialism, towards language and its significations.

Raising gender as a problematic for feminism reminds me of a formula that Gayatri Spivak has used, where gender is formed by *internalized constraint, perceived as choice* (Spivak, 1992). In a not dissimilar view, Judith Butler argues that it is far from popular to think of gender formation as a series of generative prohibitions which regulate not only sexual behaviour, but sexual desire itself. In particular Butler cites prohibitions around homosexuality (Butler, 1990). These are very useful points because in contrast to Gillick's broadcast projections, it is apparent that in everyday life in school, adolescents are actually more likely to experience sex education through the prohibitions and pressures of peer-group dynamics, than from adult teachers of either sex. Sexual ignorance is usually a very embarrassing force at school, just as sexual humiliation, as a disciplinary model, is a very powerful weapon and can provide a retreat for sexual discrimination especially when used against young Black men.

I work part-time in an administration role at a local comprehensive school where the student population is composed of a mixture of African, Caribbean and Indian descent, as well as Black British students, with a minority, in this case, of white Europeans. Male students are the gender majority by about 60 per cent. On the teaching staff the gender ratio is round about equal, with Black staff in the minority at about 25 per cent again with a relative gender balance. All women staff are ostensibly straight (except me) – just to give a picture of the rich intercultural dynamics and possibilities in a local comprehensive in London. School policy is strong on gender as a political issue for classroom management as well as teaching and learning materials. There is also, for all staff, a contractual commitment to equal opportunities policy and issues of gender equality. In practice, however, 'gender' tends for the most part to be raised by women teachers as an issue for male students. It may be needless to say that disparities between policy and practice are regularly on the agenda of school staff meetings.

The following case in point illustrates how notions of sisterhood can change dramatically from one site of conflict to another. It turns on a misrecognition of sisterhood and some dynamics of racism between white women, in a link which appears at one level to bind anti-sexism to racialized imagery and another level, it raises complications around the misconception of sexism in the context of gender politics. The case is an account of an incident and the institutional response to it, involving a white female teacher and a Black male student. The incident became a disciplinary matter resulting in the student's temporary exclusion.

Rosita Burton,[10] one-time deputy leader of education in the Inner London Education Authority (ILEA), also at the Women's Studies Network Conference 1994, mentioned that in terms of statistics accounting for student exclusions, the highest number of cases involved disciplinary proceedings with Black male students around issues of sexism and sex-related circumstances. A recent national survey (July 95) from the Department for Education, however, fails to recognize or include issues of 'race' and racism, but not of gender, in identifying policies and procedures as well as legal obligations for the provision of education to compulsory age students (under 16) who have been excluded or expelled.

The incident: A situation occurred between the teacher and student where the Black student was heard to call the white teacher 'bitch'. The disciplinary issue was 'sexism' which sparked, to my mind, a surprising amount of indignation as well as 'sisterhood' among white women teachers in the staffroom. The incident, it seems, began as a friendly encounter, initiated by the teacher, during morning break. Apparently in a light-hearted manner the teacher was chit-chatting and teasing the boy about who he was currently going out with. It seems the teacher made a comment which was a bit too personal: I don't know what that was and it didn't seem to figure in the disciplinary proceedings. The student turned to leave and as he did he uttered 'bitch' – for which he was immediately held to account and an apology was demanded by the teacher concerned. The student refused to apologise and left the situation despite the teacher's insistence that he remain where he was. As a result, the incident was taken further and reported to the deputy head. An investigation ensued, in line with normal procedures, where the student was instructed to apologise to the teacher. Since the student continued to refuse to submit, he was consequently charged with Sexism: using sexist language against a female member of staff. In accordance with the school disciplinary code he was subsequently excluded for a period of three days.

Now apart from the charge of sexism or using sexist language, the use of expletives and prohibited slang as well as terms of abuse is an extremely common phenomena of adolescent behaviour. Perhaps because I knew the student, the incident struck a chord that left me thinking there was more to it than met the 'S' of Sexism. Ostensibly, refusing to submit an apology – lack of respect for authority, which is also not uncommon in adolescents of either sex. So 'bitch' is an expletive which conveys disrespect. I then decided to look up 'bitch' in a dictionary of slang, by way of some research on the question of the offence. The connotations of 'bitch' are apparently manifold in slang, most colloquially insinuating the gender opposite of bastard. In addition, however, 'bitch' has connotations of sexual teasing, indeed, to be specific, of 'prick teasing'. The teacher's case for sexism was that he had overstepped the mark when she was only teasing. Even flirting perhaps. That's harmless enough. Isn't it . . .

Signifying Racism

Stuart Hall (1995) sees 'race' as a political fiction with no scientific base and has recently argued that when body colour is used as a *racial* signifier, (as distinct from a political one), it mistakes how the discourse of racism is a *discursive regime* operating at the level of 'race' as a socially coded screen upon which race and culture can then project its messages. Hall talks about 'race' as a system of representations where *racism* speaks in many forms. In this case, the charge of sexism can be seen to signify racism as part of or embedded in disciplinary codification. It may also be argued that the teacher's case for sexism represents racism as a disciplinary strategy which, one way or another, is available to white women in connection with Black men. Quite apart from arguing that adolescence and sexual maturity are not equivalent in status, I would also ask, in this case, can the sexist threat be issued by a sexually inexperienced, or is it that the sexual threat was turned on him as such? The Black male student, in this case, I suggest, was as if a sitting duck – both available to the white woman teacher, but also a sexist threat. These are racist representations. This is not the same as saying it's all in her mind. Taking issue with the variables involved in the incident: her sexual maturity in relation to his sexual inexperience, his adolescence, as well as the power relations operating in this particular scenario, I think it is not unfair to argue that in this case, a gross injustice was done to the Black male student.

The teacher's case for sexism was that he had overstepped the mark when she was only teasing. Must I call this white woman sister? It is at this point, I would argue, that the politics of sisterhood collapses into collusion with institutional racism and significations of 'race'. But there are also questions which remain unresolved. For example, what was the white teacher playing at and what did she expect? In questions of feminism and sisterhood, it is not enough to (mis)recognize the project of anti-sexism as one bound by sexual opposition alone with 'women' as a generalized and prescriptive antidote to sexism in particular and 'men' in general. The retreat to such a charge, in this case, as bell hooks suggested, doesn't threaten cultural imperialism, but in fact supports it. Must I call this strategy sisterhood?

In conclusion . . .

I would like to reintroduce this case in point above as a material example of political resistance: resisting racist stereotypes and images of 'race' despite the overwhelming odds against the young Black man. For me the case exemplifies shifting positions in the subject of sexism – from the white woman 'sister' to the young Black man. In light of which the question of sisterhood takes on a different level. It is not enough to issue a charge of sexism on the grounds of gender positions: that is to say, that the woman is always already the object of sexist sentiment and sexism. In questions of feminist solidarity, it is thus a mistake to presume that sexism is always bound by a gender opposition tying sexist stereotyping to men, without considering racism and signifiers of 'race', as complicating variables between *white* women. If raising the question of sisterhood should provoke rhetorical closure, then bell hooks' enquiry 'Must I call every woman sister' must be one for the record of the Women's Studies Network.

Special thanks to Judy Young for her invaluable assistance at the Centre for Extra-Mural Studies.

Notes

1 Consciousness raising.
2 Editorial *Feminist Review*, **11**, 'Sexuality', 1982.

3 *Asian Times*, 4–10 October 1985.
4 *Deadly Silence*, 1991.
5 *Daily Telegraph*, editorial, 7 July 1995.
6 *Daily Express*, 7 July 1995.
7 On 5 July 1995 The Department of Education merged with The Department of Employment which then became The Department of Education and Employment.
8 Professor of Criminology, Middlesex University, London.
9 'The Time and the Place', Carlton TV, May 1995.
10 Rosita Burton chaired the paper by Barbara Watson Powell.

References

Asian Times, 4–10 October 1985.
BHAVNANI, K. and COULSON, M. (1985) *Feminist Review*, **23**, and in EVANS, M. (1994).
BUTLER, J. (1990) *Gender Trouble*, New York, Routledge.
Daily Express, 7 July 1995.
Daily Telegraph, Editorial, 7 July 1995.
Deadly Silence – black deaths in custody, (1991) London, Institute of Race Relations.
DEPARTMENT FOR EDUCATION (1995) *National Survey of Local Education Authorities' Policies and Procedures for the Identification of, and Provision for, Children who are out of School by Reason of Exclusion or Otherwise*, July.
EDITORIAL (1982) 'Sexuality', *Feminist Review*, **11**, London, Pluto Press.
EVANS, M. (1982) (Ed.) *The Woman Question*, Oxford, Fontana.
EVANS, M. (1994) *The Woman Question*, 2nd Edition, London, Fontana.
FANON, F. (1986) *Black Skin White Mask*, London, Pluto Press.
HALL, S. (1995) 'Working with Fanon', Conference presentation, ICA, May.
HOOKS, B. (1994) 'Beyond Western cultural imperialism', Presentation at WSN(UK) Portsmouth, July, (unpublished).
MILLETT, K. (1977) *Sexual Politics*, London, Virago.
RICHARDSON, D. and ROBINSON, V. (1994) 'Theorising women's studies, gender studies and masculinity: The politics of naming', *European Journal of Women's Studies*, **1**, pp. 11–28.
SIMMONDS, F. N. (1992) 'Difference, power and knowledge: Black women in academia', in HINDS, H., PHOENIX, A. and STACEY, J. (Eds) *Working Out*, London, The Falmer Press, pp. 51–61.
SPIVAK, G. (1992) Presentation at 'Gender and Colonialism' Conference, Galway. May.
SPIVAK, G. (1993) *Outside in the Teaching Machine*, London, Routledge.
WATSON POWELL, B. (1994) Presentation at 'Women's Studies Network (UK)' Conference, Portsmouth.

WILKINSON, S. and KITZINGER, C. (1993) *'Heterosexuality': A Feminism and Psychology Reader*, London, Sage.

WITTIG, M. (1985) 'The mark of gender', *Feminist Issues* **5**, 2, (Fall), pp. 3–12.

Part II

Re-sistering a Space to Speak

Chapter 4

Deconstructing Feminist Critiques of Radical Feminism

Diane Richardson

Introduction

Why is it still necessary to discuss two (or more) categories, radical feminism and, say, socialist feminism if, as McDowell and Pringle (1992, p. 127) suggest, we have reached a point where such distinctions are both unhelpful and inaccurate? To some it may seem ironic, perverse even, to want to do this in a historical context where we are busily deconstructing categories by which to classify, a little sad and naïve perhaps to want to continue to hold to a particular identity as a certain 'type' of feminist. Others may be dissuaded from looking at this question because of fears that it may inflame past divisions and political disagreements in an unhelpful and unproductive way. I can understand both of these positions. Nevertheless I think there are a number of important reasons for wanting to examine radical feminism as a category to which certain beliefs and practices are often imputed.

First, I am weary of being labelled a political dinosaur and/or a bad fairy of feminism, or at least on the basis of what is very often inaccurate and badly informed critique. This is nothing new, as radical feminism has historically tended to be seen as beyond the pale and regarded as extremist in popular accounts of feminism. However, in recent years it would seem that radical feminism has increasingly become a position against which a new generation of feminists and queers have rebelled. For example, a number of books which purport to represent 'new feminism' have attacked radical feminism (Rophie, 1994; Denfeld, 1995) or, alternatively, have largely ignored its contribution (Findlen, 1995). In this sense radical feminism is currently being constructed as an (oppositional) category both within feminism and outside it. Arguably, this process of typologizing 'radical feminism' is part of the context for understanding the maintenance of such a category and an associated identity.

At a wider level, discussion of how feminism, in this case radical feminism, is represented as extremely important for the development of theory – not only radical feminist theory more specifically, but feminist thinking more generally. In constructing contemporary feminist theory we are informed by versions of earlier feminist theories, which are often taken as a knowledge position from which to move forward. It is therefore important to look at how

45

radical feminism is represented as well as *whether* it is, as erasure can also have a significant influence on the development of social theory (Bhavnani, 1993).

This is also linked to developments in the marketing and publishing of feminism. Thus, for example, book series which are defined primarily by their theoretical orientation, such as Routledge's *Thinking Gender* series, are currently heavily dominated by postmodernist positions and for the most part do not include radical feminist perspectives. By failing to encompass a full range of feminist perspectives in their catalogue series and lists, publishers are thereby contributing to a form of censorship of radical feminism that, inevitably, will have a significant effect on the development of contemporary feminist theory and debates (Robinson and Richardson, 1996). Related to this, we also need to consider how the predominance (or otherwise) of different feminist theoretical approaches may influence how Women's Studies is becoming defined as a subject area.

Discussion of the ways in which radical feminism is represented is important, then, in terms of having a critical awareness of the ways in which feminist knowledge is constructed and the issues which are deemed to be socially and politically relevant for feminism in the 1990s. For example, if it is the case that there is a tendency towards rebelling against a (mythical) radical feminist position as a now defunct knowledge base and political standpoint, then there is a danger that issues of crucial and continuing importance to women's lives, which are associated with radical feminism, may also be disregarded or minimized. In this sense, it is important to ask what responses to radical feminism reveal about power relations within feminism and the interests they serve. What does it mean when certain strands of feminist thought and practice get discredited and/or ignored?

Related to these earlier points, this debate also has important implications for the Women's Studies classroom. The misrepresentation of radical feminism and the erasure of its influence in certain historical accounts of feminist theory and practice (see, for instance, Lovell, 1990) has resulted in radical feminism being very poorly understood by students, who frequently paraphrase the stereotypic assumptions contained in numerous texts. In the next section I critically examine some of these stereotypes and consider their wider implications for feminist theory and practice.

(Mis)representations

One of the most common representations of radical feminist thought is that it is essentialist. Although this can usually be interpreted as implying a reductive or deterministic theoretical approach, the term essentialist is not unproblematic. As Diana Fuss (1990) and others have pointed out, essentialism and social constructionism, with which it is usually contrasted, are relative and not absolute terms. This is reflected in the different meanings attached to the 'essentialism' imputed to radical feminism. In some accounts radical feminist theory is identified as locating women's oppression in biological differences between women and men which are relatively 'fixed' (Weedon, 1987; Abbot and Wallace, 1990). In some cases the emphasis is placed on how radical feminists have supposedly appealed to a concept of 'women's nature', more especially women's biological capacity for motherhood (Ussher, 1991).

It is thus suggested that through a positive affirmation of roles and attributes typically associated with women, those roles and attributes are essentialized as female. The label 'cultural feminism', itself highly controversial, has been used particularly in an American context and is often equated with both radical feminism and the concept of the 'essential female'. Lynne Segal, for example, defines cultural feminism as a new form of radical feminism which 'celebrates women's superior virtue and spirituality and decries "male" violence and technology' (Segal, 1987, p. 3). The American writer Alice Echols (1989), by contrast, uses the term cultural feminism to distance it from what she regards as 'real' radical feminism which, she claims, ceased to exist in the US after the mid-1970s. Cultural feminism is seen as not so much a new as an aberrant form of radical feminism, unworthy of the name: hence the need to apply a different label to writings of which Echols (and others) disapprove. In this sense cultural feminism is not a term that is largely chosen by (radical) feminists themselves, but rather one which has been applied by others to their writings. Elsewhere, the focus is on how radical feminists have essentialized understandings of the male, in particular through appealing to the notion of a specific male biology which produces differences in sexuality and aggression (Abbot and Wallace, 1990).

This portrayal of radical feminist analyses as biologically determinist is somewhat surprising, as within most radical feminists' accounts it is clear that sexuality and gender difference are understood to be socially constructed and the emphasis is on challenging and changing essentialist notions of male and female sexuality as fixed. Indeed, the essentialist/social constructionist debates during the 1980s were strongly influenced by contributions from radical and other feminists arguing a social constructionist position. The question this prompts therefore, and to which I shall return, is: Why does this occur? What motivates such misrepresentation? It is also somewhat ironic when we consider the charges levelled at radical feminism for *over* emphasizing the possibilities for change and the potential for transforming our sexual practices and ideas.

The characterization of radical feminism as essentialist takes other forms besides an inferred biological determinism. In some cases, the term essentialism is used to imply that radical feminism is based on a form of cultural determinism which relies on an essentialized notion of 'woman' as an oppressed category (Weedon, 1987) and/or a view of the role of culture as one where it interacts with male biology in some inevitable and immutable way (Segal, 1987). The influence of postmodernism on feminist thinking, as well as more broadly on social theorizing, has been particularly significant in the

47

classification of radical feminists as 'essentialists' in their use of concepts like 'patriarchy' and the (problematic) category 'woman'. Such classification usually takes the form of claiming that radical feminists conceptualize women's oppression as universal and unchanging, failing to acknowledge historical and cultural difference. To quote Valerie Bryson (1992), the radical feminist theory of patriarchy 'is said to be ahistorical and based on a "false universalism" that reflects only the experiences of white middle-class women and obscures the very different problems faced by working-class, black and Third World women' (Bryson, 1992, p. 186).

Again this is surprising for, as Walby (1990) and others have pointed out, typically radical feminist analyses are historically and socially sensitive, concerned with the ways in which patriarchy impacts on women in particular sociohistorical contexts. In addition, as I have argued elsewhere (Richardson, 1996a), radical feminists are concerned to examine the interrelationship between patriarchy and other unequal power relations such as class and racial inequalities. At a theoretical level, it is also important to disentangle the issue of the universalism of women's oppression from the theorization of difference between women, rather than, as is often the case, eliding from one to the other (Stacey, 1993). It is possible to offer generalized theories of oppression *and* theorize how and why those oppressive structures affect women differently according to, for instance, class, race, ethnicity and sexuality. Equally, we may develop theories which do not claim the universality of women's oppression and still ignore important differences between women. (A good deal of feminist work on women's role as carers within the family, for example, has implicitly accepted a heterosexual framework).

There are a number of possible consequences arising from this and other versions of radical feminism as 'essentialist'. For instance, such stereotyping may, in part, explain the perception of radical feminism as overly simplistic and lacking in theoretical analysis, especially of differences between women (Eisenstein, 1984). Implicit in what I am saying is that the use of the term essentialist is value laden and can be used in such a way as to discredit writers despite the fact that their work may have stressed the socially constructed nature of gender and sexuality. To quote Teresa de Lauretis:

> Doesn't the insistence on the 'essentialism' of cultural feminists reproduce and keep in the foreground an image of 'dominant' feminism that is at least reductive, at best tautological or superseded, and at worst not in our interests? Doesn't it feed the pernicious opposition of low versus high theory, a low-grade type of critical thinking (feminism) that is contrasted with the high-test theoretical grade of a poststructuralism from which some feminists would have been smart enough to learn? (de Lauretis, 1994, p. 11)

The imputation of essentialism can therefore serve as a mechanism of social control within feminist discourse, a means of undermining the legitimacy of, in this case, radical feminist theory. If this is the case it suggests that the determination to single out radical feminists as essentialist and the unwillingness to recognize their rejection of essentialist conceptions of gender, serves as more than a theoretical critique. Indeed, it is worth asking why other feminisms have not been 'accused' of essentialism when there is clearly a possibility of doing so, the classic example being the sex/gender distinction embraced by many earlier feminist accounts (Nicholson, 1994).

The view that radical feminist theory is theoretically underdeveloped compared to other forms of feminist analyses (see, for example, Snitow, Stansell and Thompson, 1984; Hollway, 1993) and 'behind the times' is one reinforced by the tendency of many writers to illustrate the 'radical feminist position' through citing a narrow range of sources. Typically, it is the work of American writers whose cited works are usually books first published in the 1970s and 1980s. Shulamith Firestone (1970), Kate Millet (1970), Susan Brownmiller (1976), Adrienne Rich (1977, 1980), Mary Daly (1978), Susan Griffin (1981) and Andrea Dworkin (1981) are classic examples of this. This limited representation of radical feminist thought is problematic, not only because it tends to disregard radical feminist critical writing over the last ten years or more, undermining the perceived relevance of radical feminism to contemporary debates, but also because it suggests a narrow range of radical feminist views whereas there are, in fact, a wide variety (Douglas, 1990). In addition to encouraging a view of radical feminism as unitary and monolithic, it also encourages the individualization of radical feminism through its association with the work of a handful of writers. Through this process of individualization, a diverse body of work under the heading 'radical feminist' can be dismissed.

The Anglo–American context of the debates around radical feminism is interesting in other ways. Not only is it largely American writers who are associated with radical feminism, marginalizing the work of European (including, in this case, French) radical feminists, but American critiques of radical feminism have also gained prominence in the UK. A feminist writer who attacks radical feminism and/or lesbian feminists can currently expect to be both published and noticed by the mainstream media. Writers such as Camille Paglia (1992) and Katie Roiphie (1994) are classic examples of this recent trend of commercial feminism whose success depends on playing the media game and distancing themselves from or attacking lesbian and/or radical feminists (Robinson and Richardson, 1996).

In addition to being defined in ways which allow some feminist writers, and Women's Studies students, to claim that radical feminism is out-dated and conceptually weak, radical feminism has also been branded in some accounts as 'oppressive' and 'anti-woman' (for example, Ussher, 1991; Denny, 1994). This takes a number of forms. In many cases it is linked with the construction of radical feminism as narrow and judgmental, oppression practised through what Camille Paglia and others have referred to as 'prescriptive' or 'politically correct Stalinist' feminism which dictates to women what they shall or shall not do. This view is particularly apparent in critiques of radical feminist accounts of sexuality, more especially of heterosexuality but also, in recent years, examinations of sexual practices between women, which suggest that radical feminists are moralistic adherents to some kind of social purity movement (Hunt, 1990).

This construction of radical feminists as the new moralists has led to their being blamed for sexual conservatism, or at least claims that radical feminism has aided the sexual oppression of women through being useful to the Right in their conservative sexual agenda (Rodgerson and Wilson, 1991; Segal, 1994). For instance, Sara Dunn (1995) claims that 'mainstream educational institutions, the judiciary, government and the media in Reagan's US all found radical feminism relatively easy to accommodate and marginalised other feminist voices' (Dunn, 1995, p. 46). This critical view of radical feminism as the 'acceptable' face of feminism is somewhat ironic when we consider that it is radical feminism that is most often defined as extreme by those on the Right *and* the Left, most especially in relation to critiques of heterosexuality and 'the family'. It is especially ironic in an American context where the strong tradition of liberal (heterosexual) feminism concerned with civil rights is surely that which has been most acceptable to the mainstream.

Even where radical feminist arguments have been adopted by the Right, leading to charges of collusion and alliance between radical feminists and the moral lobby, this does not mean that this is necessarily sought or desired by feminists. Indeed, in the UK radical feminists have strongly denied any willingness to work with the religious right-wing on the grounds of differing theoretical positions and political aims (Kelly, 1992), some claiming that this is a strategic misrepresentation by feminists who hold different positions to radical and revolutionary feminists on issues such as pornography (Jeffreys, 1990). Moreover, where feminist arguments are appropriated by the Right it is very often the ideas of nineteenth-century feminists, and the involvement of some of these feminists in social purity movements, which are drawn on. This is not so surprising when we consider the contradictions involved for the moral right, ardently pro-family, in supporting modern-day radical feminist thought in which a critical analysis of the heterosexual nuclear family as a key site of patriarchy is central (Luff, 1996).

The criticisms made about radical feminism and its so-called association with the right are interesting in the context of recent debates on the Left about social values. Weeks (1995), for instance, has suggested that in the past the broad Left has been fearful of the 'value question' and has been reluctant to engage in battles over 'moral' issues, in part because to raise certain issues was to risk being seen as siding with the Right, itself a reflection of the Right's hegemonic hold on such debates. Weeks is highly critical of this fearfulness in arguing that what the Left should be doing is claiming such concerns, a move with which some of 'New Labour' would appear to agree.

Related to this characterization of radical feminism as reactionary and/or 'moralistic', it is not uncommon for radical feminists to be described as 'anti-sex' or 'sex-negative' (Evans, 1993), usually in contrast to other 'pro-sex' (socialist) feminists and some queers. This kind of stereotyping has given rise to another version of radical feminism as oppressive to women: in this case the charge is that it has silenced some women and made others feel guilty about their sexual feelings and desires. This has been particularly evident in debates about S/M and butch/femme, as well as in recent work on theorizing heterosexuality (Segal, 1994). Indeed, some writers have suggested that women's involvement in S/M and butch/femme, rather than an outcome of the commercialization and cultural dominance of certain sections of gay male and lesbian culture, is a consequence of radical feminism itself (Woods, 1995, p. 54).

Implicit in suggestions such as these is that radical feminist discourses have had more 'disciplinary power' to influence women's lives than other perspectives. Along with many others (for example, Ramazanoglu, 1993), I would question whether radical feminist discourses on sexuality have this hegemonic hold. Furthermore, to interpret critiques of certain forms of sexuality as 'anti-sex' is fundamentally flawed. To be legitimately described as 'anti-sex' one would surely have to declare oneself opposed to all forms of sexual experience. In the early days of the women's liberation movement a few radical feminist writers did argue against any involvement in sexual relationships. In her early writings, the American writer Ti Grace Atkinson, for instance, argued that any sexual expression perpetuated women's domination by men and emphasized celibacy (Atkinson, 1974). Similarly, feminist arguments in favour of celibacy were a feature of nineteenth-century feminism both in Britain and the US (Jeffreys, 1985). Yet it is not these earlier feminists who, as Thompson (1991) suggests, could quite legitimately be described as 'anti-sex', that are being singled out. The accusations of being 'anti-sex' are directed at feminists who have critiqued certain expressions of sexuality, especially sexuality which is violent and disempowering.

The use of the terms 'pro-sex' and 'anti-sex' by critics of radical feminism are interesting in themselves. To claim that certain feminists are not 'pro-sex' is to construct sex (and good sex) in certain kinds of ways; it is to suggest that the kinds of 'sex' that so-called 'anti-sex' feminists defend (or at least do not critique) is not sex and that 'sex' is best equated with those activities which 'pro-sex' writers celebrate/defend in their work. It is also important to recognize that radical feminists are not alone in criticizing certain forms of sexual practice and desire; so have some so-called sex radicals, queers and socialist feminists (Rubin, 1984; Nichols, 1987; Smyth, 1992; Segal, 1994). A good example of this is the derogatory use of terms like 'vanilla' and 'politically correct' sex.

The view of radical feminism as oppressive is also reflected in the view put forward by certain writers that radical feminism is a discourse which turns women into victims with little control over their lives. By contrast, some critiques of radical feminism have claimed that it has done much to counter

51

images of women as victim (Alcoff, 1988). For example, Hester Eisenstein (1984, p. xix) criticized what she saw as 'cultural' feminism's 'pessimistic depiction of women as the innocent, passive, and powerless victims of male violence'. In a similar vein, Lynne Segal (1987, p. 70) claims that: 'The identification of sexuality as "the primary social sphere of male power" was . . . disastrous in my view, because it encouraged "all women" to identify themselves as the victims of "all men".'

This perspective of radical feminism as overemphasizing the role of coercive forces and denying women's agency is influenced in part by the association of radical feminism with essentialism and social/biological determinism. However, to argue that society is structured by male domination is not to suggest that such domination may not be successfully challenged. On the contrary, like other feminisms, radical feminism sees women as active agents in the processes of social change. Otherwise, what's the point! Nevertheless, this question of depicting women as victims is one that needs addressing and is relevant to the development of feminist theory in general. How do we draw attention to the 'atrocities committed against women, while at the same time asserting women's strength' (Thompson, 1991, p. 123)? Bearing this in mind, it is interesting to ask why it is the case that if, for instance, we draw attention to conditions of high unemployment, poverty and economic 'harsh truths' facing women, both locally and globally, we are unlikely to be seen as rendering women powerless and of portraying certain groups of women as victims of institutional realities. Related to this, it seems clear that the term 'victim' rather than being carefully defined and used as a critical concept is more often imputed to certain feminist positions and issues in a simplistic manner which serves to undermine their legitimacy and relevance (Tucker, 1995).

Bearing this in mind, it is important to recognize that for some the word 'victim' can, in certain contexts, be construed in a positive sense, as an acknowledgement that they were victims and in no way responsible for what happened to them. A clearer delineation of the term 'victim' also queries the equation of victim with passivity or lack of agency. To see oneself as not to blame for something is also to begin to be able to see oneself as someone who doesn't have to feel guilty or ashamed. It potentially allows us to make sense of our experience in an active and much more positive way. In this sense victim narratives can be transformative and part of a politicization process. Similarly, Plummer (1995), discussing feminist narratives of rape, points out that this process of identifying as a victim can be a crucial and necessary step in a woman seeing herself as a person with control over her responses to the victimization, as a survivor, a woman who is 'more determining than determined' (Plummer, 1995, p. 76). It is this kind of distinction that radical feminist accounts of especially sexual violence towards women have articulated (Kelly, 1988) and which allow for an acknowledgment of a felt sense of victimization alongside the possibility of this generating personal and political change.

Conclusion

In this chapter I have sought to highlight some of the main ways in which radical feminism has been (mis)represented and misunderstood. One of the more serious consequences of this is that radical feminist thought is frequently dismissed as out-dated, irrelevant or damaging, both within and outside the Women's Studies classroom. This is not to say that there should not be criticism of radical feminism, but rather that there should be accurate and effective criticism which enables conceptual clarification and theoretical development in place of what often appears to be little more than, at best, ill-informed criticism or, at worst, a deliberate side-swipe or put down.

This process of (mis)representation also raises the question of how our political identity and chosen theoretical perspective can interact with how we are positioned as 'other' (Richardson, 1996b). Radical feminism has often been perceived within popular culture as the extreme wing of feminism, with the conflation of radical feminism and lesbian feminism serving to strengthen the view of radical feminism as both unacceptable and 'other'. Is it also the case, as Teresa de Lauretis (1994) suggests, that what motivates the misrepresentation of radical feminism on the part of some feminists, in particular the imputation of essentialism, is the challenge it poses to the institution of heterosexuality?

As feminism develops and undergoes transformation we need to continue to ask what these shifts mean. What issues may lose their political significance and what issues may gain in perceived relevance? What are the wider implications of such shifts for women's lives, their experience of and resistance to varying forms of oppression and, related to this, for the teaching of Women's Studies? What kind of feminist narratives work to empower women? If we fail to represent some strands of feminist thought in feminist discourse, does this serve to delimit the possibilities for empowerment in ways we ought to be seriously considering?

References

ABBOT, P. and WALLACE, C. (1990) *An Introduction to Sociology: Feminist Perspectives*, London, Routledge.

ALCOFF, L. (1988) 'Cultural feminism versus post-structuralism: the identity crisis in feminist theory', *Signs: A Journal of Women in Culture and Society*, **13**, 3, pp. 405–36.

ATKINSON, T. G. (1974) *Amazon Odyssey*, New York, Links Books.

BHAVNANI, K. K. (1993) 'Talking Racism and the Editing of Women's Studies', in RICHARDSON, D. and ROBINSON, V. (Eds) *Introducing Women's Studies: Feminist Theory and Practice*, London, Macmillan.

BROWNMILLER, S. (1976) *Against Our Will*, Harmondsworth, Penguin Books.

BRYSON, V. (1992) *Feminist Political Theory: An Introduction*, Basingstoke and London, Macmillan.

DALY, M. (1978) *Gyn/Ecology: The Metaethics of Radical Feminism*, Boston, MA, Beacon Press.

DE LAURETIS, T. (1994) 'The essence of the triangle or, taking the risk of essentialism seriously: feminist theory in Italy, the US, and Britain', in SCHOR, N. and WEED, E. (Eds) *The essential difference*, Bloomington, IN, Indiana University Press.

DENFELD, R. (1995) *The New Victorians: A Young Woman's Challenge to the Old Feminist Order*, New York, Simon & Schuster.

DENNY, E. (1994) 'Liberation or oppression? radical feminism and in vitro fertilisation', *Sociology of Health and Illness: A Journal of Medical Sociology*, **16**, 1, pp. 62–80.

DOUGLAS, C. A. (1990) *Love and Politics: Radical Feminist and Lesbian Theories*, San Francisco, CA, ism Press.

DUNN, S. (1995) 'Teenage mutant big-haired feminists', *Diva*, June, pp. 46–7.

DWORKIN, A. (1981) *Pornography: Men Possessing Women*, London, The Women's Press.

ECHOLS, A. (1989) *Daring To Be Bad: Radical Feminism in America 1967–1975*, Minneapolis, MN, University of Minnesota Press.

EISENSTEIN, H. (1984) *Contemporary Feminist Thought*, London, Unwin.

EVANS, D. (1993) *Sexual Citizenship: The Material Construction of Sexualities*, London, Routledge.

FINDLEN, B. (Ed.) (1995) *Listen Up. Voices From The Next Feminist Generation*, Seattle Seal Press.

FIRESTONE, S. (1970) *The Dialectic of Sex: The Case for Feminist Revolution*, London, Jonathan Cape.

FUSS, D. (1990) *Essentially Speaking: Feminism, Nature and Difference*, London, Routledge.

GRIFFIN, S. (1981) *Pornography and Silence: Culture's Revenge Against Nature*, New York, Harper & Row.

HOLLWAY, W. (1993) 'Theorising heterosexuality: a response', *Feminism and Psychology*, **3**, 3, pp. 412–17.

HUNT, M. (1990) 'The de-eroticizaticn of women's liberation: social purity movements and the revolutionary feminism of Sheila Jeffreys', *Feminist Review*, **34**, pp. 23–46.

JEFFREYS, S. (1985) *The Spinster and Her Enemies: Feminism and Sexuality 1880–1930*, London, Pandora Press.

JEFFREYS, S. (1990) *Anticlimax: A Feminist Perspective on the Sexual Revolution*, London, The Women's Press.

KELLY, L. (1988) *Surviving Sexual Violence*, Oxford, Polity Press.

KELLY, L. (1992) 'Sex Exposed: Sexuality and the Pornography Debate', *Spare Rib*, **237**, August–September, pp. 19–20.

LOVELL, T. (Ed.) (1990) *British Feminist Theory*, Oxford, Blackwell.

LUFF, D. (1996) 'Sisters or Enemies: Women in the British Moral Lobby and Feminisms', unpublished PhD., University of Sheffield.

McDOWELL, L. and PRINGLE, R. (Eds) (1992) *Defining Women: Social Institutions and Gender Divisions*, Cambridge, Polity Press.

MILLETT, K. (1970) *Sexual Politics*, London, Abacus.

NICHOLS, M. (1987) 'Lesbian sexuality: issues and developing theory', in BOSTON LESBIAN PSYCHOLOGIES COLLECTIVE (Eds) *Lesbian Psychologies*, Chicago, University of Illinois Press.

NICHOLSON, L. (1994) 'Interpreting Gender Signs', *Journal of Women in Culture and Society*, **20**, 11, pp. 79–105.

PAGLIA, C. (1992) *Sex, Art and American Culture*, London and New York, Vintage Books.

PLUMMER, K. (1995) *Telling Sexual Stories: Power, Change and Social Worlds*, London, Routledge.

RAMAZANOGLU, C. (1993) 'Theorising heterosexuality: a response to Wendy Hollway', in WILKINSON, S. and KITZINGER, C. (Eds) *Heterosexuality: A Feminism and Psychology Reader*, London, Sage.

RICH, A. (1977) *Of Woman Born: Motherhood as Experience and Institution*, London, Virago.

RICH, A. (1980) 'Compulsory heterosexuality and lesbian existence', *Signs*, **5**, 4, pp. 631–60.

RICHARDSON, D. (1996a) 'Misguided, dangerous and wrong: on the maligning of radical feminism', in BELL, D. and KLEIN, R. (Eds) *Radically Speaking*, Melbourne, Spinifex Press.

RICHARDSON, D. (1996b) 'Representing other feminists', *Feminism and Psychology*, **6**, 2, pp. 192–196.

ROBINSON, V. and RICHARDSON, D. (1996) 'Repackaging women and feminism: taking the heat off patriarchy', in BELL, D. and KLEIN, R. (Eds) *Radically Speaking*, Melbourne, Spinifex Press.

RODGERSON, G. and WILSON, E. (Eds) (1991) *Pornography and Feminism by Feminists Against Censorship*, London, Lawrence & Wishart.

ROIPHIE, K. (1994) *The Morning After: Sex, Fear and Feminism*, London, Hamish Mamilton.

RUBIN, G. (1984) 'Thinking sex', in VANCE, C. S. (Ed.) *Pleasure and Danger: Exploring Female Sexuality*, London, Routledge & Kegan Paul.

SEGAL, L. (1987) *Is the Future Female? Troubled Thoughts on Contemporary Feminism*, London, Virago.

SEGAL, L. (1994) *Straight Sex: Rethinking the Politics of Pleasure*, London, Virago.

SMYTH, C. (1992) *Lesbians Talk Queer Notions*, London, Scarlet Press.

SNITOW, A., STANSELL, C. and THOMPSON, S. (Eds) (1984) *Desire: The Politics of Sexuality*, London, Virago.

STACEY, J. (1993) 'Untangling feminist theory', in RICHARDSON, D. and ROBINSON, V. (Eds) *Introducing Women's Studies: Feminist Theory and Practice*, London, Macmillan.

THOMPSON, D. (1991) *Reading Between the Lines: A Lesbian Feminist Critique of Feminist Accounts of Sexuality*, Sydney, Lesbian Studies and Research Group, The Gorgon's Head Press.

TUCKER, S. (1995) *Fighting Words. An Open Letter to Queers and Radicals*, London, Cassell.

USSHER, J. (1991) *Women's Madness: Misogyny or Mental Illness?* London, Harvester Wheatsheaf.

WALBY, S. (1990) *Theorising Patriarchy*, Oxford, Blackwell.

WEEDON, C. (1987) *Feminist Practice and Post-Structuralist Theory*, Oxford, Blackwell.

WEEKS, J. (1995) *Invented Moralities: Sexual Value in an Age of Uncertainty*, Oxford, Polity Press.

WOODS, C. (1995) *State of the Queer Nation. A Critique of Gay and Lesbian Politics in 1990s Britain*, London, Cassell.

Chapter 5

Reclaiming Sisterhood: Radical Feminism as an Antidote to Theoretical and Embodied Fragmentation of Women

Renate Klein and Susan Hawthorne

Introduction

Twenty-five years ago 'Sisterhood is Powerful' was an enspiriting call to action for feminists. Women called for an end to women's oppression wherever it occurred and horizontal distrust of women was challenged by the sense of community that sisterhood entailed. Without the theoretical construct of 'Sisterhood' – as well as the practical implications of acting upon that theory – feminism could not exist. 'Sisterhood' is the recognition of a sense of political commitment to women as a social group and that is perhaps the reason why only radical feminists have continued to champion the idea. 'Sisterhood' does not mean that every woman should like, love or commit herself to every other woman without critical engagement. What it *does* mean is that we respect, support and encourage women's efforts to achieve freedom globally, we work to further the interests of women as a diverse group and we work with women in our own fields when this is possible. Importantly, we are honestly and constructively critical of other women's theories and practices (rather than criticizing them on the basis of looks or how well they pronounce the words). Commonality of purpose, connection, communication and community are all ingredients of sisterhood. But what we hear these days, inside and out of academia, are differences of purpose (the impossibility of commonality), fragmentation (the impossibility of connection), solipsism or the fear of speaking from any position other than one's own (the impossibility of communication) and individualism (the impossibility of community).

Postmodernism, the forces of capitalism and international restructuring, as well as the advent of new global information systems have all played their part in this process. Of these, within the field of Women's Studies, postmodernism is having a devastating effect. With its promise of glory within the institution – a degree measured by its value as a luxury item comparable to gold (promotion and publication in prestigous 'Gender Studies' series) and not threatening the territory already held and fortified by the boys – postmodernism appeals to the career-girl feminist. It is also extremely diversionary: reading your way through Foucault, Lacan Derrida, Baudrillard and Deleuze takes a long time. During that time many other feminists lost their jobs for not being able – or refusing – to speak the language (to those of us from 'the colonies' this has a familiar ring). We are called 'essentialist' (but what can be more essentialist than the idea that Queer people are determined by their genes? and yet Queers are not derisively called essentialist). We are called universalist (for the crime of organizing politically across classes, cultures, sexualities and borders; for claiming 'Sisterhood' and for excluding the boys). These days we are even called 'pious'[1] for insisting that radical feminism has remained as radical as it was in the 1970s; prurient and priggish (Garner, 1995)[2] for saying that sexual harassment, pornography and violence have got to stop; and too radical for continuing to say all of the above even after we've reached the unhip old age of 40 or 50 (Denfeld, 1995)![3]

Postmodernism is a theory based on distancing and indifference.[4] For all their talk about difference (différance) postmodernists take very little notice of the *real* experiences of people. The author is dead (she died just at the moment when women, blacks, indigenous peoples, lesbians, the disabled and anyone else marginalized by the system were beginning to be heard).[5] The author not only died but became fragmented, atomized, unable to speak as part of a group. Only one perspective is possible: that of the individual. In 1995, long-time UK feminist Beatrix Campbell tells us that the Women's Liberation Movement ceased to exist at some stage in the late 1970s when a few small groups of women stopped making resolutions.[6] This, we believe, is an insult to all the women who have continued to fight for those same goals of Women's Liberation throughout the 1980s and 1990s, many of them the same women who were there in the 1970s.

Postmodern discourse has made a virtue out of not taking a stand. Radical feminism, on the other hand, emphasizes the importance of taking a stand. We dispute the accusation that this position limits us or means that we do not understand the complexities of the issues. As Michelle Cliff so ably states in her title, *Claiming an Identity they Taught me to Despise* (1980), taking a stance and claiming identities are critical political strategies. The alternative is silence and fragmentation. But if I am a postmodernist I cannot speak for anyone whose identity I don't share, designated by postmodernists as the 'Other'. Postmodernists capitalize the 'Other' to show their disconnection. Not me, says the postmodernist, I'm not one of them. The 'Other' is anyone outside the peer group of postmodernists: an Eurocentric lot on the whole. After all, you can't be a postmodernist if you haven't read Nietzsche, Freud, Lacan, Derrida, Foucault, Baudrillard, Deleuze, Bataille. Also an androcentric lot: you can't be a postmodernist if you haven't read Nietzsche, Freud, Lacan, Derrida, Foucault, Baudrillard, Deleuze, Bataille. You *can* be a postmodernist if you haven't read Kristeva, Cixous, Irigaray, Spivak; but if that's all you've read, you're probably not a proper postmodernist.

Postmodernists prevaricate about power and in all our reading of postmodern 'texts' there is a failure to locate and understand the mechanisms of power. There is a tendency to 'disengage' from reality, to be disinterested, indifferent. The failure to take a stand has something cowardly about it, as well as a denial of our human capacity for empathy, compassion and putting oneself in another's shoes.

The only people who can afford not to take a stand are those who belong to the dominant group, those with the power to make 'choices'. As white women we have the power to make a 'choice' on whether to take a stance on racism, but if we refuse to challenge racism when it arises we cease to be feminists (Thompson, 1994); if we were black[7] that 'choice' would not exist; as committed lesbian feminists we cannot 'choose' to pass as heterosexual in order to gain heterosexual privilege without compromising our politics; many of us cannot 'choose' the things that happen to our bodies such as disabilities – whether temporary or permanent, visible or invisible. The refusal to take a stand results in confusion, results in equating truth with dogma, results in a fragmentation of self that undermines the collectivity of our politics.

Fragmentation

The fragmentation of women's bodies and souls is mirrored in the increasing technologization of women's Selves in which women are conceptualized as body parts – as immune systems, wombs, eggs, hormones – that are declared 'diseased' and in need of fixing by different experts. Gena Corea's term 'The Mother Machine' – which she coined in 1985 for her groundbreaking exposé of new reproductive technologies such as in vitro fertilization (the test-tube technology IVF) – in the 1990s encompasses the control and fragmentation of women via the medicalization of their lives from girlhood to old age.

Here are some examples. Best documented in Germany (Schüssler and Bode, 1992), there is an increasing trend to urge girls from as young as seven years to see a gynaecologist once a year for a check-up including a vaginal examination. The girl gets a passbook with her picture and is encouraged to trust 'Uncle Doctor' as her friend. The subtext is that she learns early to see her 'reproductive' health separate from herself: not part and parcel of her physical and mental wellbeing but a separate entity which is quality-checked as to its later usefulness as breeder. She also learns that there are 'averages' and 'norms' of hormonal levels, breast sizes and shapes and menstrual flow. Should she not fit these norms she is told that there are drugs at hand, dispensed and monitored by the caring expert – the doctor (mostly male, few women seem to work in this field) – who also instils the expectation in the girl that vaginal penetration by a man is 'for her own good'.

Medicalization and heterosexuality made compulsory at an early age; moulded into docility and conditioned to the habit of drug-taking because she has been told that she is prone to disease and conceptualized as breeder-stroke-sex-object: how is a young woman to develop a sense of her Self in the face of this fragmentation? Importantly, she is meant to internalize that all of this is her *individual* problem which, as a consequence, sets her apart from her friends – her sisters – who are much prettier and much better and thus become her rivals. Haven't we heard this before? Women divided and at each other's throat: the best strategy that patriarchy has ever invented, now wrapped in new/old technospeak.[8]

At the other side of a woman's lifespan, the medical fragmentation has picked up speed as well. Hormone replacement therapy (HRT) promises to save mid-life from the 'death' of our ovaries, the impending crumbling of our brittle bones and our withering and shrinking vaginas. The idea is that once again diagnosed as a 'walking disease' and suffering from a 'sex-linked, female dominant, endocrine deficiency disease' – menopause in medicospeak by Sydney doctor Barry Wren – a woman will thankfully embrace one more magic pill that makes its promoters rich (Wren, quoted in Klein, 1992). Needless to say that not even the debatable promise of eternal youth that matters within a heterosexual framework is delivered: wrinkles do not go away but are only smoothed by water retention, hence the bloated, plastic look of some women who are on HRT. Moreover, HRT brings with it a long list of short- and long-term adverse effects ranging from increased blood pressure to worsened diabetic conditions and breast problems, many of which are counteracted with yet other drugs. Most worrying, however, is HRT's potential to cause addiction. While complaining about migraine, bloating, sore breasts, weight gain, thrush and even breast lumps – which brings with it the very real fear of the increased risk of breast cancer – women still say they feel 'happier' on HRT and state that they have an increased 'sense of wellbeing' (for details, see Klein and Dumble, 1994).

A variation on the hormone theme and older women is the recent 'success' of IVF pregnancies for women who are in their sixties by means of young and 'fresh' donor eggs and massive doses of hormones. Unlike the mainstream press and right-wing moralists who deliberated that this was 'bad' because a 60-year-old woman was too old to be a mother, the point radical feminists are making is that this technological 'miracle' reduces *two* women to body parts and puts their health and even their lives at risk: the young woman whose eggs are surgically aspirated after the administration of dangerous fertility hormones and the older woman who is pumped full of hormones to enable her to carry a pregnancy to term. Add to these ordeals cosmetic surgery which tucks and nips and augments and reduces and you end up with an alarming sense of alienation and destabilization[9] – and no need for joint action to resist such debilitating techno-solutions to the threat of expired 'use-by-date' which, in spite of the many feminist analyses of the 'Beauty Myth' during the last thirty years, continues to exert power and control over women (among others see Wolf, 1991).

The dissection-cum-fragmentation ideology also includes women who are too fertile or those 'undesirables' who should not procreate at all: the poor, the genetically 'inferior' – nowadays called 'carriers of genes for genetic diseases' in the benign language of the genetic engineers – and women belonging to unwanted ethnic minorities. This development is exemplified at its most women-hating and violent in the 'anti-pregnancy' vaccine, an immunological contraceptive currently in Phase II trials in India and under the auspices of the World Health Organization (Richter, 1993; Guymer, 1995; Richter, 1996). A woman is injected with the slightly altered pregnancy hormone HCG (human chorionic gonadotrophin) attached to a diphtheria or tetanus carrier. Her body starts to produce antibodies against this 'invasion' and when she gets pregnant these antibodies attack her own pregnancy, her own future child. Without even considering the debilitating and dangerous short- and long-term adverse effects on the woman's general health and the real possibility of triggering new autoimmune diseases, the technological 'feat' of turning a woman against herself – virtually by attacking herself – mirrors the destabilization of a woman's identity and further alienates women from our bodies – ourselves.

Add this to the aim of the international Genome Project which is to reduce us to our genes – first anatomy was our destiny (with compliments to Sigmund), then came the hormones and now we're told it's all in our genes – throw in the increasing pressure on women who intend to become pregnant to 'screen for perfection' before and during their pregnancies and you've got the perfected technological fix for the atomized postmodern era, where people are split into bits and pieces that are exchangeable. The cries in the wilderness of the women who had their Selves reduced to 'Mother Machines' – and who were badly hurt in the process – are muted and often suppressed. Again we're told it's for our own good and, moreover, that these technological fixes are 'choices'.[10] Radical feminists who do not quite see it this way are accused of 'victim feminism' and of denying women agency. The fact is that 'agency' and 'choice' are meaningless concepts when *all* options available amount to violations of a woman's Self. But it is the claim to an embodied Self – the interactive unity of 'body and soul' – that is most severely denounced by postmodernists. Real live people who value togetherness, joint actions and relationships threaten the powers that structure the Gene Age.

Cultural Betrayal and Unreal Lives

Ersatz experience, virtual realities, voyeurism (Hawthorne, 1990, 1994b)[11] all take precedence over real life and real women. Instead we are faced with an array of fantasies that bear little or no relation to personal and cultural history. An example from Australia exemplifies this fragmentation. The word lesbian is one of the most powerful words in the English language. It's a word that has been despised, has created shock and still evinces (silent) reactions of dismay. Lesbians thought that we were safe using this word, that it would not be appropriated. We now have to define ourselves as women-born lesbians[12] because some men who have decided they wish to join the underclass by becoming first artificial 'women' then 'lesbians' want to use our space: a space set up specifically for lesbians to enjoy. Perhaps you think we are being unfair to the transsexuals; but would you think us unfair if a white woman self-identified as Black somewhere after the age of 20 or 30? If she then wanted to attend an all-Black women's group to get support for her new-found identity, would you support her or would you support the Black women with a real personal and cultural history of being Black?[13] To present as 'women' or as 'lesbians' when one has the personal and cultural (we mean socially constructed) history of a man is a betrayal of women. Feminist ideals would be better served if the men who 'don't fit in' with masculine culture had the courage simply to behave differently. Changing one's genitals does not change, or even challenge, patriarchy. The lives/bodies of transsexuals, gender outlaws and lesbian boys are simply another example of disembodied fragmentation: yet another example of alienation from the project of being human – body/mind/heart/soul.

Taken in another direction, the fascination with avoiding confronting the needs of and violations of *real-life human beings*, in particular women – including working for social change – becomes the fantasy of the cyborg – a peculiar blend of human and machine. Donna Haraway writes (1991, p. 149): 'The cyborg is a matter of fiction and lived experience that changes what counts as women's experience in the late twentieth century.'

But the question is: whose experience? Will it change the experience of disabled women who struggle to survive in an ablist world? Of Black women who continue to be discriminated by racism? Haraway writes about 'pleasure in the confusion of boundaries' and the goal of a 'world without gender' (1991, p. 150). But our past experience (is it worth anything?) tells us that when the word 'gender' is used, women disappear; when the word 'queer' is used, lesbians disappear (Jeffreys, 1994). Androgyny proved not to be a useful concept for women (early recognized by Janice Raymond, 1975). As Haraway (1991) puts it 'a cyborg world is . . . about the final appropriation of women's bodies in a masculinist orgy of war' (p. 154) and 'Cyborg feminists have to argue that "we" do not want any more natural matrix of unity and that no construction is whole' (p. 157). So what do 'we' want? Haraway suggests that 'The cyborg is a kind of disassembled and reassembled, postmodern collective and personal self' (p. 163) and then further endorses the Age of Body Parts by proclaiming: 'Communications technologies and biotechnologies are the crucial tools recrafting our bodies' (p. 164). Equating communications technology and biotechnology reveals the crux of radical feminists' problem with Haraway's solution.[14] Such a claim can only be made by ignoring any bodily specificities, for example pain when you are cut in surgery. Cyborg feminism is a celebration of disembodiment in a grand way and, indeed, Haraway states further, 'It is time to write *The Death of the Clinic*. The clinic's methods required bodies and works; *we have text and surfaces*' (p. 245, our emphasis). The women in India whose 'texts and surfaces' hurt and bleed from injected anti-pregnancy vaccines and implanted contraceptive rods (as in Norplant) and, indeed, the women in IVF programmes whose ovaries just burst because of hyperstimulation through fertility drugs, might have a problem understanding this postmodern cyborg world. Apart from its total insensitivity to human suffering caused precisely by these technological feats, Donna Haraway cyborg fantasies, sadly, collude with those of the biotechnology establishment who for a long time have fantasized about the total manipulation of reproduction without women.[15]

A similar theoretical position underpins the possibilities represented by the virtual reality approach to bodies. Virtual bodies have no status in the real world, light cannot pass through a virtual body, can have no impact on it. Nor is the virtual body affected by heat, rain, the smell of a rose. It is a body without heart. This array of heartless bodies, disconnected from their own history, disconnected from a reality which although we might find hard to bear at times, nevertheless creates in us a memory: body memory that we can trace. Without this we are cut loose in the universe like the astronaut in *2001: A Space Odyssey*. Such freewheeling is not the basis of a political movement. Cut loose from our history we lose the gains we have made in the last couple of decades and the next generation of feminists would have to reinvent the wheel once again.

Likewise, in our use of language and naming we need to recognize the constituency of the class of women. Terms like 'Foucauldian feminist' cut us off from that constituency; terms like 'volatile bodies' lead us in the direction of atomization and fragmentation of political objectives and away from notions of solidarity and sisterhood.

Global Issues

Globally, the move away from real people – women, children and men – and division of the world's women into 'worthy breeders' and those that must be stopped multiplying is cruelly mirrored in the latest wave of the west's – and the so-called third world's élite's – fear of the dreaded ghost of overpopulation in poor countries and among the poor throughout the world. The need for population-control policies is seen as unavoidable by many including conservation groups such as the World Wildlife Fund and other environmental groups.

Unfortunately, since the 1994 United Nations International Conference on Population and Development in Cairo it can be said that feminists too – some feminists – support this goal. In fact, euphemistically speaking of 'empowerment' and giving women 'reproductive rights' and 'choices', part of the western women's health movement – heavily dominated by US groups such as the International Women's Health Coalition which in turn is heavily funded by the population-control establishment – have become key players in the population game. In preparation for Cairo, in 1993, 'The Women's Declaration on Population Policies' was launched by a group called Women's Voices '94 Alliance. It advocated a *feminist* population-control policy.

Question: is the rhetoric of 'empowerment' and women's reproductive 'rights' commensurate with the philosophical and political stance of feminism? Is the co-optation of feminist language feminism? Is the selling out of some women for the continued luxurious lifestyles of other women feminism?

Answer: Yes: only if you believe in 'choices' and rampant individualism; only if you advocate the 'feminist version' of the survival of the fittest; only if you have declared the theory and practice of the Women's Liberation Movement dead and no longer support the aim of creating social change for *all* women. No: if you continue to believe passionately that feminism in theory and practice is committed to eliminating hierarchies of oppression and to promoting women's health and bodily integrity. Integrity as wholeness that defies hierarchies of oppression and control by outside forces such as, for example, provider controlled contraceptives like long-acting Norplant and Depo Provera and the second-rate chemical abortifacient RU 486 rather than low-tech contraception in women's hands.[16]

Bodily Integrity

There are many different ways in which bodily integrity can be approached. In January 1995 in Melbourne an extraordinary experiment was started. It is the Performing Older Women's Circus or POW Circus. All the women in this circus are over 40 and none are professional performers. The trainers are also women over 40 who have been members of Melbourne's Women's Circus,[17] established in 1991 to teach circus skills to women who were victims of sexual assault. Both circuses have been great successes, but it is POW Circus that I want to focus on here. The reason: it is a fantastic example of 'Sisterhood' in action. Women aged between 40 and 65 learn a wide range of physical skills including trapeze, rope work, juggling, stilt-walking, clowning and an imaginative array of double and group balances.

In a three-tiered group balance it is necessary to have 'bases' and 'flyers' as well as those in the middle who perform both functions. The bases need to have strong backs, good knees and steadiness (they do not have to be heavy or large). The 'flyers' need to have balance, a lightness of approach (not necessarily the same thing as light in weight) and no fear of heights. The second tier of women need to be able to combine these two approaches: steadiness and lightness of approach; strength and balance. A group balance of this kind will usually involve around 10 women. Concentration is essential, as is trust and respect for the person you are supporting or standing on. In short: Sisterhood. If one woman is unsteady the whole structure collapses. When this happens women can be hurt. The same is true for the practice of Sisterhood: the success of the enterprise depends on all of us, no matter what our role is in the overall structure of things. We are all responsible for the success of the final structure, its balance, its imaginative qualities, its steadiness, its equitable sharing of load, its consideration of individual limits. We are all standing on the shoulders or backs of women who have gone before us. And we ourselves are models and supports for the women who come after us. We need to respect those women and trust them. Trust and respect beget trust and respect. We need that concentration, commonality of purpose, connectivity, communication and sense of community if we are to forge new shapes, new structures and imaginative ways of living. POW Circus is successful and inspiring because we all need one another's support to do the things we do. We do not necessarily all like one another, but we each know that our own welfare is linked to the group's welfare.

Wild Politics

POW Circus is an example of Wild[18] Politics.[19] It is a politics that takes a clear radical feminist stance across a range of issues including economics, people, poetry and the land. Wild Politics challenges the New Intellectual World Order of Poststructuralism, Postcolonialism, Postfeminism. It challenges the enclosure policies of all kinds, whether it is the fencing in by all these Posts – or whether it be the fencing in and taming of land. The capitalist and patriarchal enclosure movement is about controlling the ideas of uppity wild people, among them women, indigenous peoples, the disabled, lesbians and anyone marginalized by limited access to the resources of wealth, power and information.

Wild Politics is a metaphor based on the notion of wild types, a term used in genetics that identifies unregulated genetic structures. Wild types occur in all living organisms and are not the result of human interference through breeding or hybridization. Wild types are the source of genetic diversity and critical to the continuing biological diversity of the planet. Wild seeds are evidence of plant diversity in a particular environment. They indicate a healthy ecosystem that returns as much as it gives.

Wild reproduction, reproduction without the interference of technologies that control women becomes rarer as the pressures to push coercive population-control policies on women are presented as 'empowerment'. All these procedures control who is born and add value to the resulting child through R&D, labour and technical interference. The intended result is that no wild children – no children with visible or hidden disabilities – be born. Wild reproduction means not knowing and refusing to know the sex or genetic characteristics of a child. Wild reproduction allows for wild types.

Wild Politics embraces a wild and radical philosophy and refuses co-option into patriarchal and capitalist institutions as outlined above. It resists the backlash and the silencing of wild women in every quarter, including in academia. It resists the eradication of meaning through the creation of stories and taking political stances seriously. Wild Politics is life affirming. It values diversity, self-reliance, creativity and the sustaining of cultural traditions that support equality. Wild Politics is rooted in the earth and in knowledge of local

65

conditions and environments and encourages respect for specificities. Wild Politics encourages productivity and exchange that gives as much (or more) as it takes and is not based on the growth and accumulation of property or power. Wild Politics is a politics of joy.[20]

Twenty-five years after the first call for sisterhood and in the face of paralysing fragmentation, we strongly believe that sisterhood can still be powerful and that there is indeed a new surge of interest in a radical feminist politics that is connected to the daily realities of the lives of women internationally. For those of us in the west who are in privileged positions, this renewed focus on wholeness as a spiritual concept avoids the mind/body split and keeps us from going insane. For other women such as poor women in western countries, ethnic minorities as well as the majority of women in the so-called Third World, the resistance to fragmentation and dystopian individualism is, quite simply, a matter of survival. The last decade has made women poorer, more prone to homelessness and forced migration. It has increased the number of girls and women subjected to male violence, trafficking and prostitution and a plethora of medical crimes. But what is growing too is renewed anger and the building of international networks to resist this oppression of many faces. So, while we cannot promise heaven on earth we nevertheless highly commend radical feminism. We are the women you have been warned against and we are taking a stand as sisters, as colleagues, as lovers, as friends. Above all we are passionate, proud and persistent – and we won't go away.

Notes

1 Reminded after her talk at the Desperately Seeking Sisterhood Conference (1995) from which this book results, by one of us (RK) that radical feminism was well and alive in the 1990s, Beatrix Campbell retorted by stating that such thinking was 'pious'.

2 In Australia, Helen Garner's non-fiction book, *The First Stone*, caused a public storm when it was published in early 1995. The book tells the story of two young students from the University of Melbourne who alleged they were sexually harassed by the Master of the College with the result that he lost his job. Helen Garner, a well-known novelist who is in her fifties, bemoaned that feminism had turned young women into 'icy cold' beings. Why couldn't they just talk it through – or kick him in the balls – rather than pursuing their rightful legal channels! Her book was hailed as 'insightful', 'brave' and a reasonable antidote to the radical fringe (meaning, the liberal feminists who keep pushing for law reforms!) and sold 50,000 copies in the first two weeks. It was as if the naming of sexual harassment (as started by Catharine McKinnon in 1979) and countless feminists' hard work to establish policies and laws had never happened.

3 US writer Rene Denfeld's *The New Victorians* caused a similar storm shortly after Garner's book. Yet her message is precisely the reverse to Garner's: 'Fifty-somethings' (a term that has acquired prominence since this debate) are obsessed with rape and man-bashing and have become bogged down in extreme moral crusades, whereas young women – Denfeld's generation – believe strongly in equal rights and reclaim feminism as equal rights feminism (which logically includes laws against sexual harassment).

4 For an analysis of indifference, see Susan Hawthorne, 1996.

5 See Barbara Christian's landmark essay on this 'coincidence', 'The race for theory' (1987).

6 From Beatrix Campbell's talk at Desperately Seeking Sisterhood Conference, see also Footnote 1. Her comments pertain to the fact that Women's Liberation meetings ceased to make singular-stand point resolutions. This also happened in Australia where, in fact, in Melbourne, in September 1976, the Women's Liberation Movement was formally dissolved at one such meeting. This does not mean, however, that the *movement* for Women's Liberation ceased (see Hawthorne, 1994a).

7 Black has different meanings in many places. In Australia it usually means Aboriginal; in the UK it is used as a political category for all non-white peoples, although it sometimes refers to African and Afro–Caribbean peoples; in the US it usually means Afro–American. 'Black' here is meant in a non-limiting sense and particularly as it applies to peoples oppressed by non-blacks. Clearly there are prejudices based on ethnicity and racism between peoples of the same colour. The argument applies equally to the relations between peoples where one group is *systematically* and *structurally* discriminated against.

8 For more thoughts on patriarchal divide-and-conquer tactics – and women's collusion – see Klein (1989a).

9 Unlike ex-Marxist feminists turned postmodernist, we do not see 'destabilization' as either exciting or promising for women. See, for instance, *Destabilising Theory* (1992) edited by Michele Barrett and Anne Phillips which was written 'to draw attention to the need to "destabilise" the founding assumptions of modern theory' (p. 1) and 'to highlight and debate the gulf between feminist theory of the 1970s and the 1990s' (p. 2).

10 For further information on the brutality of reproductive technology see Klein (1989b) and Rowland (1992).

11 *Mutant Message Downunder* by US author Marlo Morgan in which she claims to have discovered the 'real' people – a secret tribe of Australian Aborigines with whom she went 'walkabout' – is an extraordinary case of spiritual voyeurism – indeed theft (see Hawthorne, 1994b for a detailed analysis).

12 See *Newsletter* Lesbian Space Project, Sydney (November 1994) and Announcement for Lesbian Confest in Alice Springs (October 1995).

13 Indeed, this happened recently in Australia where a white man, self-identified as Koorie (Aboriginal), was expelled from the group he worked for. Despite his deep wish to be part of this group but without a confirmable personal and cultural history of Aboriginality, he was not accepted. No one uttered a word in his defence and yet many lesbians defend transsexual men who are in exactly the same political position as this white man.

14 Indeed, Haraway reaffirms this position when she states (1995, p. xix): 'Cyborgs do not stay still. Already in the few decades that they have existed, they have mutated, in fact and fiction, into second order entities like genomic and electronic databases and other denizens of the zone called cyberspace.'

15 For further thoughts on the nexus between reproductive medicine, genetic engineering and postmodernism, see Klein (1996).

16 See Klein, 1995a and 1995b for further discussion of feminism and population control.

17 For further information on the history of the Women's Circus see *The Women's Circus: Leaping Off the Edge* (1996) Melbourne: Spinifex Press.

18 Wild Politics is based on a metaphor of wild types in seeds. Its starting point is an image of diversity around which to organize. By 'wild' I do not mean the individualized and depoliticized personal solutions that are offered in recent New Age works, in particular those by Clarissa Pinkola Estes and Robert Bly, as discussed by Rosemary Du Plessis (1995).

19 An earlier version of this text was written at the People's Perspectives on 'Population' conference held in Comilla, Bangladesh, 12–15 December 1993 and published in *People's Perspectives* (1993). Many thanks to all the women at the conference whose ideas and discussions were central to the writing of this piece.

20 An extended version of Wild Politics has been published in Hawthorne (1995) and further extended in Hawthorne (1996).

References

BARRETT, MICHELLE and PHILLIPS, ANNE (1992) *Destabilising Theory: Contemporary Feminist Debates*, Cambridge, Polity Press.

CHRISTIAN, BARBARA (1987) 'The race for theory', in *Cultural Critique*, 6, Spring, pp. 335–45.

CLIFF, MICHELLE (1980) *Claiming an Identity they Taught me to Despise*, Watertown MA, Persphone Press.

COREA, GENA (1985) *The Mother Machine*, New York and San Francisco, CA, Harper & Row.

DENFELD, RENE (1995) *The New Victorians*, New York, Warner Books; Sydney, Allen & Unwin.

DU PLESSIS, ROSEMARY (1995) 'Of wild women and hairy men', in *Women's Studies Association (NZ) Conference Papers*, Wellington, August 1994, pp. 227–32.

GARNER, HELEN (1995) *The First Stone*, Sydney, Picador.

GUYMER, LAUREL (1995) 'Vaccination against pregnancy: a new contraceptive choice for women or a tool for population control?' *FINRRAGE (Australia) Newsletter*, November 1995, pp. 2–3.

HARAWAY, DONNA (1991) 'A cyborg manifesto', in *Simians, Cyborgs, and Women: The Reinvention of Nature*, New York and London, Routledge, pp. 149–81.

HARAWAY, DONNA (1995) 'Cyborgs and symbionts: living together in the new world order', in GRAY, CHRIS HABLES (Ed.) *The Cyborg Handbook*, London and New York, Routledge, pp. xi–xx.

HAWTHORNE, SUSAN (1990) 'The politics of the exotic: the paradox of cultural voyeurism', *NWSA Journal*, **1**, 3, pp. 617–29.

HAWTHORNE, SUSAN (1993) 'Wild Politics', in *People's Perspectives*, Nos 4 and 5, Dhaka, UBINIG, pp. 26–7.

HAWTHORNE, SUSAN (1994a) 'A history of the contemporary women's movement', in HAWTHORNE, SUSAN and KLEIN, RENATE (Eds) *Australia for Women. Travel and Culture*, Melbourne, Spinifex Press; New York, The Feminist Press; Munich, Frauenoffensive, pp. 92–8.

HAWTHORNE, SUSAN (1994b) 'A case of spiritual voyeurism. Review of *Mutant Message Downunder* by Marlo Morgan', *Feminist Bookstore News*, **17**, 4, December, pp. 31, 33.

HAWTHORNE, SUSAN (1995) *Broadsheet*, 205, Autumn/Ngahuru, pp. 52–3.

HAWTHORNE, SUSAN (1996) 'From theories of indifference to a wild politics', in BELL, DIANE and KLEIN, RENATE (Eds) *Radically Speaking: Feminism Reclaimed*, Melbourne, Spinifex Press; London, Zed Books.

JEFFREYS, SHEILA (1994) 'The queer disappearance of lesbians', *Women's Studies International Forum*, **17**, 5, pp. 459–72.

KLEIN, RENATE (1989a) 'Sisterhood is still powerful', *Girls Own Annual, Women's Studies Summer Institute Magazine*, Geelong, Deakin University, pp. 27–33.

KLEIN, RENATE (1989b) *Infertility: Women Speak Out about their Experiences with Reproductive Medicine*, London, Pandora Press (now distributed by Spinifex Press, Melbourne).

KLEIN, RENATE (1992) 'The unethics of hormone replacement therapy', *Bioethics News*, **11**, 3, Monash University, pp. 24–37.

KLEIN, RENATE (1995a) 'Reflections on Cairo: empowerment rhetoric – but who will pay the price?', *Feminist Forum in Women's Studies International Forum*, **18**, 4, pp. ii–v.

KLEIN, RENATE (1995b) ' "Empowerment for women": the population controllers' latest Anti-feminist rhetoric or "one can't save the earth by killing women" ', *FINRRAGE (Australia) Newsletter*, November 1995, pp. 16–20.

KLEIN, RENATE (1996) '(Dead) bodies floating in cyberspace: post-modernism and the dismemberment of women', in BELL, DIANE and KLEIN, RENATE (Eds) *Radically Speaking: Feminism Reclaimed*, Melbourne, Spinifex Press; London, Zed Books.

KLEIN, RENATE and DUMBLE, LYNETTE (1994) 'Disempowering mid-life women: the science and politics of hormone replacement therapy (HRT)', *Women's Studies International Forum*, **17**, 4, pp. 327–43.

McKINNON, CATHARINE (1979) *Sexual Harassment of Working Women*, New Haven, CT, Yale University Press.

RAYMOND, JANICE (1975) 'The illusion of androgyny', *Quest*, **2**, 1.

RICHTER, JUDITH (1993) *Vaccination Against Pregnancy: Miracle or Menace?* Amsterdam, Health Action International and BUKO Pharma-Kampagne.

RICHTER, JUDITH (1996) *Vaccination Against Pregnancy: Miracle or Menace?* 2nd edn., London, Zed Books; Melbourne, Spinifex Press.

ROWLAND, ROBYN (1992) *Living Laboratories*, Sydney, PanMacmillan; Bloomington, IN, Indiana University Press (now distributed by Spinifex Press, Melbourne).

SCHÜSSLER, MARINA and BODE, KATHRIN (1992) *Geprüfte Mädchen– Ganze Frauen. Zur Normierung der Mädchen in der Kindergynäkologie*, Zürich and Dortmund, eFeF Verlag.

THOMPSON, DENISE (1994) 'Feminism and racism', unpublished paper presented at Australian Women's Studies Association Conference, Deakin University, December 1995.

WOLF, NAOMI (1991) *The Beauty Myth*, New York, Anchor/Doubleday; London, Vintage.

The Women's Circus: Leaping Off the Edge (1996) Melbourne, Spinifex Press.

Chapter 6

RU 486: A New Reproductive Technology in the Mainstream

Sharon Tabberer

Introduction

The abortion pill RU 486[1] occupies a unique position in feminist discourse as a reproductive technology used for abortion. Its existence raises issues for feminists in relation to choice and access to abortion, as well as with respect to the use of reproductive technologies and their acceptability to women. When licensed for use in the UK in 1991, concerns were raised by some feminists about the implications for women's health. However, RU 486 was welcomed by pro-choice groups who saw it as a way of both increasing access to abortion and offering a choice of method. These two views were both developed from feminist concerns about women's health, but they had different historical and ideological perceptions of where the problem lay. For pro-choice groups the problem with provision was developed out of the 1967 Abortion Act; for those sceptical about the benefits of a reproductive technology for women the problem was with the technology itself. These groups were influential in the UK debate about RU 486 and the issues raised by them framed both how the debate was constructed and the eventual licensing of RU 486. My concern is therefore with the influence of these two groups on the UK debate about RU 486 and the consequences of this debate on the choices available to women. To understand the positions adopted by the two groups I first examine their historical and ideological antecedents; then look at the UK debate on RU 486 and the use of this technology within the contemporary NHS.

The UK Pro-choice Movement

The UK pro-choice movement was born out of the 1967 Abortion Act which legalized abortion while restricting both access and choice. Abortion was legalized with the agreement of two doctors prior to any operation, hence limiting choice as doctors were to be the gatekeepers to the service; while access was limited due to the lack of provision (Pfeffer, 1987) as doctors and nurses were afforded the option of not being involved. One of the first consequences of the Act was therefore 'geographical differences in women's access to a sympathetic, prompt abortion service' (Hadley, 1994). The haphazard and *ad hoc* development of services has been examined in respect to infertility treatments (Spallone, 1994); yet the impact of this uneven concentration of services for abortion provision is less often acknowledged. Women's choice and access were restricted within the terms of the Act. This, coupled with subsequent and regular attacks on legalized abortion, led to a post-1967 Abortion movement based on a woman's right to choose, resulting in a concentration on the role of the medical profession in allowing abortion and creating a feminist position on abortion that was uncritical of the actual choices available. In the debate on RU 486 this notion of choice was crucial to its acceptance within the UK women's health movement and is in marked contrast to the suspicion with which RU 486 was greeted with other groups concerned with women's health.

Feminism and Choice

Many writers approaching reproductive health from a feminist position have been sceptical about the idea that reproductive technologies – including those available for terminations – represent choice. Writers such as MacKinnon (1987), and Himmelweit (1988), have pointed to the legal, social and economic constraints on the exercise of choice. They have also argued that the full exercise of choice would involve a transformation of the social organization of motherhood and the eradication of ideas that link female fulfilment to birthgiving. Such constraints have particular purchase for women with disabilities or from minority ethnic backgrounds, as Farrant (1985), and Wajcman (1991), have shown. In the absence of such transformation, it is argued, the choice presented by medically controlled abortion is a superficial one. Yet it is on this choice that some feminist pro-choice campaigners have focused.

One group of feminists has taken particular issue with the development of RU 486 as a reproductive choice. The Feminist International Network of Resistance to Reproductive and Genetic Engineering (FINRRAGE) rejected reproductive technologies as being potentially dangerous for women and advise against their use. They published 'RU 486 Misconceptions, Myths and Morals' in 1991 as a 'critical, professional and feminist response to many issues raised by the research and development on RU 486/PG' (Klein, Raymond and Dumble, 1991). Through analysis of the scientific research on RU 486 the authors questioned the safety of the drug and argued for a feminist response to this reproductive technology which would take a critical view of scientific interventions of this type. The feminists involved in this critical investigation of reproductive science worked across national boundaries examining the development of treatments for women within the international science context rather than as institutional responses to individual or community demands or problems.

These critiques developed previous work which had located the medical profession as one of the pinions of patriarchy with specific consequences both for women as a group and for the individual woman in the medical environment (Oakley, 1976; Kitzinger and Davies, 1978). They argued that while developed under the guise of a beneficent patriarchal science, the covert aim of these technologies was the control of reproduction and the relegation of women to futures with 'reproductive brothels' (Corea, 1985). Technology was the latest and most imperative tool of social control working against women within society.

> But women are again assuming a benign medicine. The medical profession in fact fails to differentiate between research to aid infertility and research to change and control conception and the genetic balance. It is again using women's bodies for experimentation and using their need (social or otherwise) to have babies. Women, motivated by an intense life crisis over infertility, are manipulated by this situation into full and total support of any technique that will produce those desired children, without considering the implications of doing so for women as a social group (Rowland, 1985).

The criticisms made subsequently of the FINRRAGE position emphasized the role of the individual woman as an active participant within the medical environment, a participant exercising choice. Naomi Pfeffer (1985) argued that by emphasizing the political nature of the technologies the FINRRAGE feminists ignored the experiences of those women who want to engage with them. Michelle Stanworth (1987) pointed out that while some technologies may be harmful for women, others may have their uses. The rejection of all technologies may not be beneficial to women as not all women view their relationship with technology as problematical. As Oakley (1993) argued, women are an unhomogenous group with no one opinion. In a conference organized by the International Planned Parenthood Federation, Pro Family and the Birth Control Trust in 1992, Marge Berer developed the argument against the FINRRAGE position in the context of RU 486. She argued that existing abortion technologies are not without their dangers or difficulties and to reject RU 486 in favour of them would not be appropriate. RU 486 was therefore integrated into the wider debate about abortion access and choice.

Interestingly, these writers are based in the UK, where notions of choice with respect to reproductive processes have become part of the vocabulary of women's health activism. It is therefore not surprising that the concerns raised by FINRRAGE within an international context found difficulty in gaining credence within the UK pro-choice lobby.

Sharon Tabberer

The UK Debate on RU 486 and the Expansion of Choice

Subsequent to the licensing of RU 486 in France, stories began appearing in the UK press about the drug. These articles were prompted by a conference organized by the Birth Control Trust, a charity committed to the development of 'reproductive choice'. The conference, called 'The Abortion Pill widening the choice for women', brought together eminent UK gynaecologists with reputations in developing new methods of abortion, women involved in campaigning for reproductive choice and French scientists with experience of the drug. Thus the campaign for RU 486 to be licensed was not only located within discourses around a woman's right to choose, but was also connected with the development of medical science. Dilys Cossey, chairwoman of the Birth Control Trust, was quoted in *The Times* of 28 October:

> RU 486 is of immense potential benefit for unwillingly pregnant women, but its future in the UK hangs in the balance because of the anti-choice lobby who have made abortion a political issue. We want to ensure that the barriers of fear, ignorance and prejudice put up by this lobby are breached and that the drug is eventually available for those women who choose to use it. (*The Times*, 28 October 1989)

The conference aimed to convince the UK government that the introduction of RU 486 to the UK was a medical and reproductive rights' issue that should not be influenced by political concern. This emphasis on the expansion of choice legitimized the licensing of RU 486 as a women's rights' issue compatible with the rhetoric of consumerism which was establishing itself within the wider NHS at this time (Winkler, 1985). Choice became associated with making an informed decision based on a number of options rather than the right to an abortion on demand. Any selection would still be policed by the medical profession.

When RU 486 was licensed for use in the UK in July 1991, its availability was restricted through strict controls on its use. These requirements were in response to concerns raised by the anti-abortion movement, particularly those aimed at RU 486 by FINRRAGE members such as Renate Klein who spoke at an anti-abortion rally on issues about RU 486 and women's health during this period. By applying strict controls to the administration of the drug, the Department of Health sought to minimize any backlash against themselves either with respect to women's health or any accusations about the brokering of abortion. Notably, the licensing requirements put on RU 486 also succeeded in limiting choice as they required a lot of time and determination on the part of the woman. For example, the treatment required two visits to hospital for tablets with a follow-up and the usual visits required to access the system. In the case of the private sector, clinics were also required to inform the woman's general practitioner (GP). It is estimated that a third of women don't opt for RU 486 for this reason alone. These factors, coupled with the traditional problems with securing an NHS abortion including the attitudes of doctors, ensured that not only was RU 486 not an easy option for hospitals to provide, but also that it was not an easy choice to make.

Abortion within the Contemporary NHS

Today RU 486 is available in approximately half the NHS hospitals and a quarter of the private clinics that offer abortion.[2] While the attempts by FINRRAGE to raise issues about the safety of the drug were dealt with through the licensing requirements, the success of those women's health activists who worked for licensing as an expansion of choice was also limited. The reasons for this can be found in the post-1967 UK abortion provision, especially the concentration of the campaign on developing choice within a medical context that was traditionally dependent on the largesse of individual doctors to provide a service. For example, RU 486 has not changed the attitudes of those doctors who refuse to do abortions. It has also been problematized as a treatment by some GPs and surgeons who consider it less effective than a surgical termination. Where medical termination units using RU 486 have been set up, they are largely the responsibility of a consultant with an interest in terminations and are run by specialized nursing staff. Although these units are thought to provide a good service, offering a choice of methods, the impetus for them has come from changes in health policy rather than concerns about women's health issues.

With the White Paper 'Working for Patients' the government introduced issues of accountability into the NHS. These have had an impact on the abortion debate within the UK which has repercussions for access and choice as district health authorities and hospital management seek to provide effective services for the minimum cost. As one doctor commented during a conference on abortion in 1994:

> In the past the provision of services was dependent upon the willingness of local gynaecologists and usually had little relation to district need. Often this was purely a surgical service without counselling, contraceptive advice or follow up. Now, the internal market has given the purchasers power to specify the services required which they may purchase from local NHS gynaecologists, NHS gynaecologists in other districts or from non-NHS providers. (Catherine Patterson, 1994)

While such changes have the potential to develop the choices open to women, these choices are clearly limited by the decisions of the administrators and the doctors providing the service. A further development that is likely to have an impact on the provision of abortions, and which could also have repercussions for the methods available to women, is the devolution of abortion-contracting to GP fund holders. This imminent development will further localize the abortion debate and could have consequences for the individual woman seeking an abortion.[3]

Conclusion

The post-1967 UK abortion movement was based on the premise of abortion on demand, the main focus of which was a 'woman's right to choose'. While RU 486 was welcomed for its expansion of choice, the limits of that choice have been recognized. As Ahmad (1993) has noted in terms of race and Himmelweit (1988) in respect of disability, choices may cease to be available or are made on terms set by the wider society. In the debate over RU 486 it is clear that this rhetoric of choice was used by interested groups without reference to its limitations, it also became part of the consumerist ideology of the restructured NHS. Though this enabled gains to be made on some fronts, RU 486 will only be an available choice where contracting parties include it in their agreements and demonstrate a willingness to develop the service within their hospitals. As a result, the uneven availability and distribution of abortion will prevail.

While these issues are to some degree recognized by organizations working for the expansion of choice, their embracing of new technologies fails to give proper consideration to the abiding, if changing, influence of the medical profession on abortion provision. Conversely groups like FINRRAGE, in their rejection of all technologies, fail to address the needs of women that may want to engage with these same technologies (Stanworth, 1987). Caught between a liberal acceptance of an expansion of choice through technology and the radical rejection of this same technology, the choices available to women in this area are restricted: historically by the 1967 Act, currently by the purchasing policies of District Health Authorities or GPs and always by the attitudes and biases of individual doctors.

Acknowledgements

This paper is a revised version of one given at the UK Women's Studies Network conference 1995 at Stirling University. I should like to thank all the women who attended this session for their helpful comments and suggestions.

Notes

1 RU 486 was the laboratory code for the compound upon first discovery. It has now been branded by the pharmaceutical company as Mifegyne, while the compound has become known as Mifepristone. RU 486 is used in this paper as it is the most commonly known of these options.

2 These figures are approximate as the numbers are subject to constant change.
3 This change occurred in April 1996.

References

AHMAD, W. (1993) *'Race' and Health in Contemporary Britain*, Buckingham, Open University Press.

COREA, G. (1985) *The Mother Machine*, New York, Harper & Row.

DEPARTMENT OF HEALTH (1989) *Working for Patients*, Cm 555, London, HMSO.

FARRANT, W. (1985) 'Who's for amniocentesis? The politics of pre-natal screening', in HOMANS, H. (Ed.) *The Sexual Politics of Reproduction*, London, Gower.

HADLEY, J. (1994) 'God's bullies: attacks on abortion', *Feminist Review*, **48**.

HIMMELWEIT, S. (1988) 'More than "A woman's right to choose"?', *Feminist Review*, **29**.

KITZINGER, S. and DAVIES, J. A. (Eds) (1978) *The Place of Birth*, Oxford, Oxford University Press.

KLEIN, R., RAYMOND, J. and DUMBLE, L. (1991) *RU 486 Misconceptions Myths and Morals*, Melbourne, Spinifex Press.

MACKINNON, C. (1987) 'Privacy v equality: beyond Roe and Wade', in *Feminism Unmodified: Discourses on Life and Law*, Cambridge Mass, Harvard UP, pp. 93–116.

OAKLEY, A. (1976) 'Wisewoman and medicine man: changes in the management of childbirth', in MITCHELL, J. and OAKLEY, A. (Eds) *The Rights and Wrongs of Women*, Harmondsworth, Penguin.

OAKLEY, A (1993) *Essays on Women, Medicine and Health*, Oxford, Blackwell.

PATTERSON, C. (1994) 'Abortion provision in the NHS', presentation at Abortion Services in England and Wales, London, April.

PFEFFER, N. (1985) 'The hidden pathology of the male reproductive system', in HOMANS, H. (Ed.) *The Sexual Politics of Reproduction*, London, Gower.

PFEFFER, N. (1987) 'Artificial insemination, in vitro fertilisation and the stigma of infertility', in STANWORTH, M. (Ed.) *Reproductive Technologies: Gender, Motherhood and Medicine*, 1st edn, Cambridge, Polity Press, pp. 81–97.

ROWLAND, R. (1985) 'Motherhood, Patriarchal Power, Alienation and the Issue of "Choice" in Sex Preselection', in COREA, G. *et al.*, *Man-Made Women: How New Reproductive Technologies Affect Women*, London, Hutcheson.

SPALLONE, P. (1994) 'Reproductive health and reproductive technology', in WILKINSON, S. and KITZINGER, C. (Eds) *Women and Health*, 1st edn, London, Taylor & Francis, pp. 49–64.

STANWORTH, M. (Ed.) (1987) *Reproductive Technologies: Gender, Motherhood and Medicine*, 1st edn, Cambridge, Polity Press.
WAJCMAN, J. (1991) *Feminism Confronts Technology*, Cambridge, Polity Press.
WINKLER, F. (1985) 'Consumerism in health care: beyond the supermarket model', *Policy and Politics*, **15**, pp. 1–8.

Further reading

FUREDI, W. (1994) *Mifepristone in practice. Running an Early Medical Abortion Service*, London, Birth Control Trust.
HADLEY, J. (1996) *Abortion Between Freedom and Necessity*, London, Virago.
VAN DYKE, S. (1995) *Manufacturing Babies and Public Consent. Debating the New Reproductive Technology*, London, Macmillan.

Chapter 7

Women, 'Race' and Culture: Contexts and Campaigns

Usha Brown, Clara Connolly and Pragna Patel

Introduction: Chris Corrin

The talks in this section are presented in the style in which they were given, to retain the flavour of the plenary *Women, 'Race' and Culture*. The panel illustrated our three-layered focus on theory, practice and campaigning. Usha Brown provides the economic and political context in which the discussions of cultural and religious difference have assumed such recent importance in many parts of the world. Clara Connolly outlines the relationship between gender and dominant national cultures. She emphasizes the role that orthodox religion has played in a number of nationalisms across Europe to the detriment of women. Pragna Patel discusses the role of gender in 'minority' cultures and the struggles that Black and minority ethnic women in Britain have fought within their communities, as well as against a racist state. The latter speakers drew on their campaigning experience of Women Against Fundamentalism (WAF) and Southall Black Sisters (SBS).

Southall Black Sisters was founded in November 1979 when a small group of Asian and African–Caribbean women came together. On their tenth anniversary the group produced a bulletin *Against the Grain: Southall Black Sisters 1979–1989* detailing their early history, their reformulations after benefiting from Greater London Council funding in 1983 and the establishment of permanent workers at the Southall Black Women's Centre:

> By far the largest number of women come to the centre for advice and support in dealing with domestic violence but they stay for numerous other reasons. It's become harder and harder to help them effectively but we are compelled to go on trying. That SBS has bucked the trend to knuckle under to the new realism of the late 1980s is due in part to a refusal to play out our allotted roles. As individuals we have not been conventional wives or mothers, as political beings we have not confined our discourse within acceptable boundaries. (SBS, *Against the Grain*, 1990, p. 4)

Members of SBS work within Women Against Fundamentalism which was set up after an SBS meeting on International Women's Day in Southall in 1989. WAF continues to raise more publicly the discussion that SBS had begun. In their founding statement, launched on 6 May 1989, WAF state their challenge to the rise of fundamentalism in all religions:

> Fundamentalism appears in different and changing forms in religions throughout the world, sometimes as a state project, sometimes in opposition to the state. But at the heart of all fundamentalist agendas is the control of women's minds and bodies. All religious fundamentalists support the patriarchal family as a central agent of such control. They view women as embodying the moral and traditional values of the family and the whole community . . . We must also resist fundamentalism within British minority religions. We must challenge the assumption that minorities in this country exist as unified, internally homogeneous groups.

WAF produce a journal twice each year which covers the broad range of their work and includes debates and campaign news. The discussion generated from this panel, *Women, 'Race' and Culture*, included a focus on anti-racist work and the lack of visible support many Black women's groups gain in anti-racist struggles from other feminist groups and campaigns.

Economic and Political Contexts: Usha Brown

When we discussed this session we were conscious that we couldn't talk about culture in a vacuum: it both influences and is influenced by the context in which it occurs. So here I briefly sketch out a context, highlight some of the more disturbing trends and pick up some of the issues. It is a broad-brush approach and there are many gaps and omissions, some of which I hope will be picked up in discussion.

Context

Today's context is one of rapid and fundamental change. We are in the throes of a new industrial/post-industrial/third wave – call it what you will – revolution. The last time they had an industrial revolution in the UK, it changed the shape of the country, caused large-scale population movements, created new cities, radically changed patterns of work – separating home and work – produced new ideologies. It also had a fairly profound effect on the rest of the world. We are in a similar sort of situation. Sheila Rowbotham and Swasti Mitter (1994, p. 4) note: 'We are in the midst of a transformation in which the character of production, the composition of the workforce, the relation between state and economy, in fact the whole interaction between economic and social spheres is dramatically altering.'

This radical change has been caused by new technologies, the information explosion, the various bio-tech/engineering revolutions and it has been supported here and elsewhere in the world by government policies. Throughout the 1980s, governments (most notably here, but also in other parts of the world) set out on programmes to free the markets; they did this by a dramatic programme of deregulation and privatization, and increasingly the ideologies of the free market have become the orthodoxies of this change.

Components

All this means that information can be passed quickly and efficiently globally, that companies can make and sell products anywhere in the world. Alongside this, Charles Handy (1991, p. 72) notes that:

> organisations have realised that while it may be convenient to have everyone around them all the time, with their time at your command, because you buy their time, it is a luxurious way of marshalling necessary resources. It is cheaper to keep them outside the organisation, employed by themselves or specialist contractors, and buy their services if you need them.

Handy uses a three-leafed shamrock as a symbol of the new labour patterns. One leaf represents core workers bound to the company by what he calls 'bands of gold': high salaries and fringe benefits. The second leaf is the 'contractual fringe' to whom all non-essential work is contracted out. The third leaf is a reservoir of the 'flexible labour force' – the fastest growing part of the employment scene everywhere. Flexibility is the new key word. Rowbotham and Mitter (1994) note that 'flexibility in the organisation of work has become a key business principle.'

Because of easy movement and the new patterns of work, there is an increasing use of sub-contracting on the lines of the Benetton model: a big company with a network of smaller sub-contractors who produce the goods. Or there is the Japanese 'just in time' model: materials and labour ready just when required, not 'just in case'. Toyota apparently has 36,000 sub-contractors.

Many large companies produce nothing. Everything is sub-contracted, except marketing, the brand name and intellectual property rights. Rowbotham and Mitter (1994) state that this centralization of markets coupled with the decentralization of production, gives rise to what are known as 'hollow corporations'. It frees them from all sorts of responsibilities. The sub-contractors deal with employment problems, and because the sub-contractors themselves are competing to provide the lowest tenders, the situation for workers at the end of the line is not good. In fact, sub-contracting and free market policies have tilted the balance of power further in favour of employers. Low pay and exploitative working conditions are common.

And things could be changing radically again. Historian Paul Kennedy (1994, p. 83) notes:

> For 200 years manufacturing and assembly have been amended in all sorts of ways, but whatever the innovations of Taylor & Ford and just-in-time production, the key element was human beings coming together in a place of work; now we are witnessing a technology-driven revolution which breaks from the process by replacing factory worker with robots to increase productivity. Automation takes more and more human beings out of the factory, and perhaps only a few supervising engineers remain.

The results of all this are that shops and factories can stay open for up to 70 hours a week. A New York insurance company has its claim office in County Kerry, Ireland. Airlines in the USA have their booking offices in the Caribbean. A Swiss airline has its administrative offices in Bombay. Work in the UK can be tendered for by companies in the Philippines.

Bipolar world

Alongside the economic mayhem, the political landscape has changed and continues to change. The bipolar world is finished with the break-up of the USSR and the retreat of the USA into petulant isolationism. Old wars are reigniting, old and new nations emerging. A third of the countries represented in the UN face significant rebel movements, dissenters or governments in exile. Alvin and Heidi Toffler (1995, p. 297) point out that 'many of today's states are going to splinter . . . the most basic components in the global system are breaking down. There are more states in the system, and not all of them, despite their rhetoric, are nations.'

There are other powers, too: the UN describes 335 firms as transnational corporations. The World Investment Report to the UN Conference on Trade and Development noted 'The workplace is being shaped by the TNCs, with trade unions and national governments largely impotent to prevent the biggest companies from setting their own agenda in terms of jobs, training and industrial relations.' The money markets are also flexing their muscles as Alvin and Heidi Toffler note: 'even the most powerful governments and their central banks can no longer control their own currency rates in a world awash in unregulated tidal waves of electronic money' (1995, p. 253).

After a steady period of inroads being made into inequality and poverty, they are again on the march. In 1993 the *Guardian* magazine front cover carried the question: 'What's the difference between Tanzania and Goldman

Sachs?' The answer was: 'One is an African country that makes $2.2 billion a year and shares it among 25 million people. The other is an investment bank that makes $2.6 billion and shares most of it between 161 people' (*Guardian 2*, 10 December 1993).

According to the UN, the ratio of incomes shared between the richest 20 per cent and the poorest 20 per cent of the world population has gone from 30:1 in 1961 to 61:1 in 1991. (*Guardian Outlook*, 4 March 1995). Around 20 per cent of the population of Latin America and the Caribbean, 30 per cent of the population in the Middle East and North Africa and almost 50 per cent of the population of Sub-Saharan Africa live below the poverty line.

In the UK, economist Will Hutton (1995) notes that there has been a virtual stagnation of income for those in the bottom third of the population. In the USA, one job in five does not carry enough income to rear a family of four. Save the Children Fund notes that in Scotland, one in three children are living in poverty. The Scottish Low Pay Unit has pointed out that around three-quarters of part-time workers, the majority of whom are women, earn below the low-pay threshold. The vast majority of single parents are women, who constitute the largest group of those who are poor.

It all sounds very pessimistic. However, the process of change does not involve predicting the future with any degree of accuracy. The idea that machines would make workers obsolete goes back at least as far as the industrial revolution, but it has not happened yet. Clearly technology and science have benefited everybody and women's positions have improved. For very many women (and men) new technologies and flexible ways of working have been a 'liberation'. Anthony Giddens (1994, p. 17) says:

> Even without the corroding effects of markets, tradition and pre-established habits lose their hold ... to put things simply, our lives are less and less lived as fate; it is no longer the fate of a man necessarily to become a breadwinner. It is no longer the fate of women to settle for a life of domesticity.

Trends

That is a very broad picture of the context. I now look at some of the more disturbing trends that are emerging. Inevitably, given these huge changes there is a feeling of uncertainty, of fear. Eric Hobsbawn (1992, p. 14) sums up the mood:

> because we live in an era when all other human relations and values are in crisis or at least somewhere on the journey towards unknown and uncertain destinations. Xenophobia looks like becoming the mass ideology of the Century *fin de siècle*. What holds humanity together today is the denial of what the human race has in common.

We have seen the growth of nationalisms, and fundamentalism not just of the religious kind but also of the secular variety. We know about the emergence of fascism, neo-Nazism and the endemic racism in Europe. After all, Le Pen's National Front Party in France won 15 per cent of the vote at the local elections in June 1995.

But there are other backlashes too. Poverty is increasingly being portrayed as a result of individual choice: people remain in poverty because they choose it. The Welfare State, once seen as the tool to create a more equal society, is being viewed as a creator of poverty! – the main culprit in the dependency culture. Welfare programmes are being cut everywhere in the world. Increasingly, people see welfare as 'us' having to help 'them'. In the USA, there are reports of people on welfare being harangued in shops for buying what their accusers consider luxuries and wasting taxpayers' money. 'Cuddly' Newt Gingrich (Speaker in the US Congress) is warmly supported for his suggestion that women on welfare who continue to have children should have them taken away. The UK's Peter Lilley (Minister for Social Security) earns standing ovations for his puerile doggerel attacking the 'welfare scroungers'.

And too much apparently has been done for groups that face discrimination and inequality. Critics point out that with rights come responsibilities and it is now time to make the recipients – the clamourers and whingers for rights – deliver on responsibilities. Affirmative action is under attack from India to the United States. It is this perceived tug-of-war between rights and responsibilities that communitarians like Etzoni[1] are trying to deal with. Etzoni sees the rebuilding/resurgence of communities as part of a general moral programme: one that creates mutual dependence and balances rights and responsibilities.

This period of change is going to face us with some very difficult situations. What I have been talking about is the easy part. The discoveries in genetics and bio-engineering (see Rowland, Chapter 13, and Tabberer, Chapter 6, this volume) are going to provide the real posers. That is the nature of a warning.

Issues

I now raise some issues of concern:

1. I think it is worth remembering that the group that J. K. Galbraith calls 'the contented majority' – those of us with secure jobs and income, and those of us who are less secure but are getting by – have, here and elsewhere, consistently voted for policies that do not favour the redistribution of wealth, or radical action on poverty and discrimination. Instead we have as a group voted for policies that increase our wealth.

2. It is true that we have both rights and responsibilities, but a close examination of current arguments show that they are focused on the individual: my

responsibility for myself and my family. Put another way, today's answer to the biblical question 'Am I my brother's (or sister's) keeper?' is, 'No, they are responsible for themselves.' We are not going to build open communities or achieve the balance between rights and responsibility unless we can take responsibility for the 'other', especially the unknown 'other'.

3. I think we also need to be very aware that the trends I have described are a fairly focused attack on women. Sheila Rowbotham (1992) has pointed out that in times of change, women are presented as part of nature to be controlled, as symbols of continuity in a world of flux. Traditionally, women have been seen as the carriers of culture, those who pass on the traditions of the group to the young. Traditionally, woman as mothers carry the future of a group. In defence of the future of race/culture/creed people (men particularly) will do very dangerous and damaging things and not count the cost.

4. Finally, despite Naomi Wolf's (1993) belief that the day of power feminism has come, I would urge caution. There is no guarantee that we will continue to keep what we have achieved. If we take the area of work, for example, women were the first into factories, on the assembly line, working with information technology, but somewhere along the line we got shifted sideways or downwards – or back home.

We have achieved a great deal, but all that glitters is not gold. Alison Miller[2] points out that when women were fighting to improve health services and to gain acceptance for a holistic model of health they did not expect to find themselves with stress centres, while the medical services were rolled up behind their backs. Power to the sisters who want to power feminize but I don't think it's time to abandon sentry duty.

Dominant Cultures and Gender: Clara Connolly

Pragna Patel will be discussing women and 'minority' cultures, though she will point out that a minority in one place may well be a majority in another. This section is about dominant cultures – dominant in relation to nation-states – and their relation to gender. Nira Yuval-Davis and Floya Anthias (1989) have explained very clearly the relationship between women and nation; I cannot spell out all the dimensions here. When the 'nation' is perceived to be in crisis, women will have a particularly difficult burden to bear. Women are perceived as the bearers of the national culture over which men will fight to the death. Rape in 'fraternal' wars – where the national boundaries are not clear, such as in the former Yugoslavia and between Pakistan and Bangladesh – is only an extreme example of a bitter truth: women's bodies are literally the boundary of the nation.

Béatrix Campbell[3] spoke at this conference about the crisis of 'Englishness' and she linked it with a crisis in masculinity. I want to address the dimensions of this crisis that are particularly relevant to Women Against Fundamentalism. For Englishmen, the current enemy is Europe; football and parliamentary hooligans are equally assiduous (and equally vociferous) in defending the sacred English traditions against an inferior civilization dominated by the 'equally suspect' French and Germans. The enemies within are those people living here who are not English, though they *may* be British. Remember Norman Tebbits' cricket test?

Margrit Shildrick[4], in an eloquent and thought-provoking paper at the *Sisterhood* conference, described 'community' as defined primarily by 'exclusion'. It is so also for the 'national community'. Who are the 'others' of the English national community? They are defined most basically by colour and youth. Gender is not so commonly explored.

Muslims are most clearly the self-defined 'other', if we (the English) are other than that – i.e. Christian. Everyone knows that they are the fundamentalists. We (Christians) have the dear old fuddy-duddy Church of England. Is that so? In England, the distinction between being English and British is often ignored; 'English' is substituted for 'British'. One example is the way in which the Church of England is the established Church in Britain and maintains its privileged links with crown and State. On the issue of mandatory Christian worship in English and Welsh State schools (which is a regularly enforced legal requirement) the Church of England is divided. Some voices from within the Church – most notably the Archbishop of York – have been raised in a sense of unease, if not exactly protest. However, the most conservative elements in the Tory Party and the government – encouraged by Christian fundamentalists such as the Plymouth Brethren and the Association of Christian Teachers – show no such liberal hesitation. They are not concerned about the disenfranchisement of minority religions, of members of no religion, and indeed the tedium caused to the vast majority of English and Welsh young people, who are indifferent to religion. The most conservative elements in Christianity – a miniscule minority themselves – have been able to use the 'establishment' and the myth of England as a 'Christian' country to impose the most reactionary practices on State schools. This is particularly disturbing in the area of sex education, which has recently been considerably restricted, to the detriment primarily of schoolgirls, our daughters. They are to be reduced to the mercy of the playground and of boys' rule. Confidentiality between teachers and pupils is no longer to be respected by law.

The values of the Christian family, as defined by people such as Victoria Gillick (see also Annette Kilcooley, Chapter 3, this volume) are being protected at the expense of girls' and women's access to information and rights to autonomy. These are among the consequences of conceiving of Britain in the absence of other visible signifiers – as 'Christian' – in the teeth of all the evidence of empty pews and Sunday shopping.

Rada Boric, from Croatia, who is an activist with the Centre for Women War Victims and co-founder of the Women's Studies Centre in Zagreb, has reminded us at this conference that sisterhood is easier when lives depend upon it. She can tell, better than I, how religion is playing an increasingly powerful role in the signifying of national difference in the former Yugoslavia. Always an important cultural resource there, and a mark of difference, it has recently become a lethal boundary market between warring natons. The effects on women from all communities are tragic. The United Nations has played its part in attempting to turn 'Bosnians' into 'Muslims'. The effects of Catholic Croation nationalism and the shrinking of secular space has the same effect on women and girls as anywhere else: restricted education, and restrictiveness on access to opportunities for autonomy. Sarajevo, Tuzla and other Bosnian cities remain the threatened enclaves of pluralism. The former Yugoslavia is only one area of the world where religion has become increasingly politicized, to the detriment of women. But it is a terrifying example of how fragile secular and pluralist values are at a time of national threat and disintegration.

Feminism has usually been perceived as anti-nationalist (although it is not always so). There are good reasons for this. Feminists have less stake in national and ethnic boundary-markers and can see more in common with each other across these boundaries. This does not mean that 'sisterhood is global': there are real economic and political divisions between feminists, which make the use of a common language of communication very difficult. But feminist responses can loosen the boundaries of community and make dialogue between communities (national and ethnic) possible.

In my own country – Ireland – feminists from the North and the South are entering into a difficult dialogue – between those who support republicanism and those (usually from the 70-year-old Republic) who are suspicious of nationalism. Snippets of this dialogue are reflected in the pages of *Feminist Review* No. 50, a special issue called 'The Irish Issue: the British Question'. However important the British Question is for the Irish, it is my belief that the question of Ireland will be solved by the Irish. This is why dialogue between feminists from majority and minority communities (on both sides of the national border) is a powerful resource for the new Ireland. Whatever shape it takes on the map, we hope that it will emerge as truly secular and pluralist and that women can take an equal place in it. That vision is worth it. It seems slightly more feasible (though this may be only a moment of fragile hope) than it is in Britain, or at least in England.

Gender in 'Minority' Cultures: Pragna Patel

The focus of this contribution is on the struggles waged by Black women from within their communities. But what I have to say cannot be understood without the wider context of what Clara has spoken about. This wider context refers to the nature of the British State and the relationship between the State and minority communities. In the course of understanding those struggles, we have come to problematize the notions of community, culture, religion and identity.

But first, two recent events which occurred in the last two weeks which crystallize the dilemmas and contradictions faced by Black women in taking on a multiplicity of struggles against racism and patriarchal oppression simultaneously.

The death of Joy Gardner – this was a defining moment for Black people in Britain. It certainly left me and many others feeling frustrated and angry because the police officers who were charged with her manslaughter got off free. Prior to this, Bernie Grant, the Black MP, called on all Blacks to be patient (as opposed to taking to the streets), to allow the law to work its course. We were waiting with baited breath. Will justice be done this time? But we were cheated. The justice system was certainly in operation, but what happened? The judge at the trial had actually directed the jury to disregard race, power and politics when determining its verdict. Reality as experienced by many Blacks was actually being reinvented before our very eyes. We were made to accept the 'truth' of the police, the courts and the criminal justice system. The 'truth' we were made to accept was that the killing of a Black woman by police and immigration officers had nothing to do with race and politics. Justice, in this case, had nothing to do with Black reality or Black truth. The lives of Black people were, at a stroke, made invisible and with it a history of racism wiped out. The law and the State constructed a different reality: one in which Blacks and Black women were constructed as a 'problem'. The cultural stereotype that was invoked was that of the 'big, Black violent woman'. It was a threatening image. She needed taming and controlling. Being 'illegal', she needed to be thrown out, she did not belong. Immigration laws therefore construct Blacks as 'problems'. They were excluded from the rights and privileges enjoyed by the rest of society.

Second, the Bradford Riots. Three hundred young Asian men rioted. But the media was interested not in what led up to the riots but with the aftermath – curiosity about the 'exotic', the 'cultural' dilemmas of the youth. What was interesting was the response of the State – i.e. the police – to the riots. Both police and media collude in the construction of the community as unstable, volatile and potentially criminal. There is no serious analysis, it is merely perceived as a 'Black problem'. The police responded to the riots by talking in terms of alienation, disenfranchisement. They put it down to a problem of 'parents and elders no longer being able to communicate with the young ones'. They are seen to be estranged from their own cultures and from the majority culture. The police did not refer to themselves as key players in that disenfranchizing process. But then who do the police talk to to 'calm things down' and to negotiate? They talk to the elders – the very people they claim are no longer in touch with Asian youth culture. There are no meetings with the youth themselves. The riots also showed how Asian male youths have been criminalized in much the same way as African–Caribbean youths have been.

The police approached the event in the classic multicultural style. We in Southall Black Sisters refer to this as the 'take me to your leader syndrome'.

Another interesting aspect of the riots was that they were triggered off by an assault on an Asian woman by the police. Many black riots have been triggered off by police attacks on black women. Beatrix Campbell talked about public spaces, political discourses and criminality linked to notions of masculinity. I question the 'protection' that was attempted in this instance by the men who rioted. What does it mean for women's autonomy and self-determination? The young men were protecting their 'community' and their women. Therein lies the dilemma for black women. Black women are also being policed within the community by those same youths. A little-publicized but vital fact is that the youths were also 'cleaning' the streets of white prostitutes whom they thought to be defiling their spaces. In other words, they were protecting the community, but mainly Asian women, from 'moral corruption' as symbolized by the white prostitutes.

Now that 'religious fundamentalist identity' rests on the control of women's minds that bodies, the policing of women within black communities is also on the rise. What is the trade-off here? If women are protected from external racist threats then the borders of community must be heavily policed. But those borders cannot be crossed by the women themselves. The containment of Asian women from within reinforces images of them as passive and submissive. We are owned but we do not own ourselves.

While we can understand the youth defending community against State harassment, that same youth also control and police women and will not allow women to defend themselves against domestic violence and sexual harassment. The minority community is not therefore internally uniform, equal or even progressive, with everyone sharing the same interests. As much as the community is excluded by the State and made to feel that they do not belong, internally, those who dissent, doubt or question power equally do not belong. This leads me to the issue of multiculturalism.

Definition: It is a model based on notions of tolerance and respect for 'difference' as long as the differences are 'compatible' with the norms of the majority society. But diversity and difference have become substitutes for equality. The multicultural model rests on assumptions of homogeneity and other voices are suppressed. In Southall Black Sisters' experiences, under this model women are denied their rights. For example, take the case of a Pakistani Muslim woman fighting for custody rights of her young daughter. She has left her Muslim husband following years of violence. Her marriage had come to an end. However, her husband refused to divorce her. She went to live with her boyfriend, also of Muslim background. Her husband branded her an adulteress. In court, her husband argued that he should have custody of his daughter although she was the prime carer, on the grounds that his wife was an adulteress and therefore ostracized from the community. He argued that according to the religious laws of the community, such women would never find respect and that her shame and dishonour would be transferred on to the child, who in turn would have difficulties in having an arranged marriage. He brought in a number of Muslim clerics to verify his account. Although a Court Welfare Officer's report had stated that the child should stay with the mother, the judge was swayed by the arguments put forward by the husband and the Muslim clerics. In fact, he adjourned the case for further investigation into the religious aspects of the case.

The danger that existed here was that the judge was willing to apply different criteria to the ones he would normally apply had the woman not been Muslim. Here, he was prepared to be guided by religious laws rather than civil family law. We therefore see creeping in an end to the universalist application of civil law where women from certain minority communities are concerned. This case was about to set a dangerous precedent, but it came to an abrupt end because the man was given a prison sentence in relation to some criminal proceedings against him. The case was also alarming because it refused to recognize the woman's interpretation of her culture and religion. The judge assumed that religious laws are uniformly interpreted and applied. In such multicultural perceptions there is no room for recognizing other identities and interpretations, especially those of women who wish to construct their own identities, based on their own experiences and understanding of religion and culture.

These, then, are some of the failures of multiculturalism. It is undemocratic as it bypasses the question of unequal power relations between the State and minority communities and between different groups within a minority community. Consultation between the State and the community takes place through power-brokers, usually male, religious and business leaders. In the multicultural approach to minority communities, the British State grants communal autonomy in exchange for individual autonomy. Black women have to struggle to raise their voices from within, to move from a position of marginalization to one where their own identities are recognized as legitimate. But we also have to move away from simplistic notions of struggles based on Black/white or majority/minority identities. We may be part of a minority in this country, but elsewhere we may be part of a majority community oppressing other minority peoples.

In the course of our struggles, we have needed the support of women from other backgrounds. Those struggles have been long and hard and all sorts of accusations have been flying. Through experience we have learned to move away from notions of a hierarchy of struggles or a hierarchy of oppressions and identity politics. Southall Black Sisters has made alliances with different groups for different campaigns. Our main aim is to come to 'own' all our struggles as women, irrespective of our race, cultural and religious backgrounds.

Women Against Fundamentalism aims to do precisely this. WAF was formed because of the dangers of religious fundamentalism and its impact on women. Religious fundamentalism in the UK utilizes the multicultural discourse. Women are the primary targets, although women have also joined fundamentalist movements – this is a complex issue and there is no time to discuss this here. In WAF we attempt to move beyond solidarity because we make central the need to understand the nature of the British State, its relationship to minority communities and, through the State, the relationship of minority communities to each other. WAF is made up of Jewish, Asian, Irish, Iranian, Egyptian and English women. We oppose both racism and religious fundamentalism. This enables us to do two things: to think and act internationally and to take on a number of issues which concern us all. We have come together not because of who we are, but because of what we want to do. WAF is an example of sisterhood in thought and action.

Notes

1 Amitai Etzioni is a sociologist, writer and theorist of the Communitarian Movement. His book *The Spirit of the Community* (1993) Fontana Press, contains many of his ideas.
2 Alison Miller is a community worker with the Centre for Women's Health in Glasgow and a poet.
3 Beatrix Campbell's talk at the 'We're all Different Aren't We?' Plenary at the *Desperately Seeking Sisterhood* Conference, June 1995.
4 Margrit Shildrick 'Against Ethics: Sisterhood and Others' *Desperately Seeking Sisterhood* Conference, June 1995, unpublished paper.

References

Feminist Review, No. 50, special issue 'The Irish State: the British Question', London, Routledge.
GALBRAITH, J. K. (1992) *The Culture of Contentment*, London, Sinclair Stevenson.
GIDDENS ANTHONY (1994) 'What's Left for Labour?' in *New Statesman and Society*, 30 September.
HANDY, CHARLES (1991) *The Age of Unreason*, London, Century Business.
HOBSBAWM, ERIC (1992) *New Statesman and Society*, 24 April.
HUTTON, WILL (1995) *The State We're In*, London, Vintage.
KENNEDY, PAUL (1994) *Preparing for the Twenty-First Century*, London, Fontana.
ROWBOTHAM, SHEILA (1992) *Women in Movement: Feminism and Social Action*, New York and London, Routledge.
ROWBOTHAM, SHEILA and MITTER SWASTI (Eds) (1994) *Dignity and Daily Bread: New Forms of Economic Organising Among Poor Women in the Third World and the First*, New York and London, Routledge.
Southall Black Sisters (1990) *Against the Grain: A Celebration of Survival and Struggle*, Southall, Middlesex, Southall Black Sisters.

Part III

Re-searching Sisterhood

Chapter 8

Zero Tolerance of Violence against Women

Susan Hart

In Memoriam: Franki Raffles

The Zero Tolerance public awareness campaign was launched in Edinburgh District Council by the Council's Women's Committee in November 1992 in an attempt to tackle the issue of violence against women. The Local Authority Women's Committee is charged with the task of 'improving the lives of women in Edinburgh' and what better way than to break new ground on the issue of their safety. Many have asked what led a local authority to embark on such a campaign with a clear feminist agenda in such a public way. The answer is relatively simple but contains a number of essential components which may be useful to look at for those of us wishing to challenge traditional perceptions of women's experiences.

The use of existing and new research to justify the campaign and its 'radical' message was and still is a crucial element in gaining support for Zero Tolerance. Evelyn Gillan, a former employee of the Council working for the Women's Committee, knew this and embarked on an audit of existing research and practical initiatives both in the UK and abroad. Evelyn's confidence that the time was right to initiate a campaign was boosted by Franki Raffles, a freelance photographer and designer, whom she employed as Creative Director of the Campaign. Evelyn and Franki assisted by me, worked extremely hard during 1992 to find ways to present a feminist analysis of the causes of the violence against women, for the first time with local government backing, in the public domain. The discussions were wide-ranging but the decision to present clear research findings on the prevalence of gender violence was always central.

Using research to campaign for change seems obvious enough but how often does it happen? Particularly with feminist research, many of us seem not to have access to it or have not had the opportunity to develop the campaigning and lobbying skills needed to turn it into a clear message for change in the public domain. For me, this highlights the necessity for feminist academics to acknowledge the crucial role of campaigns and to communicate with those feminists with campaigning skills and experience, whether in political parties, single issue groups, trade unions or more non-traditional arenas and for those experienced campaigners to attempt to access or even commission research themselves. You do find women with a foot in both camps who recognize the need for campaigners to utilize academic research and for academics to actively put energy into translating what they know into action. My experience of the Zero Tolerance Campaign and other campaigns shows that when this happens sparks can fly!

The Edinburgh Experience

It was known that tackling violence against women was a high priority for women in Edinburgh because of previous research undertaken on behalf of the local authority in 1990. Women's attitudes and experiences of violence had also been documented elsewhere in the UK and abroad, but very little had been done on young peoples' attitudes to gender violence and, in particular, the attitudes of boys. A research project was commissioned in 1992 to be carried out in secondary schools in Edinburgh with boys and girls aged 12 to 16 (Falchikov, 1992) to determine adolescents knowledge of and attitudes to domestic violence. The results showed that there was a wide acceptance of violence against women among boys, some as young as 12 years old and the majority of students said they were likely to use violence in their personal relationships in the future. This information proved to be crucial to the process of convincing the local authority to commit themselves to the idea that a public awareness campaign was necessary as well as agreeing to the £15,000 needed to carry it out. The knowledge that the next generation were expecting to inflict or experience the misery of gender violence, coupled with the presentation of a concrete proposal on how to tackle it, meant that it was more difficult not to embark on a campaign than to do so.

The Canadian national strategy[1] and an adapted version of a strategy for Edinburgh convinced the local authority and subsequently many other organizations to support the Zero Tolerance Campaign. Zero Tolerance adopted the Canadian three-pronged approach and called for:

Prevention: Active prevention of crimes of violence against women and children;

Provision: Adequate provision of support services for women and children;

Protection: Appropriate legal aid for children and women suffering from violence.

The shaping of the campaign, the messages and images that it used, was the next crucial stage. Relevant women's organizations were consulted and the potential impact on their services discussed along with the key elements to success ensuring that the campaign built on the years of accumulated experience of the women's movement.

By the time they reach eighteen,

one of them will have been
subjected to sexual abuse.

Z

ZERO TOLERANCE

**FROM FLASHING TO RAPE
MALE ABUSE OF POWER IS A CRIME**

Figure 8.1 Images focus on domestic situations to highlight the prevalence of violence against women and children which occurs in their own homes.

Figure 8.2 Myth: Crimes of violence against women are only perpetuated by working-class men against working-class women.

From three to ninety three,

women are raped.

Z
ZERO TOLERANCE

**HUSBAND, FATHER, STRANGER
MALE ABUSE OF POWER IS A CRIME**

Figure 8.3 Myth: Crimes of violence against women only happen to certain women because of their age, appearance, dress or behaviour.

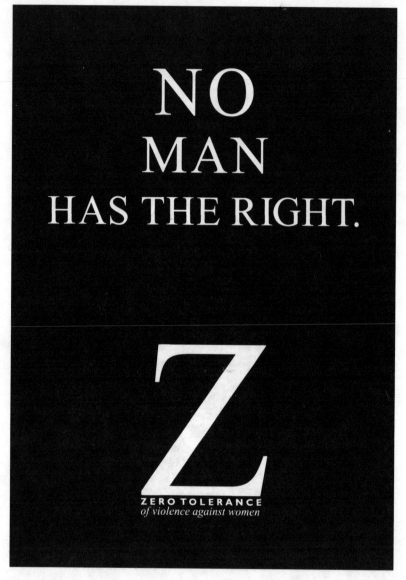

Figure 8.4 Use of a strong, unifying design theme to make links between different forms of violence against women.

Campaign

A series of posters (Figures 8.1–5) highlighting the different forms of violence against women were produced and displayed in prominent positions throughout the city. Traditional outdoor and indoor advertising sites were used such as billboards, bus shelters, pubs, shops, libraries and other community venues in a sequential way over an initial six-month period and were backed up by a local newspaper campaign and other printed information. The specific objectives of the initial campaign were to:

• Highlight the prevalence of the various crimes of violence against women and children, linking these crimes as part of a continuum of the male abuse of power;
• Promote a criminalization strategy and send out a clear message that these forms of violence should not be tolerated;
• Empower women and challenge men; and
• Debunk some of the myths about these crimes. For example, the campaign material targeted the myth that such crimes are only perpetrated by working-class men against working-class women (Figure 8.2), that they are mainly attacks by strangers out of doors and that they only happen to certain women because of their age, appearance, dress or behaviour (Figure 8.3).

The materials were developed within a distinct set of parameters, decided on in consultation with women's groups to reflect the priorities of their organizations. These included:

• No images of 'victims' to be used: only positive images of women and children;
• The images would focus on domestic situations to highlight the prevalence of violence against women and children which occurs in their own homes;
• The images should be visually appealing and reflect notions of comfort and security and contrast with the message of the text; and
• There should be a strong unifying design theme throughout the campaign to make links between different forms of violence against women.

The process by which the campaign images and messages were developed was another crucial element contributing to its success. As mentioned previously, freelance woman photographer and designer Franki Raffles was commissioned to work on the campaign, not only because of her proven track record in the design field but because of her understanding of the issue and commitment to the development of a ground-breaking campaign on gender violence. The team of committed and experienced women involved in the many months of planning, creative design and intensive consultation owe much to her drive, creative energy and clarity of thought. Franki tragically died during childbirth in December 1994 only days after some very difficult decisions and creative debate on the second phase of the Campaign. Her involvement in Zero Tolerance is still sorely missed. Many of us are still looking to replace the gaping hole that used to be her energy, consistency and acute understanding of the issues. Finding the resources, negotiating discounts and sponsorships, negotiating media coverage and keeping the politicians informed were crucial elements of the six-month planning process. Although not the most interesting of tasks to many, these were carried out deliberately and with precision.

The Response to the Initial Poster Campaign

The response of the public, politicians, professionals and the media was exciting to say the least. Enquiries flooded in from organizations and individuals, first in Edinburgh, then further afield in the UK and finally abroad. An evaluation of the public response to the Edinburgh Zero Tolerance Campaign was carried out in 1993 (Kitzinger and Hunt, 1993). It found that the Campaign was extremely successful both in attracting the attention of and gaining a positive reaction from the majority of people who took part in the study. Seventy-nine per cent of people expressed positive feelings about the Campaign and most felt that it showed that Edinburgh was forward-thinking. Although, as expected, women were consistently more supportive of the Campaign and were more likely to have discussed it, only 12 per cent of men were negative about the Campaign overall. This confirmed for us that a so-called radical message and the provision of information previously unknown or not acknowledged was not only possible, but desirable in the eyes of most of the population.

More in-depth analysis undertaken in focus groups showed that people had some very specific reasons for feeling positive about the Campaign as well as reasons for feeling negative (6 per cent negative feelings overall). Some participants felt that the Campaign challenged everyone, rather than just targeting those who are victims or perpetrators of violence. Many survivors felt it relieved them of the burden of revealing how widespread abuse is and helps those who are abused to realize they are not alone. The most common comment we received in terms of anecdotal evidence was that the Campaign asked men to consider the issue instead of asking women to change their behaviour or seek help. The Campaign was thus empowering, encouraging individuals and groups to organize against such abuse.

Some of the concerns raised by people who had negative feelings about Zero Tolerance included that it might be distressing for women who had been abused, or that it was anti-men and labelled all men as potential rapists. However, this was not the feeling of the survivors who were interviewed. Yet women were particularly pleased that the Campaign did not only target women and place the onus on women to protect themselves. They understood that the Campaign identified violence as a wider social problem and that any attempt to 'water down' the Campaign by making it non-gender-specific would

When they say no, they mean no.

Some men don't listen.

WHOEVER, WHEREVER, WHENEVER
MALE ABUSE OF POWER IS A CRIME

Figure 8.5 Poster specifically aimed at young people.

undermine the whole point of the message. In general people wanted more information on the subject of violence and specifically information directed at young people. In response to this, the Campaign produced an additional poster aimed at young people (Figure 8.5) and work is progressing in another Scottish local authority to produce an education pack for work with young people.

The results of the evaluation helped other local authorities considerably to adopt Zero Tolerance in their areas and the work of particular elected councillors and officers in some authorities gained widespread acknowledgement of the sense behind the Zero Tolerance approach. More than 70 other areas throughout the UK have run Zero Tolerance. Some have adapted it slightly to take account of the composition and history of their own areas but none have been allowed to alter the fundamental principles or parameters of the Campaign, although a few have tried!

The Next Phase

Zero Tolerance built on its success in Edinburgh by bringing together a group of committed women (mainly local authority women or equality officers) to work on the second stage of the Campaign, using slogans directly challenging the justifications used by men to avoid taking responsibility for their violence. Clarion Communications (employed following the death of Franki Raffles) developed a bus advertising campaign during 1995. For example, 'Blame the woman, blame the drink, blame the weather – domestic violence – there is no excuse' was used on the sides of buses. Large outdoor placards displaying relevant statistics and slogans were used in Edinburgh to reinforce the theme and pilot radio campaigns were launched. Other local authorities evaluated different aspects of their campaigns and we continue to share information and build on each other's developments through networking. A cinema advertisement was jointly funded and shown throughout Scotland during 1995. There is general acknowledgement that any public awareness campaign has to be long-term, well-resourced and nationally coordinated if it is to have any chance of success in changing attitudes and ultimately behaviour. Although Zero Tolerance has come some way towards this in three years, it is still some way from gathering the political and resource commitment from the government necessary to come close to the commitment of \$136 million per year given by the Canadian Federal Government to their national anti-violence initiative.

The Future

On a more positive note, the Zero Tolerance National Trust has been established which will put the Campaign on a firmer footing and give it a national focus. The trustees are currently working on sources of funding for research and staffing. After some consolidation of existing initiatives and planning of the next stage, Zero Tolerance will move on to new heights. Recovering from the death of Franki Raffles has taken us all some time and dealing with the demands of local government reorganization in Scotland with diminishing resources had brought its challenges.

However, projects such as Strathclyde Region's research into the needs of women with disabilities and the training of all social work staff in gender violence issues is definite progress. In Edinburgh we are developing a community-based strategy on Zero Tolerance in response to local demand from communities to get more involved. This also feels very much like a new phase in developments. Evaluation of these projects will be essential to enable other organizations to utilize the experience and build on it positively. Zero Tolerance of Violence Against Women is now a concept firmly embedded in the minds of many who have come across it and, as such, it is larger than the sum of the individuals who created it. This is a mark of its intrinsic value and the value of feminist analysis and implementation.

Ensuring that this or any future government adequately commits to and funds a comprehensive strategy to end violence against women will ultimately be one of the tests of feminists' ability to recognize the desperate need to free all women from the fear or reality of violence and a test on our collective strength and ability to organize and campaign for our freedom.

Notes

1 The concept of running a campaign to raise awareness of issues related to domestic violence against women was initiated in Canada in 1991. See Zero Tolerance Campaign, Edinburgh District Council 1992.
2 Photographs copyright Franki Raffles.

References

FALCHIKOV, N. (1992) *Adolescents Knowledge About, And Attitudes To, Domestic Violence*, Edinburgh, Edinburgh District Council Women's Committee
KITZINGER, J. and HUNT, K. (1993) *Evaluation of Edinburgh District Council's Zero Tolerance Campaign*, Edinburgh, Edinburgh District Council.
Summary of Canadian Initiative, Zero Tolerance Campaign (1992) Edinburgh, Edinburgh District Council.

Chapter 9

Can Commissioned Research be Feminist and Can Conflicting Interests be Served?[1]

Celia Jenkins, Maggie O'Neill and Ruth Swirsky

In the current academic climate lecturers are under increasing pressure not only to publish so as to enhance research ratings but to bring in contract research or undertake commissioned research as part of their professional activities. Louise Morley describes this process as 'coercive creativity', escalating in response to market values concerned with income generation through attracting research and publications (1995, p. 116). Similarly, professional researchers are also affected, relying on short-term contracts and having to apply for projects that they might not otherwise have considered. Moreover the competition between universities fuelled by the Higher Education Funding Council (HEFCE) research exercise creates almost unbearable pressure both for lecturers who may or may not be 'research active' and professional researchers. This chapter examines the ways in which feminist research is being affected and undermined in the current context, focusing on our own experiences of doing commissioned research.[2]

Ruth Swirsky and Celia Jenkins work at the University of Westminster, which was commissioned by British Telecommunications (BT) and Westminster City Council, together with the Metropolitan Police, to find a solution to what they perceived as the 'problem' of unauthorized advertising by prostitutes in public payphones. The research proved both an interesting and an uncomfortable experience, raising issues about compromising feminist and professional ethics in conducting contract research. Maggie O'Neill's research, first on prostitution and then on routes into prostitution from local authority care, was conducted while she was at Nottingham Trent University. This was also a difficult experience both emotionally in terms of the ethnographic work with young people and institutionally because of the internal dynamics of the research 'team'. Our aim in using our different experiences of commissioned research as case studies is to raise questions about the research process and begin to develop some guidelines so that women embarking on such research need not learn the hard way.

Despite considerable debate about what constitutes feminist research, less attention has been paid to the research process (Roberts, 1988; Purvis and Maynard, 1994). In opposition to 'sanitized', 'hygienic' research, criticized by Stanley and Wise (1993), Purvis and Maynard (1994) edited a collection of

106

articles which probe the 'silences' about the complex processes involved in doing feminist research and the conditions for maintaining integrity. One of their themes is 'the impact of involvement in research' (1994, p. 5) and it is this aspect that we explore in this chapter. In the same collection Kelly, Burton and Regan (1994) offer an excellent contemporary analysis of methodological concerns for feminists in which they state that they now prefer the concept of 'feminist research practice' to describe feminist research as a means of incorporating all aspects of the research process.

We are interpreting feminist research here as research that hopes to be useful to women in their struggles against different forms of oppression as well as informed by a feminist politics and perspective and utilizing a feminist research practice, as defined by Laws (1990); Hanmer and Saunders (1984); Stanley and Wise (1993) and Kelly, Burton and Regan (1994). Laws (1990) argues that what individual researchers gain from the process should be a secondary consideration to how the research might benefit women, whereas institutional pressures are exerted on women to make their own careers their primary concern if they are to hold their own within the academy.

The institutional context can make it difficult for women to sustain their position if they do not generate income for the university. This situation is presented in its starkest form by Kelly, Burton and Regan (1994) where their jobs at the University of North London depend on generating enough income to pay their salaries and the running costs of the Child Abuse Studies Unit (CASU). They describe the contradictory context in which they work as follows: 'Whilst we have the safety of an explicit feminism both our personal job security and the long-term future of CASU are tenuous' (1994, p. 27). Maggie O'Neill was more fortunate: as a lecturer she had job security and received support from Nottingham Trent University for her research because it generated income for the university, fitted into the requirements of a research unit and would result in publications, boosting the unit's contribution to the HEFCE exercise. However, her experience of institutional support also had negative consequences because when she left, the research unit claimed ownership of her data and told her she had no right to publish it. The deeply problematic nature of feminists undertaking research within these institutional structures and processes is reflected in CASU and Maggie's very different situations.

While the model of feminist research is applicable to any research, commissioned or contract research presents specific difficulties within different contexts. Both case studies discussed in this chapter are of research where the terms of reference and research team/process were not feminist but where we as researchers attempted to maintain feminist integrity within our work. By comparing and contrasting our respective experiences in this chapter, we hope to grasp both the specificity of our experiences and move beyond them while suggesting issues and potential guidelines for future feminist research practice.

Should we Accept Research about Women when the Terms of Reference are not Feminist?

It is difficult for women to refuse to undertake commissioned research offered to them regardless of how it relates to their ethical standpoint as feminists. One important factor influencing any decision about participation in a research team should be an assessment of the power relations to see if there is any scope to influence the direction of the research. If Ruth and Celia had refused to participate in the BT project, the research would have continued without them. They felt an obligation as feminists to try to influence the direction and outcomes as far as possible because the research might have an impact on women – both prostitutes and those using phone boxes. Their team was led by the male head of school and fortuitously he was non-directive in leading the research because this then gave them considerable scope to fulfil their own objectives. In contrast, Ann Phoenix comments that women positioned towards the bottom of the research hierarchy rarely influence its design or analysis 'a situation not generally explored in writing on feminist methodology, but one that can and does divide women researchers depending on their position in the research hierarchy' (1994, p. 57). She describes her discomfort as an interviewer when she did not agree with the direction of the questioning or the dilemma she faced when respondents gave similar critical feedback. She also cautions against the assumption that women at the top of research hierarchies will challenge the *status quo* or make the research 'for' women or empowering.

The terms of reference of Celia and Ruth's research were to establish the extent of the 'problem' of prostitutes advertising in phone boxes, to discover how and why the system worked so well and the views of interested parties (including BT, Westminster City Council and the Metropolitan Police, prostitutes, residents groups and members of the public) about possible solutions. In this respect, the research was characteristic of research commissioned by relatively powerful and overwhelmingly male-defined organizations: its aim was to use the information gained to take more effective action against the prostitutes by developing strategies to prevent them advertising in phone boxes. Kelly, Burton and Regan reiterate Law's warning that research focusing on women 'informs the powerful about an oppressed group' (1994, p. 34). However, careful consideration was given to how the information received from the prostitutes was used in the report. In any case, it would be misleading to imply that the prostitutes are powerless. Although they lack institutional power, nonetheless they maintain the upper hand insofar as they have successfully resisted all attempts to remove their cards from phone boxes.

In Maggie's case the initial work was commissioned by Safer Cities to address practically the issue of street prostitution. The residents wanted women off the streets, while probation, women's aid, health workers and social services were concerned with the walfare, health and legal needs of women and young women working as prostitutes. The police were concerned with both. With the help and support of Karen, a health professional conducting outreach work who was trusted by the women, Maggie was able to work with the prostitutes to develop suggestions and to rally support from major agencies involved with them. The work could not have developed without the support from the people representing the various agencies and the women working as prostitutes. Given the backing and support Maggie received from all those involved, it was possible for women's needs and rights to be central to the ongoing work. The relationships built up over time with the women and the agencies involved were crucial to support and involvement in further work, particularly the local authority care project.

How can Feminist Research be Conducted within a Project Commissioned with a Different Agenda?

In the local authority care project which was not defined as feminist, the ways in which Maggie worked on the routes into prostitution applied feminist ways of knowing, seeing, thinking and feeling in her work. The fact that she had responsibility for relationships with both the relevant professionals and the young people ensured that the process and progress of the research was feminist. Her commitment to feminist research practice entailed understanding more fully young people's involvement in sex work/prostitution; creating the intellectual and practical spaces for their voices to be heard; and moving towards feminist strategies of empowerment. Maggie has drawn effectively on various research methods to promote a feminist research practice (O'Neill, 1993). In her work she endeavoured to take account of the ethical and political dimensions in the social production of knowledge at the same time as validating and facilitating the shared participation of the women and young people with whom she was working.

In the BT research, Celia and Ruth had to confront the question of how to meet their terms of reference while maintaining feminist objectives. For example, the narrow terms of reference made it impossible within the timescale to investigate the relationship between this and other forms of prostitution which feminist analyses of prostitution stress as important (Jarvinen, 1993; Phoenix, 1995). The content of some cards also raised issues of pornography (Russell, 1993; MacKinnon, 1994) which were beyond the scope of the research. Nevertheless both prostitution and pornography formed a backdrop to this research.

The men in the initial research team took a liberal stance on prostitution while failing to take account of the content of the cards. Ruth and Celia redefined the issue to include the impact of the cards on women users of public telephone boxes and the damaging portrayal of women in the more pornographic cards. Their priority was to promote women's interests – both the prostitutes and women members of the public – in the hope that it might have some impact on the formulation of policy. They were also aware that participating in the research project entailed some risk for the prostitutes but that if they were not willing to talk, there would be no prospect of representing their solutions. In fact, many of them proved adept at evading direct questions about how the system worked, confining their responses to questions about strategies that would enable them to maintain their cards in phone boxes.

Ruth and Celia subverted the research as far as possible to represent the interests of the different constituencies of women. However, the sponsors rejected the recommendations, refusing to allow them to be published or discussed outside academic circles (for example with the media) and made it clear that they would not accept any strategies that entailed compromises with the prostitutes. Moreover, Westminster City Council used the report to legitimate a strategy which it had explicitly not endorsed.

The outcome of the research has not as yet been socially useful for women. So far not only have the recommendations been ignored, but some subsequent strategies introduced by BT and Westminster City Council have temporarily affected the prostitutes adversely and there has been no reduction in the pornographic content of the cards. This raised interesting questions for Ruth and Celia about whether it can be described as feminist (within the limitations of the context) if the outcomes, so far, were not. Kelly, Burton and Regan argue that feminist research should 'create useful knowledge' with the aim of making a difference for women (1994, p. 28). Some useful knowledge was gained about the activities of the sponsors and the successful counter-strategies deployed by the women to maintain their cards in the phone boxes, which belies their passivity or powerlessness. At least this representation of the prostitutes complies with Bhavnani's first principle of feminist accountability in research through her concern to make visible the agency of women being researched without reinscribing dominant representations of their powerlessness (1993, p. 98).

There will be problems and difficulties for feminists working in research commissioned towards a different agenda. The conflict and troubled progress within the case studies are indicative of this situation. However, amid the difficulties, there can be positive outcomes when women work creatively doing feminist research while conforming to the language and modes of organization of those directing the research, which are not feminist.

What Issues are Raised for Feminists Working in a Non-feminist Research Team?

Ruth and Celia work collaboratively in their daily work, continuing this practice in relation to the research. Their expectation of working collaboratively with the research team as a whole proved unrealistic. It consisted of a self-selected, disparate group, representing a range of disciplines and operating with different politics and intellectual frameworks with little common ground.

This was exacerbated by the lack of effective team leadership and within the group there was no setting of ground rules and relatively little commitment to the project. Despite allocating the research tasks, the bulk of the fieldwork ultimately fell to Ruth and Celia. The group dwindled from the ten involved in designing the research to four, with the two men working mostly in isolation and contributing little to the final research.[3] Despite the increased pressure, taking control of the research meant that they were able to steer it in the direction they wanted. In other circumstances they might have been pressurized into doing research they did not condone and attaching their names to a report they did not support.

In the local authority care project Maggie experienced teamwork as an additional pressure because she was both doing and managing the research, trying to facilitate feminist praxis (O'Neill, 1994) within a team that was not committed to it. Her central problem while involved in the research was working in isolation with minimal support from the team, especially emotional support around gathering the life-history narratives which sometimes included the most painful and traumatic experiences. She was committed to listening to these narratives in ways that were ethical and sensitive to the emotional and practical needs of the young people and individuals working with them. This was emotionally exhausting and time-consuming and support from other team members would have made it a bit easier. Instead, her major sources of support were a trusted female friend also working in a sensitive area and another woman working for Prostitute Outreach Workers (POW). The situation improved somewhat when a female research assistant was appointed who actively engaged with the process of doing feminist research.

A raft of difficulties also arose when Maggie left the project to take up a new post. These related to both control of the research and ownership of, and access to, the data. First, the action-research component which Maggie had set up as integral to the research was dropped. By no longer being involved in the final stages of the research project she could not see her hard work come to fruition nor influence the final outcomes. Second, she was informed that she had no right of access to the data as it belonged to the team and the university.[4] Third, after lengthy negotiations, it was agreed that she could publish from her part of the project only, but everything she published must first be approved by the team and not overlap or conflict with their publications. There was no question of her name being added to their publications as she had left the team and would not be involved in their production. The right of censorship of information was unidirectional, effectively silencing any criticisms she may wish to make. At the same time her name cannot be attached to a report that she does not support. However, Maggie insisted that she was referenced in all publications for her part in developing, managing and conducting the fieldwork over the first two years of the three-year project. Since then, there has been no further communication and Maggie has produced one article, with support from the female research assistant, which referenced the project but included none of its data (O'Neill, Goode and Hopkins, 1995).

Clearly, the commodification of one's work and ideas is something of which we all need to be aware. As feminists we must learn from each other's experiences to protect ourselves in future. Changes in university funding practices have also created differential use values of research and publication. The commodification of ideas may have implications for and raise questions about feminist research more generally. This commodification of our ideas and our subsequent protection of that work creates a double bind because we end up helping to reinforce the competitive 'between men culture' (Irigaray, 1993) that dominates the academy.[5] Our experiences of working in non-feminist research teams where competition, hostility and prejudice can operate as standard aspects of interpersonal dynamics leads us to consider possible strategies to protect the interests of women team members and create a collaborative or at least a non-exploitative research culture.

What Strategies can we Identify as a Framework for Feminist Practice Within the Constraints of Commissioned Research?

A major concern of feminist researchers is the management of the research process and the importance of collaborative teamwork. Morley emphasizes the benefits of teamwork: 'Paying attention to the creative process also necessitates working collectively to support one another to notice and discharge destructive patterns of internalised oppression' (1995, p. 127). For Maggie, working collaboratively in the context of the all-male research team was stressful and difficult. However, working with the female research assistant ensured her last six months on the project were improved beyond words. Working with professionals in the field and the young people involved in the project was central to the field relations. Ruth and Celia, working collaboratively with Derrick Wright, writing the report and preparing a subsequent paper (Jenkins, Swirsky and Wright, 1995), have reaped the benefits of collective endeavour through drawing on our different skills and sharing ideas and constructive feedback.

Similarly, Kaplan and Rose emphasize the benefits to be gained from collaboration, not only in dividing tasks, sharing ideas, motivating and supporting one another but also as collaborators experiencing a kind of 'intellectual and emotional synergy' (1993, p. 547).[6] Kaplan and Rose's collaboration derived from their experiences of consciousness-raising groups whereas many women are now working in an academic context where they are forced to make moral choices about competing with other women for their positions. This point is reinforced by Morley (1995) who comments that individual authorship is more highly rated in the research assessment exercise while collaborative work is less highly valued.

Research which has been designed and formulated with explicit feminist terms of reference have developed feminist approaches to teamwork and offer valuable insights for other feminist researchers. Holland and Ramazanoglu make their research process explicit, attempting to find a way of dealing with issues arising from working together. They were conscious that women occupy different positions in the research hierarchy with the consequence that the ideas of those with more power may be given more weight. Nevertheless, they tried to resolve this through regular team meetings, where there was an opportunity to discuss the negative aspects of the research (including stress, traumatic interviews, irritations with other team members). They comment that: 'The WRAP [Women, Risk of AIDS Project] team did not succeed in making all voices heard all of the time, but has tried to retain a critical consciousness of issues of power and control in the research team' (1994, p. 128). Kelly, Burton and Regan (1994) offer an impressive example of managing the research process in a way that is informed by their political perspectives. For example, they take considerable care to mobilize the particular skills of each researcher, to avoid a hierarchical organizational structure, to encourage each other and be sensitive to individual needs.

What Strategies might be Adopted in Undertaking Non-feminist Commissioned Research?

In the absence of either feminist terms of reference or a feminist research team, there may be less scope to develop the desirable models of feminist research. In these contexts, survival strategies for participants who are feminists are crucial. In terms of strategies, it is always more difficult to identify positive strategies and, understandably, researchers are reluctant to publish their failures so that others can learn from their mistakes. From our own limited experience we have learned a few strategies that we will consider when undertaking commissioned research in the future.

First, it is necessary to assess the viability of the team as a whole to work together by formulating the ground rules for participation and agreeing the ethical parameters of the research. Such a process would assist in weighing up the implications of staying in or leaving the project.

Second, an important factor influencing any decision about participation in a research team should be an assessment of the power relations to see what scope there is to influence the direction of the research towards feminist objectives.

Third, there may still be the dilemma, especially for contract researchers, that economic or 'institutional' necessity (in the current climate) may render the above strategies a luxury women cannot afford. In such cases, 'useful knowledge' and experience gained from the process of participating in the research without incurring damaging and emotionally costly consequences can still be useful.

Fourth, it is essential to negotiate the 'ownership' of the findings in the event of disputes over the outcomes and to anticipate the possibility of leaving before the project is finished to avoid the invidious position of having your name attached to recommendations you do not endorse. We need to protect ourselves from 'intellectual prostitution' and disputes over the ownership of ideas and material. However, in doing so we may be reproducing, perhaps unintentionally, competitive and individualistic practices and processes which limit truly collaborative research.

Finally it is important to understand the dynamics within the research team and also in the process of conducting the research. Being observant and noting down problems and difficulties that arise and then talking about them (if it is safe to do so) can help us to better understand our own feelings and responses and perhaps pre-empt difficult situations which leave us feeling hurt and disempowered.[7] These guidelines may be helpful for women becoming involved in contract research about women. Being open about these issues, talking about them at WSNA conferences and in our own research contexts may help us to develop shifts in our own practices that are women-centred and which feed into and help to change competitive, masculinist practices and processes.

We can never look at developing, doing and managing feminist research through 'rose-coloured spectacles'. The process of 'doing' feminist research within what Luce Irigaray (1993) calls the 'between men culture' isn't easy. The personal, material and emotional struggles are hard to work through but as women who live our feminism, these are important steps in addressing inequalities in the research process. Frigga Haug contends that the marginalization of women from 'masculine spheres of production and administration' and the ways in which 'hopes for the quality of life are otherwise displaced to the margins' can serve to immobilize (1992, p. 86). She reminds us that 'the ability to bring about change grows out of people's own activity' (1992, p. 204). Our aim has been to raise questions about the micropolitics of the research process and explore the conditions of possibility for achieving a feminist research practice. We hope that others will extend this debate by adding their experiences and suggesting other strategies that will assist feminist researchers through the pitfalls of contract research.

Notes

1 This chapter is based on a workshop presented at the Stirling WSNA (UK) 1995 Conference. The original idea for this arose from discussions between the three of us about our experiences of commissioned research deriving from our shared interest in the issues of prostitution. We have gained much from working together and from sharing and clarifying the problems and possibilities of maintaining feminist integrity in our research practice.

2 Maggie's first research project was commissioned by Safer Cities. Her second project on routes into prostitution from local authority care was funded by Nottingham Trent University.

3 Derrick Wright joined the team at a late stage. We are grateful to Derrick for typing this chapter.

4 Matters relating to ownership and control of research findings were never discussed by the managers of the local authority care project – a common mistake particularly in teams unused to conducting commissioned or funded research. We need to be very clear about the contractual obligations at the start of a project, indeed, even at the project's design stage. We also recognize that difficulties relating to ownership and control of research data may be present in feminist research teams. Ruth Swirsky has had somewhat similar experiences in accessing material from a feminist research project conducted in the 1980s.

5 The 'between men culture' which Irigaray writes about is exemplified in *je, tu, nous* (1993) as well as in numerous feminist publications, for example Dale Spender (1988) and Dorothy Smith (1978).

6 In a different context, Celia experienced this kind of 'intellectual and emotional synergy' while she, Lemah Bonnick and Mary Hickman were completing their PhDs. They presented their model of collaborative work at a workshop at the British Sociological Association Annual Conference on 'Research Imaginations' at the University of Essex (Bonnick, Hickman and Jenkins, 1993). See also Chapter 10 by Pamela Cotterill and Gayle Letherby in this volume.

7 At the same time we are concerned that we may be accused of whinging and whining or even a lack of 'ethics' by speaking out about our experiences, or perhaps even being complicit in the problems as we were part of the process of the research. Being 'other' is always a difficult position in which to exist and to work.

References

BHAVNANI, K. (1993) 'Tracing the contours: feminist research and feminist objectivity', *Women's Studies International Forum*, **16**, 2, pp. 95–104.

BONNICK, L., HICKMAN, M. and JENKINS, C. (1993) 'Washing down critiques with food and wine: collaborative work towards the completion of our PhDs', paper presented at the British Sociological Association Annual Conference 'Research Imaginations' at the University of Essex, April 1993.

HANMER, J. and SAUNDERS, S. (1984) *Well Founded Fear*, London, Hutchinson.

HAUG, F. (1992) *Beyond Female Masochism: Memory Works and Politics*, London, Verso.

HOLLAND, J. and RAMAZANOGLU, C. (1994) 'Coming to conclusions: power and interpretation in researching young women's sexuality', in PURVIS, J. and MAYNARD, M. (Eds) *Researching Women's Lives from a Feminist Perspective*, London, Taylor & Francis.

IRIGARAY, L. (1993) *je, tu, nous: Towards a Culture of Difference*, London, Routledge.

JARVINEN, M. (1993) *Of Vice and Women: Shades of Prostitution*, Oslo, Scandinavian University Press.

JENKINS, C., SWIRSKY, R. and WRIGHT, D. (1995) 'De-vicing public payphones: contesting the use of public telephone boxes to advertise sexual services', paper presented at the British Sociological Association Annual Conference 'Contested Cities' at the University of Leicester, April 1995.

KAPLAN, C. and ROSE, E. (1993) 'Strange bedfellows: feminist collaboration', *Signs*, **18**, 3, pp. 547–60.

KELLY, L., BURTON, S. and REGAN, L. (1994) 'Researching women's lives or studying women's oppression? Reflections on what constitutes women's oppression', in PURVIS, J. and MAYNARD, M. (Eds) *Researching Women's Lives from a Feminist Perspective*, London, Taylor & Francis.

LAWS, S. (1990) 'Issues of blood', *Trouble and Strife*, **20**, Spring.

MACKINNON, C. (1994) *Only Words*, London, Harper & Row.

MORLEY, L. (1995) 'Measuring the muse: feminism, creativity and career development in higher education', in MORLEY, L. and WALSH, V. (Eds) *Feminist Academics: Creative Agents for Change*, London, Taylor & Francis.

O'NEILL, M. (1993) 'Feminist research and women's lives: problems, dilemmas and transformative possibilities', paper presented at the British Sociological Association Annual Conference 'Research Imaginations' at the University of Essex, April 1993.

O'NEILL, M. (1994) 'Feminising theory/theorising sex: researching the needs of young people in care', paper presented at the British Sociological Association Annual Conference at the University of Lancashire, April 1994.

O'NEILL, M., GOODE, N. and HOPKINS, K. (1995) 'Juvenile prostitution – the experience of young women in residential care', *Childright*, January.

PHOENIX, A. (1994) 'Gender and "race" in the research process', in PURVIS, J. and MAYNARD, M. (Eds) *Researching Women's Lives from a Feminist Perspective*, London, Taylor & Francis.

PHOENIX, J. (1995) 'Prostitution: problematising the definition', in MAYNARD, M. and PURVIS, J. (Eds) *(Hetero)sexual Politics*, London, Taylor & Francis.

PURVIS, J. and MAYNARD, M. (1994) 'Doing feminist research', in PURVIS, J. and MAYNARD, M. (Eds) *Researching Women's Lives from a Feminist Perspective*, London, Taylor & Francis.

ROBERTS, H. (1988) (Ed.) *Doing Feminist Research*, 2nd edn, London, Routledge.

RUSSELL, D. (1993) *Against Pornography: The Evidence of Harm*, California, Russell Publications.

SMITH, D. (1978) 'A peculiar eclipsing: women's exclusion from Man's culture', *Women's Studies International Quarterly*, **1**, 4.

SPENDER, D. (1988) 'The gatekeepers: a feminist critique of academic publishing', in ROBERTS, H. (Ed.) *Doing Feminist Research*, London, Routledge.

STANLEY, L. and WISE, S. (1993) *Breaking Out Again: Feminist Ontology and Epistemology*, 2nd edn, London, Routledge.

Chapter 10

Collaborative Writing: The Pleasures and Perils of Working Together

Pamela Cotterill and Gayle Letherby

Introduction

This piece is autobiographical in nature and centres on our experience of collaborative writing. This debate is ongoing. Among the most recent contributions is an article by Carey Kaplan and Cronan Rose (1993) and a comparison between their experience and ours forms part of this piece. We are driven to write about the collaborative work we do together because we believe that collaborative work and particularly that undertaken by women is misunderstood and underrated. It is politically important for women to write and to write together. As Gail Chester and Sigrid Nielsen (1987) write:

> Learning to organise thoughts on paper, to express feelings, to re-spond to others, is an enormous extension of women's power. It allows communication over time as well as distance. (p. 11)

> Collective writing is an important feminist tradition, and writing collectively can help to develop a fluid intermingling of many voices, giving confidence to its participants and creating opportunities for a wider range of people to appear in print. (p. 17)

This is important, for as Kaplan and Rose (1993) note, 'marginalized voices need to be heard' (p. 545). This is important both in terms of women's position in the academy and in terms of the production of academic knowledge.

Thus, writing individually and together is something that we feel strongly about, like many others. It is also something we find pleasurable and, in part, we write this piece as a celebration of our own and other working relation-ships. We are unable to distinguish between work and friendship within our relationship and, indeed, we no longer try. We share the same political convic-tions and we are fortunate that our means of expression are compatible. Writing together is therefore 'easy'. Also, like other collaborative writers, we find it impossible to write about our academic relationship without reference to our personal autobiographies (Kaplan and Rose, 1993).

Centring Ourselves

We are both white and able-bodied and originate from working-class backgrounds. We each came to academia as mature students and, consequently, came late to our professional careers. Pam is a lecturer in Women's Studies and Sociology at Staffordshire University. She completed her doctoral research into mother and daughter-in-law relationships in 1989. Her teaching interests are in feminist epistemology and methodologies and in social policy and her current research interests focus on issues of autobiography and biography in feminist research. Gayle is a lecturer at Coventry University. Her teaching interests are in women's studies, crime and deviance, health and medicine and research methods. She is nearing the completion of her doctoral research on experiences (predominantly women's) of 'infertility' and 'involuntary childlessness'. We met as undergraduate student (Gayle) and teacher (Pam) but later became friends. Friendship led to animated discussions about our experiences of sociological research and although we continue to pursue individual projects, we share thoughts and ideas all the time. Our collaborative writing, however, is only a fractional aspect of our relationship. We live near to each other and meet frequently and our conversations and shared activities are not confined to the academic. We socialize together with mutual friends and family members. We support each other through good times and bad and, in short, neither of us can imagine not having the other around.

Kaplan and Rose (1993) highlight that in relation to the 'institution' our position as women is marginalized, but this was not the basis of our feminism nor the reason we started to write together. Indeed, shared oppression on the basis of gender does not necessarily lead to collaboration. It is well-documented that other variables divide women and that experiences that result as a consequence of gender are not always sufficient to override the structural barriers of status, class, sexual orientation, age, ethnicity and disability (Ramazanoglu, 1989; Stanley, 1990; Cotterill, 1992). Kaplan and Rose (1993) note that they both began their careers in the 1970s. This, they argue, was a critical period for women as academics and students in higher education. In their view the marginalization they experienced was instrumental in the development of their working relationship. However, we recognize that women were and continue to be at the lower levels of the academic hierarchy and that some women, by virtue of their sexuality, ethnicity and other aspects of their identity may be more marginalized than others. Therefore it is politically important for women to write together but this was not our original motivation. We began to write together because we shared interests and importantly because we liked each other. The positive outcomes of this, both political and academic, were a bonus. Furthermore, in our own discipline of Sociology the marginalization of female academics in the 1970s did not noticeably lead to a plethora of collaborative writing from women.

Pamela Cotterill and Gayle Letherby

When we started to write together our statuses within the university where we both worked at the time were similar (we were women) and different (one of us was a lecturer, the other a postgraduate student). We recognize that, objectively, there was a power differential but in practice our relationship was (and is) of reciprocal support and sharing. Colleagues appeared to recognize and respect this and thus we did not encounter the problems identified by other collaborative writers. For example, Liz Kelly, Linda Regan and Sheila Burton (1991) state:

> The existing differences and confidences were reinforced by external responses, even from other feminists. At times what we managed to create internally was undermined by these interactions. Exploring these issues explicitly and systematically also threatened the collectivity we managed to maintain most of the time. (p. 14)

Neither did we have the problem of 'long-distance collaboration' (p. 549) referred to by Kaplan and Rose (1993) but like them we were often frustrated by the fact that other commitments can interfere with opportunities for joint writing. For example, although daily discussion of ideas was fairly easy for us, finding compatible blocks of time to sit and work together was more difficult.

Five years on in our collaborative relationship there have been some changes. Gayle has just completed her second year as a full-time permanent lecturer at Coventry University so although we still live near to each other daily contact at work is no longer an option. We both work in 'new' universities and have experienced the tensions associated with this new 'status'. The expansion of higher education has led to increased teaching and administrative loads for both of us. Alongside this, as Broughton (1994) argues, we like all academics find ourselves 'caught in a cycle for which "publish or perish" is rapidly becoming a frozen metaphor' (p. 114). Thus it is necessary, as Broughton adds, to publish 'often, in the right forms and in the right places, or be punished, by having your teaching and administrative loads increased' (p. 114). All this creates a number of dilemmas for us. First, how we can find the space to meet, talk and write? Second, our careers are dependent simultaneously on our work within the institution as teachers and administrators and within the discipline as researchers and writers. Third, writing together has always had an element of enjoyment for us which is currently being eroded by all these pressures.

Yet working together has developed into a strategy to combat some of these dilemmas. Making a commitment to meet another person, having done some preparation around a particular issue, is harder to break than a commitment to oneself. And working together challenges the experience of isolated academic existence.

120

Collaborative Writing and Inclusion of the Self: Academic Texts or Self-indulgent Ramblings?

Collaborative work is not always given high status. Chait argues that 'Despite rhetoric that honours collaboration, co-operation, and shared authority, most colleges and universities neglect or underutilize group rewards for group performances' (Chait cited in Kaplan and Rose, 1993, p. 558). We have experienced this first hand. At many of the conferences we have attended there have been 'Getting into Print' sessions and invariably speakers on these occasions have warned against writing collaboratively. The consensus view appears to be that such work invokes questions around the equality of input and the division of labour. It is appropriate here to apply and extend Catherine Itzin's (1987) work. Her theory on the social construction of aesthetic divisions within the art of non-fiction is applicable both to writing which includes reference to the self and pieces which are written collaboratively. She argues that a hierarchy exists in literature in which fiction is of higher status than non-fiction and further within the 'working-class' non-fiction area there are subdivisions of status. For example: 'Authors of cookery books or gardening books are definitely not in the same class as the academics (whatever their discipline), and the writers of "how to" books are hardly regarded as writers at all' (p. 67).

Like Kaplan and Rose (1993) we would argue that feminist collaboration and/or that which includes explicit reference to the personal is likely to be even less valid. At a conference on 'Auto/biography in Sociology' it was clear that some participants felt that the inclusion of self in the writings resulting from research was inappropriate. Again, we have experienced this first hand. An article we wrote together for the journal *Sociology* (1993) was 'reviewed' by Gary Day (1993) who attacked our assertion that research involves the weaving together of the researched and the researcher. He considered our piece to be both 'grossly self-indulgent' and 'sickly self-advertisement'.

Clearly, some would argue that work which involves inclusion of self and/ or is written collaboratively comes low down in the academic hierarchy. We disagree strongly. We know that the work we do together is wholly collaborative and within it the inclusion of aspects of ourselves, our relationship and our individual academic and research experiences reiterate this. As Tillie Olsen (1980) argues the product is part of the conditions of its production and we cannot leave ourselves out of our writing. With us, some ideas start as Pam's or Gayle's and become 'ours', some which come to us independently we subsequently discover we share. When we look at the finished piece we can recognize our individual contributions, while at the same time there are places where our ideas are so completely interwoven that it is difficult for us to determine their original source. We also believe that the inclusion of self enables the reader to recognize us as people within the work. In this we agree with Chester and Nielsen (1987) who argue: 'Good collective writing is like good individual writing – it does not flatten out the individual voice and the new thought' (p. 11). This is particularly important since like Kaplan and Rose

(1993) we deplore academic styles which aim to mystify rather than clarify. These styles we would add are both exclusive and excluding and maintain academic power relations and hegemonies.

Our first joint endeavour was prompted by a flyer inviting contributions to a methodology text. We quickly developed a working routine that we both find enjoyable. Our pattern of work varies a little depending on what we are doing but is generally a variation of the following. After some individual preparation we meet and make a plan. We divide the work into sections and then decide on the division of labour. Neither of us want to do some of the sections, so we usually leave those areas and do them together later. We also leave the introduction and conclusion and write them together at the end. After some work apart we meet at one of our houses to piece together what we have so far. We each bring our computer disk and transfer what we have on to one and then rework what we've got together. This part feels very much like doing a jigsaw. At this point, we should mention the importance of food to the whole process. We always have nice things to eat on these occasions and, consequently, we eat a lot and find it impossible to write without treats.

Having completed our first draft we seek the assistance of 'significant others' in our academic life. These are people who read and comment on our work and whose opinions we value and trust. This process is not unique to us as almost every book and article we read acknowledges the comments made by others on earlier drafts: a clear example of how even individually written pieces are in some small way collaborative. We then rewrite incorporating suggestions and if the paper has been written for presentation we practise both privately and to colleagues and friends. Finally, we tidy up, finish off and either formally present our finished piece or send it to the relevant journal.

At the end of our first collaborative piece we wrote (Cotterill and Letherby, 1995):

> Writing has been something we do alone, private and isolated, although we have always shared thoughts and ideas with each other and others whom we trust. Now we have learned to write together too. We have found it intellectually stimulating and extremely enjoyable. Indeed, (dare we say it) it has been fun! (p. 133)

Several collaborations later we confirm this view. Indeed, if a tape recording of the afternoon(s) in which we wrote this piece accompanied the text you would hear the helpless laughter alongside the academic and literary angst. As well as stressing this enjoyment, it is also important to emphasize the academic development which has resulted for both of us from our work together. For example, we have found new ways of writing individually and have become interested in topics we would perhaps not have come across if not for each other. Collaborative writing has also led to joint presentations: a new development and an acquired skill for both of us. Again, along with anxiety about academic vulnerability comes the fun of doing it together.

Once written, any academic piece intended for presentation and/or publication becomes the subject of peer revision. Khun (1975) cited in Spender (1981) suggests that those who have established reputations often have a vested interest in preserving the authority of their knowledge and work. Dorothy Smith (1987) supports this, arguing that the dominant ideas in any society are mediated through language – in written texts and in verbal communication – and these are created by those in positions of power. She adds that, as these are occupied almost exclusively by men, women have been excluded from the making of knowledge and culture. Recently, with the growth of feminist scholarship in academia there have been huge developments in feminist research and theory and associated publishing opportunities. This is not to suggest that feminist work is no longer considered a challenge to more traditional forms of knowledge and it may be reviewed unfavourably in this light. However, collaborative writing challenges not only the substance of traditional knowledge but the style of presentation. This is evident with regard to the previous UK Research Assessment Exercises. Collaborative pieces written by two people counted for half the worth to the individual as a piece written alone, suggesting that academic production is measured in terms of quantity rather than quality. Perhaps some of the negative response to collaborative work is the common assumption that working relationships are often based on exploitation involving an uneven distribution of labour. We acknowledge that exploitation is possible but we also know that it is not inevitable.

With respect to inclusion of the self, the 'personal is political' is central to feminism. Thus the feminist writer needs to acknowledge her intellectual and personal biographies (Stanley, 1990; Cotterill and Letherby, 1993, 1995). This sometimes brings criticism. Yet as feminist researchers committed to theorizing beyond the personal, this inclusion has political as well as academic importance. As women committed to feminist principles we need to be careful not to misinterpret the experiences of women who are not. As feminist academics we need to challenge stereotypical images of women's place in the world.

Some Conclusions

Collaborative writing is now a significant part of our lives. Both of us have collaborated with others on various pieces and again this allows us to develop our interests and expertise as well as our writing skills. But this does not mean that we have moved away from our original partnership with each other. Indeed, although we enjoy writing with others we find it is not always so easy. Working relationships always involve compromise to a greater or lesser extent. Others have highlighted the tension collaborative writing sometimes involves (Holliday *et al.*, 1993; Bell *et al.*, 1994). For example: 'The construction of the paper has taken place over nine months and has involved constant negotiation (and arguing)' (p. 45). However, as we and others have highlighted, collaborative work has political benefits which outweigh individual personal divisions. It is also important to point out that 'the embattled nature of collaboration' (Kaplan and Rose, 1993, p. 558) which is part of some joint endeavours is not necessarily detrimental to both the process and the product. Indeed, differences of perspective may lead to creative ways of writing and presentation. Pile and Rose (1992) deal with this by writing the main body of their article on modernism and postmodernism in geography in parallel columns.

So complete harmony is not essential for good collaborative work. Although we sometimes disagree, the differences between us are never insurmountable and there is little tension in our personal and working relationships. Despite this, we feel that it is politically impossible for us to adopt the metaphoric use of 'lesbianism' as do Kaplan and Rose (1993). We would argue that our relationship is both supportive and creative but as heterosexual women we feel uncomfortable with the lesbian metaphor. As women who are committed to each other and to other women generally, we prefer to call our relationship 'woman-centred'. For us this recognizes that '"sisterhood" is both powerful and mutually empowering' (Kaplan and Rose, 1993, p. 557), yet also acknowledges that lesbianism may have an erotic element and that the label 'lesbian' carries a stigma that we are free from as heterosexuals. Another danger with the term 'lesbian collaboration' is the implication that lesbian relationships are always non-exploitative, some lesbian relationships are abusive. Several writers have commented that this abuse may be physical, verbal and emotional (Kelly, Regan and Burton, 1991; Hall, 1992; Mann, 1993).

Feminist work of any kind gives a voice to women with different experiences, expresses feminist ideas and shapes the way we view our individual and collective lives. Feminist collaborative writing does all of this as well as replacing the isolation of working alone with the empowerment that comes from mutual support. This type of working together also has possible implications for woman-centred teaching and learning. Yet many of the obstacles faced by feminist academics who seek to work collaboratively will also be experienced by their students. At all levels of the academic hierarchy the value of the product that is collaboratively produced is likely to be measured by traditional standards. We think it is important to keep writing and talking about the positive aspects of working together.

Acknowledgements

We should like to thank all the people we have written with collaboratively: Ruth Holliday; Lezli Mann; Karen Ramsay; Gillian Reynolds; Ruth Waterhouse and Dawn Zdrodowski. Our thanks also to the people who attended our presentation at the Women's Studies Network Conference in Stirling. Some of their comments have been included in this piece. We should also like to acknowledge how much we appreciated those who told us of their own positive experiences of collaborative work and those who gave us more ideas about nice things to eat while working. Thanks also to Liz Stanley for her comments on an earlier draft of this chapter.

References

BELL, D., BINNIE, J., CREAM, J. and VALENTINE, G. (1994) 'All hyped up and no place to go', *Gender, Place and Culture*, **1**, 1, pp. 31–48.

BROUGHTON, T. (1994) 'Life lines: writing and writer's block in the context of women's studies', in DAVIES, S., LUBELSKA, C. and GUINN, J. (Eds) *Changing the Subject: Women in Higher Education*, London, Taylor and Francis, pp. 111–23.

CHESTER, G. and NIELSEN, S. (Eds) (1987) *In Other Words: Writing as a Feminist*, London, Hutchinson.

COTTERILL, P. (1992) 'Interviewing women: issues of friendship, vulnerability and power', *Women's Studies International Forum*, **15**, 5/6, pp. 593–606.

COTTERILL, P. and LETHERBY, G. (1993) 'Weaving stories: personal auto/biographies in feminist research', *Sociology*, **27**, 1, pp. 67–79.

COTTERILL, P. and LETHERBY, G. (1995) 'The "person" in the researcher', in BURGESS, R. (Ed.) *Qualitative Methodology*, Vol. 4, Middlesex, Jai Press Inc.

DAY, G. (1993) 'Review . . . special issue biography and autobiography in sociology', *Times Higher Education*, 20 October 1993, p. 37.

HALL, A. (1992) 'Abuse in lesbian relationships', *Trouble and Strife*, **23**.

HOLIDAY, R., LETHERBY, G., MANN, L., RAMSAY, K. and REYNOLDS, G. (1993) '"Room of our own": An alternative to academic isolation', in KENNEDY, M., LUBELSKA, C. and WALSH, V. (Eds) *Making Connections: Women's Studies, Women's Movements, Women's Lives*, London, Taylor and Francis, pp. 180–94.

ITZIN, C. (1987) 'The art of non-fiction (or the social construction of aesthetic divisions)', in CHESTER, G. and NIELSEN, S. (Eds) *In Other Words: Writing as a Feminist*, London, Hutchinson, pp. 67–72.

KAPLAN, C. and ROSE, E. C. (1993) 'Strange bedfellows: feminist collaborations', *Signs: Journal of Women in Culture and Society*, **18**, 3, pp. 547–61.

KELLY, L. (1991) 'Unspeakable acts: women who abuse', *Trouble and Strife*, **20**.

KELLY, L., REGAN, L. and BURTON, S. (Eds) (1991) 'Defending the indefensible?: quantitative methods and feminist research', presentation at Women's Studies (UK) Annual Conference, July.

MANN, L. (1993) 'Domestic violence within lesbian relationships', presentation at British Sociological Association Conference, University of Essex, April.

OLSEN, T. (1980) *Silences*, London, Virago.

PILE, S. and ROSE, G. (1992) 'All or nothing? Politics and critique in the modernism-postmodernism debate', *Society and Space*, **10**, pp. 123–36.

RAMAZANOGLU, C. (1989) 'Improving on sociology: the problems of taking a feminist standpoint', *Sociology*, **23**, pp. 427–42.

SMITH, D. (1987) *The Everyday World as Problematic*, Milton Keynes, Open University Press.

SPENDER, D. (1981) 'The gatekeepers: a feminist critique of academic publishing', in ROBERTS, H. (Ed.) *Doing Feminist Research*, London, Routledge, pp. 186–202.

STANLEY, L. (1990) 'Feminist auto/biography and feminist epistemology', in AARON, J. and WALBY, S. (Eds) *Out of the Margins: Women's Studies in the Nineties*, London, The Falmer Press, pp. 204–20.

Chapter 11

Disability Issues in the Politics and Processes of Feminist Studies

Cathy Lubelska and Julie Mattheaws

This chapter developed because of our joint interest in Women's Studies and a desire to introduce disability issues and politics to the curriculum, based on two converging perspectives, those of two women: a non-disabled research supervisor and a disabled postgraduate student. The issues that we explore in this paper have therefore arisen partly from lengthy discussions at a general level, of the most appropriate ways in which to address disability within Women's Studies; while ensuring, most specifically, that Julie successfully completes her postgraduate research. We intend through our accounts to highlight both the opportunities and obstacles encountered in the processes and priorities of feminist study. In recent work, for example pertaining to feminist research methods, the complexities and durability of the power relationships between the researcher and the researched is a recurrent theme. Yet the influence and the interaction of the student/researcher and supervisor and of the wider contexts which shape the nature and quality of feminist research and pedagogy, is comparatively neglected. We also anticipate that in sharing our different experiences and standpoints with regard to research issues and relationships, we might be able to identify appropriate ways of developing a collaborative framework for the development of a feminist politics of disability in higher education. While recognizing the complexities of the issues which we attempt to unravel here, we share the aim of promoting a positively inclusive and empowering approach to impairment and disability issues within the curriculum and research. Our tactics and perspectives around these issues are both practical and political. As women we both struggle to survive within a patriarchal institution. As a disabled student, and now postgraduate, whose principal research is conducted outside the academy, Julie has to survive and deal with many obstacles imposed on her by a disabling environment.

In what follows we start by indicating our own, individual standpoints in relation both to our engagement with disability issues and our collaboration. We then go on to jointly consider why and how Women's Studies can make a positive contribution to the development of a feminist politics of disability.

Julie: As a disabled postgraduate student in an institution which purports to be and I quote 'positive about disability' one might optimistically suppose that my specific needs and working environment had been adapted to facilitate a successful and rewarding postgraduate career: a shift, hopefully, from 'disabling barriers to enabling environments' (Lunt and Thornton, 1994, p. 232). However, as disabled people are underrepresented in higher education, it is highly unlikely that my institution would have a consultative strategy to meet the needs of disabled postgraduate student. As J. Preece reports: 'only 1 per cent of all disabled adults under pension age are involved in education or training' (Preece in Martin, White and Meltzzer, 1989).

As women we are used to having our experiences ignored or devalued. For feminists working within the academy we have an obligation to each other to make our experiences and work visible and accessible, thus breaking the silence and helping to validate our experiences. Tom Shakespeare reports: 'The role of nature, and the way women are identified as both body and nature, women hence as Other, are crucial to my understanding of disability' (Shakespeare, 1994, p. 292). In other words, if I fail to convey the complexity of my experiences, then someone else will do it for me, often in a negative and misleading manner. Ultimately I then fail to challenge or disrupt non-disabled people's knowledge and opinions about disability. As David Hevey (1992, p. 54) reports: 'Disabled people are represented but almost exclusively as symbols of "otherness" placed within equations which have no engagement to them and which take their non-integration as a natural by-product of their impairment'.

While this chapter is not in any way trying to promote an essentialist view of disability, we hope to explore a number of strategies and suggestions which would be useful for disabled and non-disabled women, in particular, women engaged in feminist studies. As a disabled woman it is assumed that I am able, as a disabled female postgraduate student, to benefit and participate in academic research on the same terms as non-disabled researchers. Julia Preece (1995, p. 87) records in her article 'Disability and adult education – the consumer view', that: 'The collective evidence of adult education participation rates, perceptions of disability as a particular form of disadvantage and a growing body of recommendations for practical and attitudinal improvement, all highlight the need for direct consultation with disabled adults.'

In assessing my needs, I need to identify the constraints that are imposed on me because of the 'disabling environment'. A programme of study needs to be realistically designed which will not be detrimental to my health. Important here is the relationship between myself and my supervisor. We have tried to share responsibility for my successful completion, thereby attempting to neutralize any issues of power in the decision-making process. For a disabled person this is crucial, precisely because for the most part many of us have been excluded from any decision-making processes regarding 'our life', for example, when non-disabled people make decisions on my behalf without any consultation or input from me. Fundamental to the understanding of disability are the social, economic and cultural inequalities we face. As Tom Shakespeare most rightly states: 'People with impairment are disabled, not just by material discrimination, but also by prejudice. This prejudice is not just inter-personal, it is also implicit in cultural representation in language and in socialization' (Shakespeare, 1994, p. 296).

Many people do not notice my disability, and therefore one could argue that I have a choice as to whether I disclose my impairment. But where I simply cannot emulate other women, such a choice can compound my difficulties and be more apparent than real. Often the concealment of impairment is not an issue of choice at all but in response to the disabling attitudes encountered:

> Disabled adults frequently provoke anxiety and embarrassment in others simply by their presence. Although they become very skilful at dealing with this, it is often achieved at great cost to themselves by denying their disabilities and needs. It is not unusual for disabled people to endure boredom or distress to safeguard the feelings of others. They may, for example, sit through lectures without hearing or seeing rather than embarrass the lecturer, or endure being carried rather than demanding an accessible venue. (French, 1994, p. 73)

However, as a researcher a great deal of my time is spent in libraries searching for information, often in inaccessible places. Lifting, bending and standing at the photocopier for an unlimited amount of time can cause me a great deal of discomfort, often resulting in me having to go home without the information I sought, feeling very frustrated. It is therefore my responsibility to discuss this with my supervisor as I may fall behind or have difficulty in completing my research. There has to be a recognition that my impairment causes me a great deal of pain, and exposing this pain as a constant occurrence in my life is crucial. As Ann MacFarlane (1994, p. 86) states: 'For disabled people there is a block in knowledge and understanding and pain relief is often withheld or there is the need to wait.'

An essential aspect of my postgraduate research is the conduct of inter-views. However, there is a strong possibility that the environment in which this occurs could create potential obstacles for a disabled researcher. I have found it desirable to conduct the interview where the interviewees feel most comfort-able, usually in their own home, which in many instances will be inaccessible to me as a disabled person. I then have to be very clear about the limitations which can restrict my choice of interviews. If I seek alternative arrangements, thus sidestepping the disabling environment, I am in a sense colluding in the oppression of disabled people by disguising or overlooking the difficulties that exist and will continue to exist by my own compliance.

Recently I had to go into hospital, where the treatment I received has caused me to have more problems than I had prior to medical intervention: for example, I now rely on a walking aid and also need physiotherapy twice weekly. Despite the extra pain and inconveniences this has caused, I had prior commitments to fulfil. Recently I attended a conference in Bristol which I felt was relevant and necessary to my postgraduate work. However, I realized that the journey would be impossible to make without support. Although my partner was only too willing to accompany me, the extra cost and difficulties that this creates causes additional stress.

Postgraduate work is often isolating, particularly in my own situation where most of the work is conducted outside the institution. Conferences, therefore, are important because they give me the opportunity to network and to share ideas and developments relating to my work. Insufficient income, restrictions on the personal assistance available and inadequate facilities can all be important in contributing to the dependency which is forced on disabled people. For example, having to rely on the support and goodwill of parents, partners and friends. 'Disabled people in Britain, in the rest of Europe and the USA, have been campaigning for some years for proper provision of personal assistance services. However, such services are not generally available in a way that gives us autonomy and maximises our control over our lives. It is the lack of these services which creates our dependence' (Morris, 1991, p. 144). Becoming involved in the politics and interests of disabled women demands that we engage in research and teaching within the academy through which disabled and non-disabled feminists can together develop an action-orientated feminist epistemology. Our experiences can be used, by ourselves and other women, to begin positively to change an educational environment which currently both reinforces and creates dependency for disabled people and many others.

The challenge for us, then, is to inform as many people as possible of the difficulties and potential of disabled people. To do this we need to enlist the cooperation and support of all women, disabled and non-disabled. Keeping the information to ourselves and pointing out the inadequacies in the system without positive action will not generate the support necessary to successfully undertake postgraduate work. Where support is given, it must be on the disabled person's terms. Academia is not a safe place free of disablism, sexism, heterosexism, racism and classism. The promotion of disability perspectives, in writing, teaching and research, at events like the *Desperately Seeking Sisterhood* conference held in Stirling together with other women, can help to promote a positive consciousness and understanding of disability and impairment.

Cathy: At the outset, and in keeping with good feminist practice, I need to say something of how I come, as a non-disabled woman, to be writing this piece with Julie. At the simplest level it is because she asked me, but in doing so I actually felt very challenged about the idea of entering what, for me, is relatively uncharted terrain, while acknowledging that my trepidatious attitude, in itself, made clear why I must take up, indeed, welcome that challenge. As a feminist I am acutely aware that we need to move forward on this issue, not least because of what I know of Julie's own experience of being a disabled student and researcher within the context of Women's Studies.

I first encountered Julie some years ago, when she was on crutches and an access student in Women's Studies. The issues which she has insistently and persistently raised regarding disability have become more and more visible to me and have been the subject of much discussion with Julie and others, yet I still feel that to some extent I am talking around them. Until recently my engagement, and I suspect that of may others, has been at an essentially practical and, in some senses, very objective level: tackling the most obvious difficulties like trying to ensure physical access to classrooms, that brailling facilities and hearing loops are available, that my language, and that of others, is politically correct around the issues – and often feeling that this is all I can and need to do. It is all too easy to lure oneself into the comforting delusion that you have done your bit, once disabled students are present in the classroom, equipped with a range of customized teaching materials and aids. What I now increasingly recognize is that once disabled students enter the classroom, and gain 'access' to the curriculum, the experience of disability is often compounded rather than diminished and this is where the real problems start.

At the beginning of her book, *Independent Lives*, Jenny Morris (1993, p. x) includes a note on terminology where she says:

> Disability therefore refers to the oppression which people with physical, sensory or intellectual impairments, or those who are mental health system survivors, experience as a result of prejudicial attitudes and discriminatory actions. People are disabled by *society's reaction* to impairment [my emphasis] this is why the term disabled people is used rather than people with disabilities.

The crucial point here is that society creates disability through the ways in which it reacts and responds to those with impairments of one kind or another. In allowing or actively encouraging disabled students into higher education and in using the frameworks and rhetoric of equal opportunities policies as the principal means of addressing, or failing to address disability issues, most universities complacently sidestep or even fail to notice the fact that the curriculum, defined in its broadest sense, continues to be disabling. By ignoring, or at best marginalizing disabled people's experiences in the content of and approaches to teaching and research, the particular oppressions suffered by those with impairments remain invisibilized, unnoticed and unchallenged.

Similar concerns among feminists about the oppressive effects on women of the omission and distortions of our knowledge and experiences was a key impulse in the creation of Women's Studies. Feminist academics are particularly well placed, in terms of the resources – of knowledge, experience and political consciousness – we now possess, to take a lead in tackling disability issues in higher education. It is also evident that we cannot claim to be adequately addressing women's oppression, wherever we find it, if disability remains marginal to the feminist agenda. The issue affects so many of us, directly or indirectly, permanently or temporarily, to the extent that it can be argued that disability is central to the experience of women. The sexism evident within the disability movement to which Susan Stewart (1995) has referred reinforces the need for feminists to act here, particularly as most recent published academic work on disability has been by men.

Many of the recent debates and areas with which we have been engaged in our writing and research can help to reveal which issues are of concern to feminists and why, as well as indicating how we might seek to address these. The aim must be to incorporate disability issues into the curriculum in a positively inclusive way which can serve as a basis for the greater empowerment of disabled women and, by implication, ultimately lessen the experience of disability as an unavoidable concomitant of impairment.

In considering together, briefly, the resources on which we might draw it is important to note that much recent feminist work has been reflectively self-critical in its approaches and outcomes. The shift of emphasis from earlier notions of an all-inclusive sisterhood, where commonalities which apparently constituted a shared, global experience of all women were both asserted and assumed, has been replaced by a greater emphasis on the differences between women, especially in relation to the diversities of oppressions and identities which distinguish us from each other (Spelman, 1988; Ramazanoglu, 1989). Here the work of Black and lesbian feminists, in particular, has been crucial not only in bringing new dimensions of thought and knowledge into the arena of Women's Studies, but also in exposing the prejudices and inequalities which had hitherto been inherent within it. The claim that feminism and Women's Studies have fundamentally been the preserve of white, heterosexual, middle-class women and the problems and exclusions which this has created have come most forcibly from those women who did not fit into this dominant category. Central within their critiques has been a focus on the hierarchical tendencies of the women's movement and of Women's Studies, where the voices and agendas of the already relatively privileged are seen to have been ascendant and to have served to silence, ignore or marginalize the concerns of others (hooks, 1989; Hill Collins, 1990; Wilton, 1993). Where advantaged groups have claimed to be inclusive in their perspectives, this has all too often resulted in an insistence on speaking for other women, on reflecting and interpreting their lives, presumptuously, from the outside; and, by implication, of knowing what is best for them (Hill Collins, 1990, p. 10). Such approaches actually enhance the power of the privileged and actively disempower, still further, those deemed to be disadvantaged. They have rightly been seen as elitist and, especially in relation to issues of race and ethnicity, imperialist in their impulses and effects (Morris, 1991, p. 130). The parallels with prevailing social and professional attitudes towards disability are all too obvious.

These powerful critiques of academic orthodoxies have begun to profoundly reshape and improve Women's Studies. They not only highlight what is wrong and what needs to be done, but also how. This is not the place to embark on a detailed discussion of the impressive array of recent relevant work. But it is pertinent to acknowledge some of its cumulative effects and how they are of direct relevance to a positive feminist engagement with disability. By foregrounding difference, and in the explicit articulation of the voices and concerns of those previously disenfranchized within dominant academic discourses, such work has generated new knowledge which explicitly challenges the legitimacy and accuracy of what might be termed the feminist 'mainstream'.

Fundamental to this challenge has been the exposure of omissions and gaps within the Women's Studies curriculum and of the inadequacies of its approaches to teaching and research. The dubiousness of methodologies and a pedagogy which was failing either to make explicit or to confront both difference and inequalities has been made clear (Welch, 1994).

There has been a growing recognition of the range and interplay of the variables which shape and change our experiences as women which has led to a greater appreciation and understanding of the differences between us. Deconstructionist methodologies, for example, have been helpful in the development of an increasingly refined appreciation of our diversities and of the dangers of unitary categories (Riley, 1988). The list of ways in which we differ keeps growing: the trilogy of race, class and sexuality may expand to include ethnicity, age, nationality and religion and very often also disability. The danger here is that the list becomes no more than a litany, where the mere mention of a word or the odd, one-off lecture is seen to deal effectively with particular differences. Where the worst excesses of postmodernism or multicultural political correctness are at play, this can result in an uncritically celebratory attitude towards difference which both neatly overlooks and reinforces the continuance of inequalities and hierarchies within both society and Women's Studies (Evans, 1991). A couple of examples illustrate how oppressive and disabling such attitudes can be to those who still continue to experience inequalities.

First, bell hooks (1989) and others have drawn our attention to the pitfall of tokenism. When an individual who somehow embodies difference is asked to speak from her own experience, this may serve to reinforce rather than to challenge the objectified otherness of the person who is cast as different in relation to the rest of the group, especially if this is to be as far as the engagement goes. Where the difference 'under the spotlight' is related to impairment of some kind, this can intensify the oppressive experience of disability and militate against integration. Second, many equal opportunities policies rest on the comforting and convenient assumption that equality can be achieved simply by facilitating access to apparently authoritive, privileged knowledge which itself perpetuates inequalities predicated on difference.

The critical recognition that even within the context of Women's Studies, difference is an experience of inequality for many women has again come most clearly from those on the receiving end. The perspectives, theoretical insights and methodologies which their critiques employ have been crucial in raising consciousness of the ways in which feminism and Women's Studies can still

133

perpetuate rather than challenge internal and wider social oppressions. The development of methodologies which centre on the reclamation and articulation of experiences and voices which have remained silent or been cast as 'other' in orthodox accounts has been particularly important (Stanley and Wise, 1993; Maynard and Purvis, 1994). These have helped to generate new knowledge and ways of seeing which challenge and disrupt the assumptions on which such orthodoxies are based. As a principal site of feminist knowledge, Women's Studies can and should be instrumental in crafting an inclusive feminist politics of value to all women. This is only possible if the methodologies which are employed in pursuit of this aim work both to expose and to rectify oppressive and exclusionary practices within the production and dissemination of knowledge and within the research processes which underpin this. Central to this enterprise has to be the recognition of the implications and role of knowledge-as-power in relation to those who are accorded, at best, marginal status and significance. More specifically within Women's Studies, we need to identify who defines and possesses academic knowledge, how this is accomplished and with what consequences for the power relationships between women, as well as between women and men, within the institution and beyond.

In relation to differences around race, sexuality and disability, for example, methodologies have been utilized which attempt to make visible the lived realities of difference and oppression and of responses to these. The increasing revelation of the nature and consequences of racist, homophobic and disablist attitudes has been accompanied by a growing insistence that Women's Studies should actively and self-consciously address its own culpability here. One reflection of this priority has been an emphasis on the need reflexively to identify, unpack and situate whiteness, heterosexism and non-disabled perspectives in order to understand and, eventually, to overcome our prejudices, (Frankenberg, 1993; Kitzinger and Wilkinson, 1993). Central to these processes are methodologies which seek critically to unravel and redress those ways in which Women's Studies still reflects rather than challenges social oppressions.

The methodologies which have been most influential here, and through which we can reshape approaches to teaching and research, have centred on, for example: feminist standpoints and grounded theories; reflexivity, subjectivity and power in the research process, issues of identity and their interplay with difference; critical perspectives on experience; participant research (Morley and Walsh, 1995).

Some of the outcomes of utilizing these methodologies in relation to disability can be indicated by brief reference to the issue of women's reproductive rights. These have consistently been an important theme in feminist politics and Women's Studies in general, within which the voices of disabled women have been notable by their absence. Where perspectives are articulated and grounded in the standpoints of disabled women, the extent of feminist neglect becomes clear. In demonstrating how and with what consequences their reproductive rights have been denied or curtailed, often without consent, through, for example, sterilization and contraception, disabled women have exposed the gaps and inequalities evident in feminist involvement or non-involvement with these issues, as well as the prejudicial assumptions on which engagement has been based (Finger, 1990; Boylan, 1991; Morris, 1991). The increased and relatively unsupervised use of genetic screening and engineering by the medical profession means that more foetuses are likely to be denied the right to life in keeping with society's disablist attitudes. If we take on board the profound influence of eugenicist perspectives in shaping oppressions associated with disability, the relevance of these issues in relation to other differences and inequalities between us becomes clear. Oppressive practices here are now well-documented in relation to race, class, sexuality and nationality.

'For domination to be challenged it has to be, in principle, possible to develop an inclusive, liberatory feminism which encompasses the range of differences between women, where what we share is a politics within which experiences can be located, explained and struggled with/against' (Kelly, Burton and Regan, 1994, p. 30). In seeking to include disability within such a project, issues and relations of power between disabled and non-disabled – particularly where these are teachers and students respectively – need to be carefully disentangled, addressed and neutralized wherever possible. Disability is created by the disempowerment of a minority by a society which both stigmatizes and ignores impairment, while purporting to know what is best for those affected. Equal opportunities and access strategies do not disrupt the structures of power and inequality but they may serve to precipitate their recipients into stark and unmitigated encounters with power as manifest in the curriculum, procedures and relationships within the institution. In attempting to empower disabled students, their issues and experiences need not only to be visible and articulated within the classroom, but to actively contribute to the creation of new knowledge, epistemologies and pedagogies through which feminists can expose, challenge and dismantle relations of power. As Julie commented earlier, support has to be given on the disabled person's own terms. A positively inclusive approach to disability actually requires the reversal of normal/accepted relations of power, where the student not the lecturer defines her own needs, demands and experiences, becoming herself a source of knowledge and an instigator of change.

In this chapter we have attempted to address some of the ways within which we can ensure that differences in relation to disability are positively incorporated into the wider feminist project. Our starting point has been Julie's own experiences of disability and a shared commitment to tackling disabling barriers within both the academic institution and Women's Studies. We believe that disability concerns should permeate the curriculum and research and be integral to our engagement with difference and inequality. Where feminist methodologies have been employed and honed in our teaching and research to bring disability out of the margins, it quickly becomes apparent that the issues affect all of us to some degree.

A comprehensive definition of disability would be very broad, encompassing mental-health issues, the temporary disabilities experienced by many women at periods during their lives, ageism and attitudes to 'disfigurement' in relation to, for example, mastectomy. If we also consider the impact of disability on women's roles as carers, dependents and professionals, the pervasiveness of the issue and its centrality to understanding and improving the experience of all women is obvious. So too is the fact that Women's Studies has resources and methodologies, themselves born of much angst over differences, inequalities and oppressions among women, through which to make a positive and political contribution to the empowerment of the impaired and the eradication of disability. As an Australian Aboriginal woman once said, 'If you have come to help me, then you can go back home. But if you see my struggle as part of your own survival then perhaps we can work together', quoted in (Morris, 1993, p. 179).

References

BOYLAN, E. (1991) *Women and Disability*, London, Zed Books.

EVANS, M. (1991) 'The problem of gender for Women's Studies', in AARON, J. and WALBY, S. (Eds) *Out of the Margins: Women's Studies in the 1990s*, London, Falmer Press.

FINGER, A. (1990) *Past Due: A Story Of Disability, Pregnancy And Birth*, London, The Women's Press.

FRANKENBURG, R. (1993) *White Women, Race Matters. The Social Construction of Whiteness*, Minneaplis, MN, University of Minnesota Press.

FRENCH, S. (1994) 'Can you see the rainbow? The roots of denial', in SWAIN, J., FINKELSTEIN, V., FRENCH, S. and OLIVER, M. (Eds) (1994) *Disabling Barriers, Enabling Environments*, London, Sage.

HEVEY, D. (1992) *The Creatures Time Forgot*, London, Routledge.

HILL COLLINS, P. (1990) *Black Feminist Thought*, London, Unwin Hyman.

HOOKS, B. (1989) *Talking Back. Thinking Feminist, Thinking Black*, London, Sheba.

KELLY, L., BURTON, S. and REGAN, L. (1994) 'Researching women's lives or studying women's oppression?' in MAYNARD, M. and PURVIS, J. (Eds) *Researching Women's Lives from a Feminist Perspective*, London, Taylor & Francis.

KITZINGER, C. and WILKINSON, S. (Eds) (1993) *Heterosexuality: A Feminism and Psychology Reader*, London, Sage.

LUNT, N. and THORNTON, P. (1994) 'Disability, and employment: towards an understanding of discourse and policy', *Disability & Society*, 9, 2.

MACFARLANE, A. (1994) 'Short forms of abuse and their long term effects', *Disability & Society*, 8, 1.

MARTIN, J., WHITE, A. and MELTZZER, H. (1989) Social Survey Divison Report 4. *Disabled Adults; Services*, Transport and Employment, London, Office of Population Census and Surveys.

MAYNARD, M. and PURVIS, J. (Eds) (1994) *Researching Women's Lives from a Feminist Perspective*, London, Taylor & Francis.

MORLEY, L. and WALSH, V. (Eds) (1995) *Feminist Academics: Creative Agents for Change*, London, Taylor & Francis.

MORRIS, J. (1991) *Pride Against Prejudice*, London, The Women's Press.

MORRIS, J. (1993) *Independent Lives: Community Care and Disabled People*, London, Macmillan.

PREECE, J. (1995) 'Disability and adult education – the consumer view', *Disability & Society*, **9**, 3.

RAMAZANOGLU, C. (1989) *Feminism and the Contradictions of Oppression*, London, Routledge.

RILEY, D. (1988) *Am I that Name? Feminism and the Category of Women In History*, London, Macmillan.

SHAKESPEARE, T. (1994) 'Cultural representations of disabled people: dustbins for disavowal?' *Disability & Society*, **9**, 3.

SPELMAN, E. (1988) *Inessential Woman. Problems of Exclusion in Feminist Thought*, London, The Women's Press.

STANLEY, L. and WISE, S. (1993) *Breaking Out Again*, London, Routledge.

STEWART, S. (1995) '*We Are All Different, Aren't We?*' Panel talk presented at Women's Studies Network Annual Conference *Desperately Seeking Sisterhood*, Stirling, June 1995.

WELCH, P. (1994) 'Is a feminist pedagogy possible?' in DAVIES, S., LUBELSKA, C. and QUINN, J. (Eds) *Changing the Subject: Women in Higher Education*, London, Taylor & Francis.

WILTON, T. (1993) 'Queer subjects: lesbians, heterosexual women and the academy', in KENNEDY, M., LUBELSKA, C. and WALSH, V. (Eds) *Making Connections: Women's Studies, Women's Movements, Women's Lives*, London, Taylor & Francis.

Chapter 12

'How Was It For You?' Talking about Intimate Exchanges in Doing Feminist Research

Yvon Appleby

Various feminist methodological debates have focused on ways of conducting feminist research which is ethical, non-exploitative and which accounts for power. Although it is possible to work towards conducting feminist research which attempts to address these issues, it is less possible to know whether as a researcher one has achieved these goals within the research process itself. Focusing on this consideration, I discuss participants' responses to the question 'How was it for you?' which I asked the participants within my study of lesbian women and education. I discuss their responses in relation to my research aims.

Introduction

In reading through the literature on feminist research it is possible to see, particularly with regard to the abstracted nature of much of the discourse, the basis of the claim that the focus is upon what we aim for in feminist research rather than what we actually do. Indeed, some feminist researchers are critical of what they perceive of as 'the romance with epistemology' (Duelli-Klein, 1983) and feel that the literature has created an impenetrable 'supermethodology' (Kelly, Burton and Regan, 1994). The separation between textually debated methodological aims and their actual practice and implementation prompted Mary Cook and Margaret Fonow (1990, p. 71) to ask, 'Is feminist methodology that which feminist researchers do or that which they aim for?' The emphasis on writing about what we are aiming for, which often serves to eclipse discussion of what we do, is also captured by Mary Maynard and June Purvis (1994, p. 1). They argue:

> Despite the high profile now given to discussing feminist research, however, much of the material published, with a few exceptions, tends to focus on the principles involved in a rather abstract way.

This can sometimes be at the expense of exploring the dynamics of actually doing research in the field.

In recognizing the existence of a discursive distinction (at least) between feminist research aspiration and feminist research implementation, it therefore becomes essential to question whether the practices of feminist research are congruent with, and do not themselves impede, feminist methodological concerns.[1] Or, more simply put, we need to ask ourselves within our research processes if we have attained what we set out to achieve. Clearly, this is not unproblematic as one of the difficulties that exists in the relationship between the aims and actions of feminist research lies in knowing how to assess this within the research process itself.

Within much feminist research an openly reflexive research position has been adopted which has lead to questioning the issues of power within research, the relations between researcher and researched and issues of exploitation and appropriation (Finch, 1984; Bhavnani, 1988; Cotterill, 1992; Opie, 1992; Phoenix, 1994; Bola, 1995). And yet within these discussions the subject 'voice' containing the reflexive perspective of the participant is often strangely absent. This absence clearly raises the question of whether as feminist researchers we are concerned with how the participants experience our efforts at doing feminist research or whether we mainly focus on our own reflexive process concerning the aim of producing ethical research.

Where research participants are discussed (Finch, 1984; Opie, 1992) they do not appear to have a reflexive 'voice'[2] of their own with which to comment on questions of their own disempowerment and appropriation within either the research process or product. Moreover, any such imbalanced power relationship, where the researcher can contemplate actions (both their own and those of the participants) and interpret the consequences of these on both the research and the researched, has striking similarities with the 'repressive myth' (Ellsworth, 1992) and the normalizing tendencies (Gore, 1992, 1993) contained in the notion of empowerment within feminist pedagogy and feminist research.[3]

What is missing, and what would provide the other more 'hidden' aspect within this process of knowledge construction, is the reflexivity of the participants.[4] Building on Sue Wilkinson's (1988) important identification of different reflexivities within research (she identifies personal, functional and disciplinary), I would argue that it is also important to consider the reflexivity of the participants. This would enable a two-voiced dialogue, rather than a one-sided philosophical monologue, which could potentially encourage the grounding of debates surrounding the process of knowledge production in feminist research. In what follows I present both my side of the dialogue, containing some aspects of my methodological concerns and aims and also the 'other side' which contains reflections of some of the participants describing how they experienced the research process.

139

Yvon Appleby

Reflections on my Feminist and Lesbian Methodological Aims

My doctoral research, from which this chapter draws, is a small qualitative study looking at the experiences of lesbian women in relation to education. I talked with 21 lesbian women from different geographical locations who were teachers, students and mothers with school-age children. This drew on my experiences and observations of being a lesbian teacher in an FE college, a lesbian mother and a lesbian postgraduate student. As a lesbian and a feminist I made what I now consider to be two relatively unquestioned assumptions at the outset of this research. First, that I would use interviewing as a 'safe' method with lesbian women and second that this method would be congruent with my feminist methodological concerns.

Julia Brannen (1988) suggests that in-depth interviewing is especially suitable for the study of 'sensitive subjects' which Raymond Lee (1993) identifies as research which potentially poses a threat to those involved. Given the heterosexist nature of the education system (Trenchard and Warren, 1984; Warren, 1984; Sullivan, 1993; Clarke, 1994; Epstein, 1994a, 1994b) this was an important methodological concern in studying lesbian women. I also considered that the method of interviewing was 'woman friendly' following various feminist steps towards its rehabilitation (Ribbens, 1989; Oakley, 1990). However, while it may be considered to be 'woman friendly', I questioned the fit between my feminist methodological aims (ethical, non-exploitative research which accounts for the means of its production) and its use with lesbian women. I explain this in detail elsewhere (Appleby, 1994) but in brief I have two concerns. The first is that although attempts have been made to rehabilitate the interview for feminist use with women subjects, by challenging the internal power dynamics, this micro-approach does not acknowledge the central position of this method of data collection within both historical and current medico/scientific enterprises: that is, the relationship with larger medical, scientific and therapeutic perspectives and discourses. Lesbian women have historically been constructed, shaped and controlled by these powerful discourses (Faderman, 1981, 1991; Jeffreys, 1987) and the 'knowledges' they have produced. Feminist rehabilitation of the interview does not necessarily make it 'lesbian friendly' for use with lesbian women as there are many issues surrounding identity and power which are inextricably associated with these models which remain largely unexamined.

My second concern was actually knowing how to incorporate my Self as a lesbian woman (what Stanley and Wise, 1993 describe as my 'auto/biographical I') at the point of data production when using an interview. What I have described, very briefly, is my concern that my aim of producing ethical and non-exploitative feminist research about lesbian women would have been impeded by using the method of interviewing. To overcome some of these problems I explored the use of a conversational approach to gather the information for this study. This method had the potential for overcoming the close

140

association with medico/scientific models contained within the interview and could also more easily allow for the incorporation of my 'auto/biographical I' at the point of data production.

Participant Reflections: 'How was it for you?'

I have outlined the tension between my general feminist research aims and finding a way of doing the research which was not disempowering for the lesbian participants. This, so far, has been my voice in the dialogue of the construction of knowledge. What follows is the 'other side' in that dialogue: how it felt for the participants.

At the beginning of each research conversation I explained what I would use a 'conversational approach'. This provoked three quite different responses. The first was of polite interest and non-comprehension as to what this meant and why it was important. The second was of fear and anxiety where the participants became anxious that they would be expected to assume the responsibility of shaping the conversation. Many participants expressed anxiety about being able to talk at length about these experiences, commenting that they rarely discussed their relationship/experiences as a lesbian woman to education and felt that they lacked confidence and practice. The third reaction was where participants expressed an interest in the possibilities that a conversation held; several of them double-checked that they could also ask questions of me.

At the end of each conversation, which lasted on average two hours, I asked the question 'How was it for you?' explaining that I would like to hear the other lesbian woman's thoughts, comments and feelings about the conversations. Most of the participants responded to this question, which is a verbal parody of intimate exchanges in heterosex, with amusement and laughter. Apart from incorporating the participants' reflexivity, the question also enabled me to check with each participant that she was not being left to deal with any difficult or painful emotions. The level of intimate exchange within the conversations, which was reasonably deep, operated through irony, introspection, discussion of emotions, humour, analysis and breathtaking honesty. The participants reported that the level of intimate exchange was partly because of my lesbian identity.

There was a recognition of the importance of our shared lesbian identification, which was tested for meaning and which unfolded within the conversations themselves. This (inter)active subject negotiation surrounding identification and intimacy appeared to be in contrast to Janet Finch's (1984) fears surrounding a simple and potentially exploitative gender commonality. When asked about issues of responsibility, several participants replied quite indignantly that they were quite aware of what they were saying and why they wanted to say it. Generally they were quite clear in expressing their feelings and reasons for their involvement and there were many instances of what Pat

McPherson and Michelle Fine (1995) call 'sameness discourse' and 'difference discourse' between us. Importantly the conversations were, and were acknowledged by most of the participants to be, full of laughter and celebration showing instances of resistance and ways of survival as well as pain and isolation.

Responses to the question ranged across reported feelings of embarrassment, excitement, pride, stimulation, intimacy, pain and vulnerability. The reports of difficulty (they were not necessarily seen or felt simply as negative) which included embarrassment and vulnerability, were in response to both individual performance and the content of the conversation. In terms of her performance within the conversation Nicky (pseudonyms are used) spoke of her embarrassment:

> N. Mmm, oh well what I thought about it was that I seem so inarticulate because I haven't got any proper sentences and I kept going off at a tangent, and there are lots of dashes and things, and you don't put all of that in when you type it out, you know. It must be rather hard for you to actually work out what I was saying.
>
> YA. No, I thought it was OK.
>
> N. Could you understand it?
>
> YA. Mmm.
>
> N. Because it just seemed very, um, I, there were lots of unfinished sentences, and then whizzing off somewhere else, and I thought oh I don't sound, if they interviewed me on the radio I'd sound awful because I wouldn't say anything coherent in sentences at all.
>
> YA. Yes but the flow was there, you know, its not like questions and answers, is it?
>
> N. Mmm, mmm.

Nicky was both expressing her embarrassment at what she felt was an inarticulate performance, while simultaneously checking that I could understand her. Although she considered her performance, this was secondary, within the conversation, to making sense and clarifying understanding which she did with irony and humour. I noted after the conversation, although she herself questioned her level of articulateness, Nicky's descriptions of her physical embarrassment at dealing with lesbianism in class, which she said made her blush profusely, and her descriptions of her feelings of looking unattractive and 'like a man' as a teacher, were, I found, breathtakingly honest. It made me question my own level of disclosure and the type of (possibly articulate) language which I perhaps used for my own self-protection.

Kate also spoke of her embarrassment at not being able to present a clear and articulate picture of herself and her experiences. However, she acknowledged this as a limitation of research generally, as illustrated by the following extract in response to my question of how it had been for her:

K. OK, OK. It was fine. It was a bit embarrassing.

YA. Why was it embarrassing?

K. Well (pause) I don't know, its difficult to talk about, you know, stuff out of context. That's a bit difficult. Um, and I think there is also a notion that you can present your life but you can't. That's kind of a bit 'Well when I was three I was a lesbian and decided . . . ' To me it would be lovely to have this kind of vision of your life where you could say (noise outside) but you can't. So it's fine.

Kate was able to express her feeling of embarrassment about her performance and she was also able to contextualize this within the more general limitations of the research act. From both Nicky and Kate's responses I considered whether the more informal conversational structure interfered with existing management strategies, which may be of particular significance to lesbian women (Moses, 1978; Woods and Harbeck, 1991). Nicky and Kate's responses raise interesting questions about vulnerability and identification within the research process itself. In both cases, however, Kate and Nicky felt able to discuss their feelings of difficulty alongside other positive comments about the research process.

Another area of difficulty reported by several of the participants was of feeling vulnerable in response to the content of the conversation. Jude said that she had found the conversation mentally and emotionally tiring as it had stirred up difficult things for her particularly about her feelings of not being out as a lesbian teacher. She balanced these difficult feelings, which she described as guilt, with being a lesbian mother where she said she was more able to be herself with her son. Jude discussed her feelings of cowardice about not being out as a teacher and said that having talked about it openly in the conversation she felt that she must either resolve this or change it, acknowledging that both would be difficult to accomplish. Becky, a lesbian mother with a teenage daughter, also remarked how she had confronted her feelings of cowardice about not wishing to be a parent governor at her daughter's school which had been discussed within our conversation. She spent some time in answering the question by tackling this feeling and questioning why she had felt that way in the conversation. When I asked whether this had raised difficult issues for her, Becky said that her negative reaction had made her think and made her realize that she wanted to be stronger. Nicky had also mentioned that the conversation had brought to the surface her anger about what she considered to be her cowardice about not being out as a lesbian teacher.

So what of my aim in doing research about lesbian women that was ethical and non-exploitative as these difficulties could indicate that I have not achieved this end by using a conversational approach. In response I think there are two points to consider. First, as many of the participants explained, these difficulties were not necessarily experienced as overwhelmingly negative. They could be interpreted as a reflection of living as a lesbian woman and feeling the expectation of being able to articulate exactly what that meant to another person. Although the social conditions of oppression were felt to be negative (causing fear, embarrassment and uncertainty) the ability to discuss the negative feelings attached to oppression (guilt and cowardice) were seen as a valuable if painful and uncomfortable opportunity. I would not describe this opportunity as either empowering or consciousness-raising. I would describe it as self-reflexive and participant-centred. The second point is that I have not uncovered something that is not there in other studies; I have merely illuminated it from a different perspective, one that I hope will challenge participants being viewed simply as research victims.

The majority of the participants, including those who discussed the difficult aspects, reported feelings of excitement and stimulation about the conversations. Ella, a college lecturer, described her enjoyment and stimulation at being able to talk in depth about issues which she had not recently had the chance to discuss:

> E. I enjoyed talking about it. Um, I have talked about it at that sort of level in the past but not recently. I've quite enjoyed our depth of conversation and working out. Yes, and bringing it up and talking about it. But at the moment I would't normally do that. So I miss that, yes. Normally it's just an even keel and you go shopping, do your normal things and you don't get into that depth of conversation. I actually enjoyed the depth of conversation, the discussion and the feedback.

> YA. You said that you had it before but you don't have it now. What is it that you miss?

> E. Um, (pause) I think I miss, it's different, it's different the depth of conversation is different with different people, and I enjoy that kind of depth. It's just relationships and what you have, that's different.

Hillary also said that she found the conversation stimulating and felt that her transcribed copy of the script would provide her with much material for her to think about and develop. She also commented on the joint aspect of the conversation:

> H. Yes I mean it's a dialogue and I actually feel there is some, there are things that I have said tonight on the tape that I haven't clearly articulated to myself before ... the stuff around homophobia and oppression and how one experiences oppression. Some of that stuff is

kind of stuff that is lying there somewhere, but this is actually having the opportunity to articulate it in this way. So it feels like a kind of synthesis of ideas coming together. Um, but you know, it's more than the sum of its parts, as it were. You know . . .

YA. Mmm, yes.

H. It's kind of different ideas sparking off.

Both Ella's and Hillary's positive reports that the conversation was enjoyable and interesting fitted my own perception of them. I was extremely surprised when several participants expressed their positive feelings by likening the 'safe' environment and joint construction to therapy. For example, Sarah, a primary teacher, asked me whether I had counselling experience. This textual representation does not fully capture my surprise and consternation at her observation:

S. But I think actually you are quite good, and again here, I don't know, have you ever counselled people?

YA. Um, no, no.

S. Because you are actually quite good at making positive statements which again a counsellor usually does. Like, you know, I can say 'Oh, I feel like a real coward, you know, not coming out at work' and you have said 'But why are you making yourself feel negative?' or whatever. Which is actually a positive way of looking at it by saying 'No, you shouldn't feel negatively.' I mean that is obviously just the way that you are personally. Um, but I actually think that you have been, I don't know whether you have done it consciously, but you have been very responsive about, as we have been going along, not letting me feel bad about myself.

Pauline, an FE lecturer, and Wendy, a college student, also to my surprise described the therapeutic and cathartic effects of our conversations. Pauline explained that she had not talked about what she called issues of her sexuality for 12 years and likened our 'private' conversation to a therapeutic setting. Wendy who had only recently, as she described it, accepted her sexuality felt that the chance to discuss the issues with another lesbian was cathartic. At the time of our conversation Wendy had experienced extreme harassment from other students, was experiencing a difficult time with her parents and was supporting her girlfriend whose lesbian mother had attempted to commit suicide.

I did not anticipate that the participants would describe the conversations in this way, especially as I had rejected the method of interviewing lesbian women because of the implicit relationship to medical and scientific models.

However, this would support Celia Kitzinger and Rachel Perkins (1993) in their claim that psychology has increasingly replaced feminism as a way of seeing and understanding the world:

> These psychological approaches teach us to privatise, individualise and pathologise our problems as women and as lesbians rather than to understand these difficulties as shared oppressions. (p. 5)

Maureen McNeil (1993) also notes that contemporary feminism has become 'a pre-eminent torch bearer of the humanist imperative to "know thyself"' (p. 154) which includes the rise of the professional to achieve this end. It is perhaps not surprising, then, that the participant's other life experiences, which included positive attitudes to therapy and therapeutic concepts, were used to describe what they felt as a 'private' and safe environment in which to discuss aspects of their lives.

Concluding Remarks

I have examined briefly the spaces between my feminist research aims and my doing research with other lesbian women. Alongside my part of the dialogue about the construction of knowledge within the research process I have also included some of the participant's moments of self-reflexivity. This has provided a glimpse of the 'other side' to the dialogue of knowledge production and one that raises many further questions for me as a researcher, especially the gaps between my aspirations, aims, and practice and what was experienced and made sense of by the participants themselves.

Within feminist methodological concerns of conducting ethical and non-exploitative research, the question of 'How was it for you?' provided me with both direct and tangible access to some of these issues within the research process itself. I am not suggesting that by itself this question will provide answers. More modestly it attempts to illuminate the space between our research aims and the impact and meanings of what we assume and what we do. In considering the problems that universal sisterhood, based on essentialistic notions of sameness (Moraga and Anzaldua, 1983; hooks, 1984, 1992; Spelman, 1988; Begum, 1992; Phillips, 1992; Mason and Khambatta, 1993) has created, it is important to find ways of talking about and building on our assumptions and our differences. It is imperative that even before the process of theorizing difference feminists consider difference, commonality and sameness, and what this means for researcher and researched within the research act and at the point of knowledge construction (Phoenix (1994) and Bola (1995) both provide excellent examples of this questioning). If we are to create transparent and fully reflexive feminist research, which accounts for the means of its production, this needs to be more fully a joint dialogue.

Notes

1 Feminist methodological concerns cover a wide spectrum depending on differing epistemological and theoretical positions. Cook and Fonow (1990, p. 72) identify what they view as five recurring themes within feminist methodology. These are: the need to continuously and reflexively attend to gender and gender asymmetry; the centrality of consciousness-raising; challenging objectivity; concerns with producing ethical research; and an emphasis on empowerment. See also Olsen (1994), Stanley and Wise (1991) and Maynard and Purvis (1994) for historical and contemporary discussions.

2 Although I suggest that the participants do not have a voice in these research writings, I am not suggesting a simple inclusion of 'voices' to create authenticity. As Kum Kum Bhavnani (1988) points out, the inclusion of 'voices' in an attempt to empower participants is flawed and leads rather to their disempowerment.

3 Empowerment within feminist research has been critically challenged because of its strong reliance on unexamined power relations, assumed essential identity characteristics and unified forms of oppression. Feminists involved with liberatory pedagogy have discussed both pedagogical empowering possibilities for women (Lather, 1986, 1991) and its limitations and repressive nature (Bhavnani, 1988; Ellsworth, 1992; Gore, 1992).

4 I suggest the usefulness of participant reflexivity within qualitative research designs generally although there would be some covert observational situations where it would not be applicable or relevant.

References

APPLEBY, Y. (1994) 'Listening and talking: interactive conversation as a feminist research method in studying lesbian women', paper presented at BSA Conference 'Sexualities in Social Context', Preston, 28–31 March.

BEGUM, N. (1992) 'Disabled women and the feminist agenda', *Feminist Review*, **40**, Spring, pp. 70–84.

BHAVNANI, K. (1988) 'Empowerment and social research: some comments', *Text*, **8**, 12, pp. 41–50.

BOLA, M. (1995) 'Questions of legitimacy: the fit between researcher and researched', *Feminism and Psychology*, **5**, 2, pp. 290–3.

BRANNEN, J. (1988) 'The study of sensitive subjects', *Sociological Review*, **3**, pp. 552–63.

CLARKE, G. (1994) 'A hidden agenda: lesbian physical education students and the concealment of sexuality', paper presented to BSA Conference 'Sexualities in Social Context', Preston, 28–31 March.

COOK, J. and FONOW, M. (1990) 'Knowledge and women's interests. Issues of epistemology and methodology in feminist sociological research', in

NIELSEN, JOYCE MCCARL (Ed.) *Feminist Research Methods*, Boulder, CO, West View Press, pp. 70–93.

COTTERILL, P. (1992) 'Interviewing women: issues of friendship, vulnerability and power', *Women's Studies International Forum*, **158**, 5, 6, pp. 593–606.

DUELLI-KLEIN, R. (1983) 'How to do what we want to do: thoughts about feminist methodology', in BOWLES, G. and DUELLI-KLEIN, R. (Eds) *Theories of Women's Studies*, London, Routledge.

ELLSWORTH, E. (1992) 'Why doesn't this feel empowering? Working through the repressive myths of critical pedagogy', in LUKE, C. and GORE, J. (Eds) *Feminisms and Critical Pedagogy*, London, Routledge, pp. 90–119.

EPSTEIN, D. (1994a) 'Keeping them in their place: (hetero)sexist harassment, gender and the enforcement of heterosexuality', paper presented to BSA Conference 'Sexualities in Social Context', Preston, 28–31 March.

EPSTEIN, D. (Ed.) (1994b) *Challenging Lesbian and Gay Inequalities in Education*, Buckingham, Open University Press.

FADERMAN, L. (1981) *Surpassing the Love of Men*, London, The Women's Press.

FADERMAN, L. (1991) *Odd Girls and Twilight Lovers*, Harmondsworth, Penguin Books.

FINCH, J. (1984) 'It's great to have someone to talk to: the ethics and politics of interviewing women', in BELL, C. and ROBERTS, H. (Eds) *Social Researching, Politics, Problems and Practices*, London, Routledge.

GORE, J. (1992) 'What can we do for you! What can "we do for you": Struggling over empowerment in critical and feminist pedagogy', in LUKE, C. and GORE, J. (Eds) *Feminisms and Critical Pedagogy*, London, Routledge, pp. 54–73.

GORE, J. (1993) *The Struggle for Pedagogies: Critical and Feminist Discourses as Regimes of Truth*, London, Routledge.

HOOKS, B. (1984) *Feminist Theory: From Margin to Center*, Boston, MA, Southend Press.

HOOKS, B. (1992) (reprinted) *Ain't I a Woman? Black Women and Feminism*, London, Pluto Press.

JEFFREYS, S. (1987) (reprinted) *The Spinster and her Enemies*, London, Pandora Press.

KELLY, L., BURTON, S. and REGAN, L. (1994) 'Researching women's lives or studying women's oppression: reflections on what constitutes feminist research', in MAYNARD, M. and PURVIS, J. (Eds) *Researching Women's Lives from a Feminist Perspective*, London, Taylor & Francis.

KITZINGER, C. and PERKINS, R. (1993) *Changing Our Minds: Lesbian Feminism and Psychology*, London, Only Women Press.

LATHER, P. (1986) 'Research in Praxis', *Harvard Educational Review*, **56**, pp. 257–77.

LATHER, P. (1991) *Getting Smart: Feminist Research and Pedagogy with/in the Postmodern*, London, Routledge.

LEE, R. (1993) *Doing Research on Sensitive Topics*, London, Sage.

MASON, J. V. and KHAMBATTA, A. (1993) *Lesbians Talk: Making Black Waves*, London, Scarlet Press.

MAYNARD, M. and PURVIS, J. (1994) 'Doing feminist research', in MAYNARD, M. and PURVIS, J. (Eds) *Researching Women's Lives from a Feminist Perspective*, London, Taylor & Francis, pp. 1–9.

MCNEIL, M. (1993) 'Dancing with Foucault: feminism and power knowledge', in RAMAZANOGLU, C. (Ed.) *Up Against Foucault: Explorations of some Tensions between Foucault and Feminism*, London, Routledge, pp. 147–75.

MCPHERSON, P. and FINE, M. (1995) 'Hungry for an us: adolescent girls and adult women negotiating territories of race, gender, class and difference', *Feminism and Psychology*, **5**, 2, pp. 181–200.

MORAGA, C. and ANZALUDA, G. (1983) *This Bridge Called My Back: Writings by Radical Women of Color*, New York, Kitchen Table Press.

MOSES, A. (1978) *Identity Management in Lesbian Women*, New York, Prager.

OAKLEY, A. (1990) (reprinted) 'Interviewing women: a contradiction in terms' in ROBERTS, H. (Ed.) *Doing Feminist Research*, London, Routledge, pp. 30–61.

OLSEN, V. (1994) 'Feminisms and models of qualitative research', in DENZIN, N. and LINCOLN, Y. (Eds) *Handbook of Qualitative Research*, London, Sage.

OPIE, A. (1992) 'Qualitative research, appropriation of the "other" and empowerment', *Feminist Review*, **40**, Spring, pp. 52–70.

PHILLIPS, A. (1992) 'Feminism, equality and difference', in McDOWELL, L. and PRINGLE, R. (Eds) *Defining Women: Social Institutions and Gender Divisions*, Cambridge, Polity Press/Open University, pp. 205–22.

PHOENIX, A. (1994) 'Practising feminist research: the intersection of gender and "race" in the research process', in MAYNARD, M. and PURVIS, J. (Eds) *Researching Women's Lives from a Feminist Perspective*, London, Taylor & Francis, pp. 49–71.

RIBBENS, J. (1989) 'Interviewing: an unnatural situation', *Women's Studies International Forum*, **12**, pp. 579–92.

SPELMAN, E. (1988) *Inessential Woman: Problems of Exclusion in Feminist Thought*, London, The Women's Press.

STANLEY, L. (1991) (reprinted) 'Feminist praxis and the academic mode of production', in STANLEY, L. (Ed.) *Feminist Praxis*, London, Routledge, pp. 3–19.

STANLEY, L. and WISE, S. (1991) 'Method, methodology and epistemology in feminist research processes', in STANLEY, L. (Ed.) *Feminist Praxis*, London, Routledge, pp. 29–60.

STANLEY, L. and WISE, S. (1993) *Breaking Out Again: Feminist Ontology and Epistemology*, London, Routledge.

SULLIVAN, C. (1993) 'Oppression: the experiences of a lesbian teacher in an inner city comprehensive school in the United Kingdom', *Gender and Education*, **5**, 1, pp. 93–101.

TRENCHARD, L. and WARREN, H. (1984) *Something to Tell you*, London, London Gay Teenage Group.

WARREN, H. (1984) *Talking About School*, London, London Gay Teenage Group.

WILKINSON, S. (1988) 'The role of reflexivity in feminist psychology', *Women's Studies International Forum*, **11**, 5, pp. 493–502.

WOODS, S. and HARBECK, K. (1991) 'Living in two worlds: identity management strategies used by lesbian physical educators', *Journal of Homosexuality*, **22**, 3/4, pp. 141–66.

Part IV

The Trick is to Keep Sistering

Chapter 13

The Politics of Relationship: Reproductive and Genetic Screening Technology

Robyn Rowland

The debates within feminism around the danger or usefulness of reproductive technology to women have basically revolved around a political difference: supporters of reproductive technology embedded in a rights-based analysis and those opposed, constructing a power analysis of the technology and its use. My own work fits into the latter category but I have recently wanted to explore the difference further and develop a stronger ethical and political base for my own opposition to reproductive technology and genetic screening. Work in feminist ethics provides a new way forward which prioritizes relationship as a way of constructing the ethical politics crucial to our continuing analysis of reproduction.

To develop this thinking here I first critique 'rights' as a concept, looking briefly at its necessity as well as its flaws. I consider some examples from reproductive technology and genetic screening which expose the logical or illogical outcomes of rights-based analysis. I then use current feminist ethics to propose the use of a politics of relationship and what I call 'anticipatory vision'.

Emerging within the context of the later 1960s and early 1970s, women's use of a rights-based analysis has been crucial in many of the advances, particularly legally, that we have known since. Along with the push for Black rights and gay rights, this stress on individualism and liberalism brought forth slogans such as 'a woman's right to choose'. This slogan has, for most of us, encapsulated the demand that women must determine their own lives and that women must be in control of their fertility and reproductive capacity. Yet even in this area, the decisions become harder and more complex. Is it right to select for termination on the basis of the sex of the foetus? Does genetic screening, which embraces selective abortion, introduce eugenics in a more subtle way than National Socialism did in Germany?

I have argued elsewhere that a woman's right to choose actually meant a woman's right to control her bodily integrity, her autonomy and her moral being (Rowland, 1992). Yet situated, as most Western countries are, within a current liberal tradition, the issue of choice has been used by opponents of woman in order to argue similar cases with respect to the access of women, for example, to dangerous contraception. We need to reconsider the concept of choice.

153

The notion of individual rights comes from a liberal stream of philosophical thought particularly prominent currently in the US and more familiar as contractarianism in Australia and Europe. The 'individual' in these philosophies is paramount, sexless and resides within social relationships driven by patriarchal values which rarely address the responsibilities of men, either to each other or to society as a whole, or to women.

It is understandable that in a society where so much has been denied to individual women, we turn towards individualism in a desire to find autonomy and integrity. Yet individualism, closely tied to ownership, is also 'the fulcrum on which modern patriarchy turns' (Pateman, 1988, pp. 14–15). Within patriarchal values, rights becomes skewed towards the social group in power: men. For example, they might include the right to 'free trade'; the right to exercise power over others; the right to privacy (often including the rape or beating of your wife); the right to use and create pornography; the right of women to work as prostitutes but not as company managers; and finally the right to use force to get what you want ('might is right'). We obviously cannot address the real rights of women without recognizing that for those rights to be equitable, there must be an enormous change in the power balance between women and men. Similar relationships of oppression and powerlessness need to be addressed with respect to indigenous and Third World peoples.

Yet for women, the list of rights might also include the right to dignity and bodily integrity; freedom from coercion in child-bearing; economic security through the opportunity to work for equal pay; a safe workplace and environment; quality child care; personal reproductive control through access to safe abortion and contraception; health education and medical care; control over birth; freedom from discrimination due to sexual orientation; freedom from assault, fear and terror (Hartmann, 1987; Rowland, 1992).

Though rights' rhetoric has led to some advances within the structure of Western democracies, women are still far from experiencing autonomy and integrity. Indeed, the rhetoric of rights and equality has often led to the institutionalization of unequal outcomes. In her analysis of the law in the US, Catherine MacKinnon points out that though there has been legislation guaranteeing pay equality, women are still the greatest number of the poor and pay is far from being sex-equal. Though feminists have been part of the move for making divorce easier, more women are losing custody of their children. Though rape is constantly increasing, convictions for rape are not. Though some legal advances on being made against sexual harassment and domestic violence, MacKinnon argues that the 'string of defeats and declines' which feminism comes up against makes us realize that liberal thinking and liberal law go only part way towards the struggle for women's equality: 'the abstract equality of liberalism permits most women little more than does the substantive inequality of conservatism' (1987, p. 16).

If society is viewed as merely a collection of individuals, all of whom have their rights, there is no concept of the public good or interdependent relationships with other people. Women have been quite rightly wary of 'interdependence' because it has always been defined in patriarchy as women's economic and men's emotional dependence. When people in our society are asked to put their own individual desire aside for the public good, it is women who usually put their needs to one side while the wellbeing of men has been defined as the 'public good'.

Trying to define a way around these dilemmas in her own work on abortion, Beverley Wildung Harrison (1983, p. 197) argues that '"rights" in a moral sense, then, are shares in the basic conditions of human well-being and, therefore, reciprocal accountabilities that are binding for all persons'. Surely the concept of rights, then, must be tempered with this accountability and responsibility to the social group. But how to do this without disempowering women further? Though this form of responsibility has traditionally been defined unjustly in such a way as to make women alone ultimately responsible for the wellbeing of the social group while denying themselves (Rowland, 1988), we need to develop a theory and a practice based both on individual integrity and social accountability, particularly to women but also to society. Women's relationships with themselves, their bodies, with men and indeed with their children are influenced by the way we develop our moral position and ethical politics with respect to reproduction.

There are crucial differences between arguments for the right to reproductive freedom with respect to abortion/contraception and the so-called right to use reproductive technology couched in the same rhetoric. Women must have the right *not* to reproduce and mother because the alternative would mean that they are *compelled* to do so. Coerced motherhood is an assault on woman and child. As Susan Himmelweit (1988, p. 50) writes in her analysis of the feminist position on abortion: 'to deny her that opportunity [abortion] is therefore to risk her health and possibly her life; the alternative that she continues unwillingly to allow the foetus to grow within her is effectively enforcing her participation in a process that, like all nurturing, cannot be properly carried out by the unwilling.'

Access to safe contraception and abortion, as yet not achieved by all women in any country, is essential to a woman's autonomy. She must have the right to reproduce free from enforced sterilization or forced abortion. On the other hand, there can be no concomitant right to have a child: the right to live without bodily coercion is not the same as the 'right' to draw on community funds or resources as if one were owed a child/product. Similarly, a man does not have the 'right' to use a woman as a so-called surrogate because he claims a right to a child/product. As Rosalind Petchesky (1984, p. 395) has noted, 'there will remain a level of individual desire that can never be totally reconciled with social need.'

Women often mistake individualism for autonomy and believe that using the terminology of rights will achieve this. But it is ultimately a self-only approach, a solipsistic and isolated picture of social relationships. As Susan Sherwin puts it (1987, pp. 25–8):

As I understand feminism, it is committed to developing a spirit of cooperation, fostering healthy human interaction, and ensuring a sense of mutual responsibility among persons. The autonomy feminism embraces is a freedom from dominance, a liberation from aggression, and not mere isolation and separation.

In analysing the constraints on women's so-called choices, I'm not saying that women are weak and manipulated: I am not denying women integrity and agency. Rather I am recognizing the way power works and the masculine values which determine the so-called free choices available to women. The arguments that 'I have a right to' and 'I'm capable of making choices' are very seductive in our current ideological framework. Choice itself is often an illusion: we choose within fairly rigid constraining influences. The term itself has been used in interesting colloquial ways: as in 'Hobson's Choice' – taking the first horse in the stable or none at all, or 'Sophie's Choice' – choosing between equally unpleasant or negative alternatives. As Robin Morgan wrote (1982, p. 4):

We are told that freedom is synonymous with choice, yet what is choice to the shopper in the supermarket who can have her pick of twenty different breakfast cereals (all made by the same company) or to the student who can train for any career but (depending on the shape or shade of one's skin) have access to few? What is choice to the Hindu widow who faced either death on her husband's funeral pyre or a life of ostracism and slow starvation? What is choice to the voter in a one party election – or in a two party system where both parties articulate virtually the same politics, but with ingeniously different rhetoric? Who defines the choices among which we choose?

In reproductive technology, the choice often presented to infertile women is either to live the life of the infertile with the associated social stigma and negativity which is currently attached to that, or to undergo procedures which can be quite violent and dangerous to a woman's health in an attempt to have a child. Is this free choice or Sophie's Choice revisited?

We all make decisions within a social context, constrained and shaped by the forces of economics, social ideology, personal psychology and established power structures. These decisions are hedged around by structured constraints depending on a woman's race, class, age, marital status, sexuality, religion, culture and able bodiedness. The constraints are greater for women than they are for men. We live in a world which is structured around power imbalances; a world with hierarchies where some people are deliberately given more advantages than others. How can Western feminists possibly discuss women's 'right' to contraception in Third World countries, when we know that, manipulated by international monetary funds, groups of women in various Asian countries are *targeted* for differing kinds of contraceptive use. Some groups receive Depo Provera, some receive IUD's, some receive Norplant. On the whole, women are not given a choice of a range of contraceptives. Time and again, activists in Third World countries tell us that the Western rhetoric of rights is of no use to them in gaining free access to information about *safe* contraception or in fact older forms of contraception which have worked before Western imperialism with commercially driven, provider-controlled contraception.

Too often recently, feminists are engaged in discussions of 'power feminism' which revolves around what 'I' as a woman can get out of the world rather than what 'we', women as a social group need in order to survive with a maximized quality of life. As Naomi Wolf writes (1993, pp. 149–50), power feminism 'encourages a woman to claim her individual voice rather than merging her voice in a collective identity, for only strong individuals can create a just community.' If this aphorism were true, a just community would surely have been established long ago: we have a long and impressive history across all cultures of strong women. A strong individual is patently not enough in order to create social change for more than that individual's wellbeing.

The nature of the rights' analysis we currently use is tied firmly into concepts such as justice, liberty and equality. Extraordinarily abstract terms, these form part of what feminist ethicists define as masculine notions of morality. Abstracted from circumstance and context they are notably disconnected from relationship. As with the nature of masculine science which is increasingly more narrowly focused and expert at tunnel vision, the hallmark of masculine morality is its pride in being *above* emotion or connection. As with traditional ethics, rights' conceptualizations rely heavily on universalizing principles with little attention to the ways in which these principles might fit with reality. This is not to say that universal principles are not useful and moral. For example, it is wrong to rape women. It abuses a woman's bodily integrity, her dignity and sense of self. Yet universalizing principles can also draw us into contentious battles about prioritizing rights themselves.

The rights' analysis we are currently using is deeply flawed in its failure to look at conflicting rights; its neglect of the role of relationship and community; the invisibility of the necessity for responsibility not just to the self and the integrity of the self, but to those with whom we live in relationship. Currently much feminist theory displays these faults. Some feminists still seem to believe that we live in a 'just world' and that choices are free and available for all. They ignore the power dynamics and hierarchies within which we live. Simplistic claims to personal autonomy and choice fail to illuminate the limits of those so-called choices. Yet there is in fact no equality in the alternatives offered to people as choices and no equality between those who are choosing. This is not to say that we are not able to make decisions within our own lives. There is an enormous flexibility and the boundaries can and are frequently pushed. But some boundaries cannot be moved. If a woman has four children to feed, she has four children to feed. This will necessarily constrain the so-called choices she has with respect to the kind of work she might do, the kind of money she needs to earn, the availability of social security, the need for a breadwinner in the family. Certainly within those constraints she will make decisions about her life, but this should not be confused with the rhetoric of 'free choice'. To say we have it is not to have it.

I look now at some examples from the area of reproductive technology and genetic screening with respect to the way in which a rights-based analysis has failed women. I will use examples where rights conflict, where rights cancel out relationship, or where rights become a potentially oppressive form of obligation.

Perhaps the clearest example of a conflict of rights mingled with the cancellation of relationship lies in the development of the so-called surrogate mother industry. Operating internationally, its commercial arm is most strongly felt in the United States. During a surrogacy arrangement, a woman contracts to carry a child for another person or sometimes a couple. In many cases she uses the sperm from the commissioning man. In most cases where couples are involved the commissioning couple are infertile, but because this is a commercial transaction, single women and men, transsexuals and homosexuals have been involved in commissioning surrogates and donor sperm is often used. The women entering surrogacy contracts are screened, but commissioning couples or people are not screened. The purchaser therefore has the power while the employee begins to lose her rights under the terms of the contract (Rowland, 1992). Perhaps the best-known case is that of Mary Beth Whitehood in the US who lost custody of her child created through a surrogacy contract arrangement. Noting that she was only 'an alternative reproduction vehicle' and not the mother of the child, Judge Harvey Sorkow described the commissioning man, Stern, as the 'natural father'. The legal debate revolved around the prioritization of rights. Sorkow awarded custody to the 'father', even though this man had no relationship with the birth mother or the child at this stage. He said: (Arditti, 1988, pp. 54, 56)

> The fact is, however, that the money to be paid to the surrogate is not being paid for the surrender of the child to the father, and that is just the point – at birth, mother and father have equal rights to the child absent [sic] any other agreements. The biological father pays the surrogate for her willingness to be impregnated and carry his child to term. At birth, the father does not purchase the child. It is his own biological, genetically related child. He cannot purchase what is already his . . . This court therefore will specifically enforce the surrogate parenting agreement to compel delivery of the child to the father and to terminate the mother's parental rights.

On appeal Whitehood regained parental rights though not custody and the child remained with the commissioning couple, yet this case set the precedent in surrogacy for the definition of father as the man from whom the sperm came. It had important implications for the concept of parental *relationship* as opposed to rights. Stern had no relationship with the child apart from the fact that the baby was genetically from his sperm. Yet Whitehood had an existing relationship with the child through pregnancy and birth. This relationship was cancelled out in favour of biological rights.

The prioritizing of the biological and genetic is followed through in what is termed in Australia 'altruistic' surrogacy. In Britain, it goes unnamed and is often termed egg donation. These terms are misleading. Through *in vitro* fertilization programmes, a sister or a friend is encouraged to act as the 'surrogate' for an infertile woman. The infertile woman produces an egg which is fertilized and placed within her sister or friend who carries the child through to term and relinquishes it to the infertile woman from whom the egg came. A social debate in Australia around this issue has been quite strong. Medical scientists involved in the field continue to stress that this is a purer form of surrogacy which eliminates the problem of relationship. As Professor John Leeton of Melbourne says: (Cited in Rowland, 1992, p. 165)

> This IVF surrogacy is superior to any other surrogacy because the child will totally be theirs genetically – her egg, his sperm – and the risk of the surrogate mother bonding to the child after that pregnancy is less . . . This is the point that everyone is missing, the vital point.

Because genetic connection is being prioritized over a relationship and defined as parental right, the woman donating the egg would have prior rights over the child. In one case in the US this has already resulted in tragedy. Anna Johnson carried a child for Mark and Christina Calvert, using their egg and sperm. To quote an article entitled 'The product of a rented womb' (Goodman, 1990, p. A25):

> The court has declared that she is not his mother, though he grew in her womb, though he came down her birth canal, though her breasts filled with milk for him. Anna Johnson is now officially, legally, unrelated to the boy she bore. A Judge in California has ruled that Johnson was just a prenatal 'foster parent' to Mark and Christina Calvert's foetus. She nurtured it, fed it, housed it – but it always belonged to them. The womb was merely rented: when her work was done, the boy product belonged to his genetic owners. Giving birth to a child is no longer proof that you are its mother.

In the conflict of rights in these situations, paternal right is obviously impeding any maternal right which comes through the relationship of pregnancy. Anna Johnson was legally forced into giving up her child. Here, maternity became defined as paternity: where the egg or sperm comes from. Yet the primary relationship of every person – the relationship developed during pregnancy and birth – is cancelled out. Surrogacy has facilitated this process enormously and the term itself, meaning substitute, reinforces the status of the birth mother as merely a carrier.

As with many of these new developments in reproductive technology, the implications are far from thought through. For example, many people on *in vitro* fertilization programmes use donated eggs or donated sperm or indeed donated embryos. Does this mean that somehow a woman who carries a child from a donated egg or donated embryo on IVF is not the 'real' mother? Indeed, if the logic of so-called altruistic surrogacy were carried through, the woman who donated the egg through *in vitro* fertilization, probably herself infertile and because of the extremely low success rates (still 5–10 per cent per attempt) probably childless, could claim the child. Both women have used donated eggs or a donated embryo: how can medical science justify differing definitions of the 'real mother'? Indeed, in the case of donated sperm, is it possible that those who have donated sperm through IVF or donor insemination programmes might use the same legal precedent to claim their children? Where rights override relationships, the unethical situation of the disempowerment of birth mothers follows.

But if birth mothers appear to be consistently disempowered, the lack of attention to children's rights in this area amounts to an appalling abuse. In many countries, no adequate legal system of keeping information about donor gametes or procedures is currently operating. Particularly in Australia, we seem to have failed to learn from the adoption experience. Socially we go on lying to people about their origins. In many cases internationally if parents do not tell their children about the nature of their conception, they may never know. If they do know, they may never be able to find out information about their genetic origins.

It is crucial that children born through reproductive technology do not continue to be infantilized as if they will never be adults with strong opinions about their rights to access information about their origins. In spite of the fact that genetic donors are not involved in the relationship of parenting, they are indeed connected to the child through their genetic donation. It is up to the child/adult born this way to take up or ignore a potential relationship with the genetic donor. The emotional impact of that knowledge will only be known as a generation of children grow up.

In terms of the rights' analysis, children's relationships seem to be consistently under threat. In a recent US case, a 4-year-old child was handed to his biological mother and biological father by the courts, in spite of the fact that he had been adopted at the age of 30 days and had resided within a happy family relationship for 3-and-a-half years. Although the child had formed a continuous nurturing relationship within his adopted family, the courts finally decided that the biological 'father' had the right to take the child from his family. He had been mothered and fathered by non-biological parents and yet the rights granted by the courts to biological connection severed this child's relationships. As the adopted father had said in an interview before the final decision: 'If our son is taken away, he loses his whole life – his grandparents, his brother, his friends, everything he knows is gone.'[1] In emphasizing parental rights, the child's existing relationships had been ignored.

The rights claimed on behalf of women in the reproductive area can also easily become an oppressive form of obligation. There is an enormous risk in the area of genetic screening that in order to be the good citizen or the good mother, women will be more and more coerced into using screening techno- logy for the purposes of terminating the 'imperfect' child. It is very difficult now for a woman to get through pregnancy without screening procedures of one kind or another. Ranging from ultrasound to chorionic villi sampling to amniocentesis, these screening procedures have already introduced a form of eugenics into our social relationships.

The issue of screening and termination is obviously complex. In some countries, women are encouraged or in fact coerced into terminating because the foetus is the wrong sex. The most obvious example of interference in a woman's reproductive life is the one-child policy in China, where recent policy now also determines mandatory termination of an 'abnormal' foetus before birth. But other countries have also embraced eugenics legislation. There is a history of such legislation in the US, for example. More importantly, however, are the attitudes we are developing towards the use of technology. Now if a woman has a Down's Syndrome child, the first question she is likely to be asked is: 'But didn't you have the test?' In 1971, the retiring President of the American Association for the Advancement of Science, Bentley Glass (Scutt, 1988, p. 218) said:

> In a world where each pair must be limited, on the average, to two offspring and no more, the right that must become paramount is ... the right of every child to be born with a sound physical and mental constitution based on a sound genotype. No parents will in that future time have a right to burden society with a malformed or mentally incompetent child.

Some studies have indicated that a level of coercion operates with respect to the use of procedures such as amniocentesis. One study in England indicated that 75 per cent of obstetricians would refuse to carry out amniocentesis unless the woman agreed to a termination if the child was genetically abnormal (Farrant, 1985). Women are already receiving the definite message that it is unacceptable to produce anything but the 'perfect' child. Georgie Hill, the wife of the British Formula One Driving Ace, Damon Hill, contemplated suicide after learning that her first baby had Down's Syndrome. She says (Taylor, 1994, p. 19):

> I was left holding this beautiful boy, who to me looked absolutely like a peach, and yet the doctors made me feel like a failure that I hadn't

161

produced a proper baby. They made me feel embarrassed that I brought one of 'those' babies into their wards.

Laura Hershey (1994, pp. 26–32), a disability rights activist with a rare neuro-muscular condition, has indicated that women's access to abortion at the moment is primarily due to the argument that women must be able to abort to avoid disability or 'deformed babies'. Defending women's access to safe abortion on demand, she argues that we also need to look at educating women about what that demand may entail. Abortion on the grounds of disability, she says, implies certain beliefs: that 'children with disabilities (and by implication adults with disabilities) are a burden to family and society; life with a disability is scarcely worth living; preventing the birth is an act of kindness; women who bear disabled children have failed.' Even the language we use reveals the discomfort people feel with the idea of difference in ability or 'normality': 'foetal deformity', 'defective foetus', 'abnormal' are all terms carrying powerful negative images.

What is difficult about the development of screening techniques is that once genetic problems are more easily diagnosed, structures come into place which reinforce the attitude that a responsible citizen should go ahead and use them: in other words, that women should use them. This is in spite of the fact that only 3 per cent of genetic abnormalities can be detected at this stage and that amniocentesis involves a late termination and usually a full labour and delivery of a stillborn, quite well-developed foetus. Many women are not told of the implications of undergoing amniocentesis in the first place.

The very availability of these tests alone changes our consciousness in ways of which we are mostly unaware: what I have previously called the 'softening up process' (Rowland, 1984). They begin to construct a benign attitude to the idea that selecting people is appropriate but they can also generate a threat to women's rights to carry a child to term without intervention and screening and negate, impede, or interfere with possible relationships between those children who are not 'perfect' and their families and society around them. The danger is that social policy developed around screening will mean a withdrawal of funds to support those differently abled and their carers.

New developments and future developments in the area of reproduction and technology may take the destruction of relationship which begins with *in vitro* fertilization and moves through surrogacy to its logical conclusion. Through *in vitro* fertilization women became fragmented and dismembered into body parts: ovaries, eggs, wombs. The logical movement into commercial surrogacy was already set up by this fragmentation. Now women were merely the 'uterine environments' or 'host womb' or 'gestational carrier' of the foetus and then child.

More recent discussions about the use of brain-dead women as surrogates would eliminate the most problematic aspect of surrogacy: the relationship between the birth mother and the child. Referred to as the 'pregnant cadaver', the woman's body is ventilated and kept operating with standard hospital life-support equipment and low-cost technology (Murphy, 1989). The precedent has already been established in situations in which children have been born from pregnant women who are kept 'alive' for around seven weeks in order for a baby to be delivered by Caesarean section. These are women who were already pregnant and had died because of brain haemorrhage or car accidents, for example (Rowland, 1992). Implanting embryos into a brain-dead woman would create the 'silent surrogate'. Within the scientific literature, discussions of this procedure seem to raise few eyebrows. A specialist in reproductive physiology at Monash University was reported as saying that 'I can't see any reason why the pregnancy shouldn't go ahead normally, as long as the female incubator is receiving the appropriate nutrients and care.' Australian bioethicist, Dr Paul Gerber, was reported as saying: 'It's a magnificent use of a corpse. It has my complete support' (Allender and Courtney, 1988; Miller, 1988).

The invisibility of relationship is also expressed in recent discussions concerning the use of immature eggs extracted from foetal tissue, matured *in vitro* and fertilized ready for donation. The development of the concept of 'foetal mothers' again ignores a wider range of issues concerning relationships. The British Medical Association discussed the possibility of donated ovaries being used in a similar fashion to other organs. Dr Michael Crowe was quoted as saying: 'donations would allow grieving relatives to feel that a young woman's death could give infertile couples the chance to share in that young person's creative potential.' The Chair of the BMA Ethics Committee, Dr Stewart Horner, was quoted as saying that no lower age limit should be fixed and that even 13 or 12-year-old girls' ovaries and eggs could be used.[2] Ignoring the fact that an ovary contains the specific genetic makeup of another person which would be carried on into the next generation, scientists seem unable to grasp that most people might find it horrifying that a non-living person, a foetus, could generate the beginning of life for an individual.

The impact on that individual of being born from donated ovarian tissue or in fact from discarded foetal material during terminations, can only be guessed at. The psychological and emotional impact of the relationship between an individual and the method of their creation is erased. The issue of the fragmentation of identity as well as the fragmentation of origin are not dealt with. The concept of a right to bodily integrity which could be applied to the person from whom the ovary and tissue are taken, or the person who is created, are ignored. But certainly the right of infertile couples to access these techniques and technologies is the social rhetoric used to move us towards acceptance of this procedure.

Within this constantly changing minefield of scientific development, can we find a way of dealing with these issues that encapsulate feminist principles? Feminism itself has a moral and ethical base. Its politics are firmly rooted in its care and concern for women and relationships, not just for individual women disconnected from their social relations.

Developments in feminist ethics have been strongly influenced by Carole Gilligan's work. Gilligan (1982) argues that men tend to use abstract thought and therefore develop abstract rules. From this emerges an ethic of justice which is characterized by masculinity. Juxtaposed to this is a contention that women tend to act on compassion and feeling, applying context. They concentrate on a protection from harm and develop an ethic of caring. Avoiding the trap of possible essentialism, what is important from the recent work in feminist ethics is the understanding that the value of caring is often left out of our ethics which primarily focuses around issues of justice. Considering the differing socialization and development of women and men in terms of their growth toward or away from relationship and connection, we know that men are encouraged to be emotionally distant and so-called objective, while women are taught that although their subjectivity is suspect, their role is to perpetuate nurturance. Though a possible trap, this emphasis on educating women for caring also brings the strong bonds of love between women and children and between women and other women. It has problematized relationships between women and men.

Further developments in an ethics 'grounded in the distinctively feminine moral experience' (Jaggar, 1991) emerge from Nell Nodding and Sarah Ruddick's work. Though Nodding sees women as 'natural carers', Ruddick on the other hand aims for a feminist ethic based in the maternal. Maternal experience is supposedly a basis for a moral sensibility based in nurturing and caring, with an emphasis on maintenance and growth rather than militarism and destruction. All three writers have drawn towards them criticisms of essentialism. Yet the value of bringing the reality of women's private experience of connection and care into morality cannot be overestimated.

Within feminist ethics, political and power analyses are crucial basic principles. Because of our belief in the necessary relationship between theory and practice, many of the ethical positions developed within feminism have occurred outside the academy or in conjunction with it, for example, Robin Morgan's book, *The Demon Lover. On the Sexuality of Terrorism*, Andrea Dworkin's, *Right Wing Women* and Sara Hoagland's *Lesbian Ethics. Toward New Value*. The development of the feminist position on reproductive and genetic engineering developed by The Feminist International Network of Resistance to Reproductive and Genetic Engineering (FINRRAGE) is a good example of the interrelationship between activists and academics. With an active membership in 32 countries, this Network has proved crucial in developing feminist theory around reproductive and genetic engineering; strategizing and developing feminist activism around the issues; publishing in book or journal form material in this area; and playing an active role in the development of legislation in many countries.

The crucial issue is that feminist ethics and feminist politics cannot be divorced: the unifying principle underlying feminist ethics is an interest in social transformation and social change with respect to the power relationship between the sexes. As Jaggar (1991, p. 98) has pointed out, the feminist ethical approach explores a belief that the subordination of women is morally wrong and the belief that the moral experience of women should be treated as respectfully as the moral experience of men. These generate a theoretical and a political agenda which lead to action:

> These assumptions generate a certain practical and theoretical agenda for feminist ethics. On the practical, these are, first, to articulate moral critiques of actions and practices that perpetuate women's subordination; second, to prescribe morally justifiable ways of resisting such actions and practices; and, third, to envision morally desirable alternatives that will promote woman's emancipation.

My own work has been part of and influenced by the development of feminist bioethics. It is grounded in the principle that the subordination of women and the power imbalance that exists between the social groups men and women is morally wrong. It begins with a women-centred perspective, basing all analysis on the questions: Where are the women? What effect does this have on women? How will this influence relationships between people? With these as the core questions, the development of a concept of society follows, based in the development of integrity-enhancing relationships. It includes the necessity to acutely attend to the relationships between children and adults, particularly as children express their justifiable dependence. I have argued that the individual, the social and the relationship between the two needs to be understood and explored. There are obligations each individual has to self and there are obligations that individuals have to others; and then there are obligations to a larger sense of community. A power analysis is crucial in this understanding. As outlined earlier, societies are based on power inequities. The challenge, then, is to change that set of imbalances, moving towards a position where women are no longer subordinate and where other delineations of power and powerlessness are similarly challenged and changed. This analysis is much more complex than the label 'a conspiracy theory' allows and is also much more complex than 'a woman's right to choose'. It is the development of the reproductive technologies and genetic-screening technologies themselves that force our analysis to move beyond the simplistic issue of rights towards a more complex understanding of human relationships. Within this analysis, the operational concepts of coercion, collusion and resistance are focal.

While using a power analysis at the macro-level, we cannot ignore the influence of ideology nor what I would call the 'politics of intimacy'. Where the structural analysis of patriarchal power deals with ideology and institutions of power, the politics of intimacy deals with interpersonal power and the development of coercive practice. So, for example, in discussions of so-called family or altruistic surrogacy, I argue that the power dynamics that operate within families, emphasizing the powerlessness of some members in comparison to the power of others, makes invalid arguments that women within these social structures can 'freely choose' to become so-called surrogate mothers and to relinquish their children to others.

If we emphasize relationship and community as well as individual need, we need to find a way of balancing the desire of individuals and the welfare of the social group. Limits can and should be imposed on what human beings can do to one another. Reproductive technology is not just concerned with medical experimentation. It is concerned with institutionalizing fragmented human relationships. How else could we describe a medicine which proceeds to tell us that the experience between a birth mother and the child she is carrying is non-existent because the egg originally belonged to someone else? How else can we explain the developing capacity of our society to ignore the power dynamics in families, the possibilities of emotional coercion, the pain of relinquishing mothers historically, the feelings of rejection and insecurity already recorded by children involved in surrogacy and the powerful effect of institutionalizing these procedures? Reproductive technology is concerning itself with constructing and changing human relationships. It is unethical to experiment with human beings medically. It should also be unethical to experiment with them emotionally and socially. If we consider the 62-year-old woman in Italy who gave birth to an IVF child using a donated egg, the increasing number of post-menopausal women pregnant through IVF, the Black woman who used a 'white embryo' for the purposes of racial selection, the daughter who gave birth to a child after carrying her mother's embryo, the grandmother in South Africa who gave birth to triplets for her daughter, we have to ask what it is we are doing in the construction of these human relationships. What is moral is not always what we find when we look at society, but rather it is what we seek. We need an 'anticipatory vision' as part of our ethics and this should then lead to the development of feminist 'participatory action'. These are inclusive terminologies which attribute agency to individuals, as well as forcing our focus on the future and where we are developing as a community. Feminist analysis has always sought to predict the direction science is taking so that we can attend and direct that future. Years ago many of us predicted that the discussion of the maturing of immature eggs would lead to the possibility of 'foetal mothers'. Now science is doing the job for us. By discussing morals and ethics, I do not mean an empty moralism: setting up rules and learning them by rote. There is a distinction between prescriptive moralism and what Andrea Dworkin (1978, p. 53) has called a 'moral intelligence'. As Dworkin sees it, moral intelligence constructs values and exercises discernment. It demands 'a nearly endless exercise of the ability to make decisions: significant decisions; decisions inside history not peripheral to it; decisions about the meaning of life; decisions that arise from an acute awareness of one's own mortality.'

It is the obligation of agents of social change to look beyond the self and engage in this moral activity. This often means dealing with painful decisions and taking a stand which is not terribly popular. Feminism is an activist and optimistic philosophy. It seeks to construct a society in which there is fulfilment for individuals, balanced with a reciprocal responsibility to the social group. Most importantly it concentrates on relationships between people. We need the politics of relationship and we need anticipatory vision to forge a more just future. If we forget that in these discussions we are linked each to each other, we call into question our human as well as our feminist obligations.

Notes

1 See for example, 'Adoptive parents hand over boy in four year custody fight', *New York Times*, 1 May 1995.
2 Quinn, Sue, 'Dead could give hope to the infertile', *Sunday Times*, UK, July 1994.

References

ALLENDER, JACKIE and COURTNEY, ADAM (1988) 'Surrogacy proposed for "dead" women', *The Australian*, 25 June.

ARDITTI, RITA (1988) 'A summary of some recent developments on surrogacy in the United States', *Reproductive and Genetic Engineering, Journal of International Feminist Analysis*, **1**, 1.

DWORKIN, ANDREA (1978) *Right Wing Women: The Politics of Domesticated Females*, London, The Women's Press.

FARRANT, WENDY (1985) 'Who's for Amniocentesis? The Politics of Prenatal Screening', in HOMANS, HELEN (Ed.), *The Sexual Politics of Reproduction*, Aldershot, Gower.

GILLIGAN, CAROL (1982) *In a Different Voice: Psychological Theory and Women's Development*, Cambridge, MA, Harvard University Press.

GOODMAN, ELLEN (1990) 'The product of a rented womb', *San Francisco Chronicle*, 25 October, A25.

HARRISON, BEVERLEY and WILDUNG (1983) *Our Right to Choose. Toward a New Ethic of Abortion*, Boston, MA, Beacon Press.

HARTMANN, BETSY (1987) *Reproductive Rights and Wrongs. The Global Politics of Population Control and Contraceptive Choice*, New York, Harper & Row.

HERSHEY, LAURA (1994) 'Choosing disability', *Ms Magazine*, July–August, pp. 26–32.

HIMMELWEIT, SUSAN (1988) 'More than a woman's right to choose?', *Feminist Review*, **29**.

HOAGLAND, SARA LUCIA (1988) *Lesbian Ethics. Toward New Value*, Palo Alto, California, Institute of Lesbian Studies.

JAGGAR, ALISON M. (1991) 'Feminist ethics: projects, problems, prospects', in CARD, CLAUDIA (Ed.), *Feminist Ethics*, Kansas, University Press of Kansas.

MACKINNON, CATHARINE, A (1987) *Feminism Unmodified. Discourses on Life and Law*, Cambridge, MA, Harvard University Press.

MILLER, CALVIN (1988) 'The brain dead could be surrogates, say scientists', *Herald*, 24 June, p. 1.

MORGAN, ROBIN (1989) *The Demon Lover. On the Sexuality of Terrorism*, New York, W. W. Norton.

MORGAN, ROBIN (1982) *The Anatomy of Freedom. Feminism, Physics and Global Politics*, Oxford, Martin Robertson.

MURPHY, JULIEN, S. (1989) 'Should pregnancies be sustained in brain-dead women? A philosophical discussion of post-mortem pregnancy', in RATCLIFF, CATHRYN S. *et al.*, *Healing Technology. Feminist Perspectives*, Ann Arbor, MI, University of Michigan Press.

PATEMAN, CAROLE (1988) *The Sexual Contract*, Cambridge, Polity Press.

PETCHESKY, ROSALIND (1984) *Abortion and Woman's Choice. The State, Sexuality, and Reproductive Freedom*, New York, Longman.

ROWLAND, ROBYN (1984) 'Social implications of reproductive technology', *International Review of Natural Family Planning*, **8**, 3, pp. 189–205.

ROWLAND, ROBYN (1988) *Woman Herself. A Transdisciplinary Perspective on Women's Identity*, Melbourne, Oxford University Press.

ROWLAND, ROBYN (1992) *Living Laboratories. Women and Reproductive Technology*, Australia, Sun Books; UK, Cedar Press.

SCUTT, JOCELYNNE (Ed.) (1988) *The Baby Machine*, Melbourne, McCulloch Publishing.

SHERWIN, SUSAN (1987) 'A feminist approach to ethics', *Resources for Feminist Research* (RFR/DRF), **16**, 3, pp. 25–8.

TAYLOR, PHIL (1995) 'Race ace's greatest challenge', *New Idea*, 5, November pp. 18–19.

WOLF, NAOMI (1993) *Fire with Fire. The New Female Power and How It Will Change the 21st Century*, London, Chatto & Windus.

Chapter 14

The Political Economy of the Gendered Language of Technology Transfer to Eastern Europe

Anne Gatensby and Nora Jung

In the spirit of sisterhood and in an effort to combine two seemingly disparate areas of study, we began our analyses of the gendered language of technology transfer between Eastern Europe and the Western industrialized nations. Prior to our collaboration, Nora's work focused on one facet of European feminist research – the case of Hungarian women's movements – and Anne was involved with the field of feminist critiques of science and technology. One of us, then, had little experience with women's studies in the European context, and the other had little experience with the theme of technology. Yet we shared a common approach and attitude to women's studies in general and felt that by undertaking a joint project where we could draw on each other's special knowledge, we might be able to add something to the field in terms of the understanding of the importance of gender in representing the world of technology transfer.

At the beginning, we were faced with the task of trying to combine the themes of technology and gender and Eastern Europe. The first thing we did was a literature search combining these themes so that we could see what kind of work had already been done by feminist scholars. We thought there might be some theoretical gaps in the literature from which we could start to see if we could develop some interesting reflections on the ways in which gender and technology were intertwined in Eastern Europe following the collapse of State socialism. What we found, however, was a little unexpected. Although we knew that much had been written about the prospects for Eastern Europe post-1989, what we discovered was that virtually all the material that reaches us in North America appears in journals and trade magazines that are geared towards the interests of practising scientists and technological managers. That in itself was not surprising for we know about the links between international capital and technological interests and about the enormous stakes that different groups have in the future of Eastern Europe. But what we did find extremely interesting was the particular pattern of representation that emerged. We found that writers typically represent Western industrialized countries as active agents of history with unquestioned authority to make decisions about Eastern European technology policies and, which is even more intriguing from

169

our point of view, such a pattern of representation is achieved through the use of profoundly gendered language, particularly as regards the choice and use of metaphors.

In the past, it has been well demonstrated by feminist scholars that the most prevalent metaphors that appear in science and technology writing are ones that evoke images of control and domination over nature (Griffin, 1978; Merchant, 1980; Collard and Contrucci, 1989). It has been further suggested that changing the dominant metaphors in a society is a way of changing the power relations that are fundamental to it (Haste, 1993). This call for a shift in thinking about science and technology towards a more emancipatory project, through the creation of a new set of metaphors which call on more inclusive imagery, imagery which better fits ideas that emanate from within feminism, is rooted in the notion of science as 'a contestable text and a power field' (Haraway, 1991).

We had no particular argument with this line of reasoning yet what we discovered in the course of our analysis was that much of the writing about technology transfer between Eastern Europe and the West does not, in fact, appeal to the metaphors of control and domination, although control and domination is clearly what the Western industrialized nations are after. Rather, what we see is an overwhelming use of metaphors that we, as feminists, might think we own: the metaphors of caring, cooperation, reciprocity, benevolence, altruism, parenting and nurturing. In the literature that we examined, the processes of technology transfer between East and West are usually depicted as being based on a mutually beneficial partnership or, alternatively, as being defined by a relation of dependence, as a child is related to a parent. In both cases, the aim is to promote the Western model of scientific and technological development in the East. The Western model is portrayed as being faultless and therefore it is assumed to be the most desirable approach for Eastern Europeans to take. Since the Western system is working perfectly, according to these accounts, there is little reason to question multinational efforts to influence Eastern European science and technology policies. Yet we know, through feminist and other critiques of science and technology, that all is not well within the Western model. From exclusions of women, the disabled and racial minorities from the practice of science, to the separation of social concerns from the content of scientific and technological knowledge, we know intuitively that such an approach is not going to work any better in Eastern Europe.

Further, we believe that the Western model should not be adopted without question in Eastern Europe simply because they have become vulnerable to the neo-liberal ideological position that currently characterizes much discourse about economic growth or globalization. However, it is taken for granted in most of these articles that the neo-liberal market economy model is the only option for post-1989 Eastern European nations. This taken-for-grantedness is primarily achieved through the use of metaphor, since metaphor is the link, in language, 'between individual thinker and social context, between existing ideas and new ideas, between where one person is and where the interlocutor wants to take that person' (Haste, 1993). Metaphors, in this sense, are the foundations on which our taken-for-granted assumptions about the world are based. The added power of gendered metaphors arises from the mapping of other dualities on to gender thereby entwining notions of masculinity and femininity with other conventional opposites such as activity and passivity, public and private, dependent and independent, East and West.

It is in this way that those writing about technology transfer between the West and Eastern Europe achieve their aims. Through the use of gendered language, the authors reinforce the taken-for-granted idea that the Western model of scientific and technological development is best. For example, much of the popular literature employs the rhetoric of equity by using such terminology as 'opportunity', 'cooperation', 'collaboration', 'partnerships', and 'joint venture' (Rich, 1989; Aldhous, 1990; Feller, 1990; Palca, 1990; Sietmann, 1990; Stevens, 1990; Johnson, 1991; MacKenzie, 1992; Mitchell, 1993; Steele, 1991; Charles, 1992; Holden, 1992; Hughes, 1992; Rhea, 1992; Richardson, 1992; Seltzer, 1992a, 1992b; Weimer, 1992; 'Doing Business . . .', 1992; 'Reforming . . .', 1990; 'The great . . .', 1990; 'United States . . .', 1992) which on the surface denote relations of equality.

However, the reality of the situation is quite different given the economic and social contexts in Eastern Europe where any pretence of equitable relations are a sham. Nonetheless, Western representations often portray Eastern Europe and the West as having something to offer each other. The usual scenario is that the West can offer much-needed capital to Eastern Europe, while Eastern Europe can offer much-lauded scientific and technological expertise with the added benefit of cheap labour costs. Thus, the 'partnership' depends on the exploitation or trafficking of scientific and technological workers from Eastern Europe. This agenda fits neatly into the kind of neo-liberal economic restructuring that has already taken place in North America where economic managers have succeeded in finding opportunities to subvert the protections gained for workers by organized labour, thus enabling them to seek labour where it is most vulnerable.

One of the most straightforward descriptions of Western interests in the development of Eastern European science and technology is in the Bromley report. In 1992, D. Alan Bromley, science advisor to then US president George Bush, compiled a report for the Federal Coordinating Council for Science, Engineering and Technology. In this report, Bromley maintains that the major objective for Eastern European science and technology policy is to 'increase access for the American science and technology community to unusually talented scientists, special facilities and unique research opportunities' (Lepkowski, 1993). Apparently, from this report (as well as from many others) Westerners want to shape not only Eastern European science and technology in a purely technical sense, but they also want to exert power over scientists and engineers who are currently working in Eastern Europe. An important aspect of this process is to provide employment for Eastern European scientists, either at home or in the West, thereby discouraging them from selling their skills to countries that are suspected of producing nuclear weapons and that are not yet under the Western sphere of influence.

Several articles report how poorly paid scientists are forced to leave their fields and how some of the better-connected ones head for the West. The migration of Eastern European scientists, what is commonly known as 'brain drain', is acknowledged by many authors, but it is evaluated in various ways (Feller, 1990; Dickman, 1992; Richardson, 1992; Lepkowski, 1993; 'The true . . .', 1992). Instead of using the term 'brain drain', one author calls this process 'brain push', suggesting that the main reason for scientists to leave Eastern Europe is shortage of money (Lepkowski, 1993). This in turn is blamed on the mismanagement of economies during State socialism. Western institutions, the beneficiaries of brain drain, are not held responsible for the negative effects of this migration. Nor is there any recognition that such programmes disproportionately favour male scientists and technologists from Eastern Europe since their female counterparts tend to have greater family obligations which curtail their mobility and thus constrain their opportunities to find work in the West.

Thus, Western control over migration is manifested both in terms of who is able to emigrate to the West and also in terms of preventing Eastern European scientists from selling their expertise to 'outlaw nations' or 'terrorist groups' (Lepkowski, 1993). Clearly, not all scientists are welcome in the West. The hidden message in some articles is a covertly xenophobic one, a fear of a flood of unwanted immigrants. To deal with them, Bromley, for example, suggests incentives for scientists and engineers to remain in their home countries. He insists that 'science has to be done in the east by easterners' as a means of 'improving the health and productivity of Eastern European people', thus avoiding charges of promoting brain drain from the East ('The true . . .', 1992). This appears to be merely lip-service to the wellbeing of Eastern European economic autonomy since the real issue is the transference of control over science and technology from the remnants of State socialist regimes to Western corporations. This transfer is justified and promoted by using imagery of an abusive father to stand in for State socialism and a caring father to stand in for the West. In other words, the metaphors and analogies chosen by different authors reflect a positioning of Eastern Europe as subordinate in a structure which is parallel to the patriarchal family.

We found that in the symbolism that emerges from the literature, Eastern Europe is assigned the role of the dependent, childlike or passive recipient of aid, in need of guidance and direction from an adult. The helping adult is the West, possessed of knowledge about what is best for childlike Eastern Europe. One author describes government officials who urged more and faster action from the US administration as 'itching to get involved in one of the most exciting moments of history' (Lepkowski, 1993). Depicting the West as the active agent of history and Eastern Europe as the passive recipient of aid fits perfectly with the metaphor of the patriarchal family. Clearly, the active, masculine, paternal role is assigned to Westerners although the social and political changes of 1989 were initiated, undertaken and completed by Eastern European nationals. Indeed, the majority of the work to be done in the transition period has to be done by Eastern Europeans themselves, yet most articles describe Eastern Europe as a passive recipient. The only active role they are assigned is in imitating the West by restructuring their scientific institutions and technological practices based on US models.

Eastern European countries are also often referred to as 'fledgling democracies', invoking the image of a young bird that is about to fly on its own for the first time (Aldous, 1990; Palca, 1990; Lepkowski, 1992). They are depicted as emerging out of infancy (dependence on the Soviet Union, the abusive father) and approaching a stage of adulthood (independence). However, what is obscured with such language is that State socialist control is merely being replaced by Western corporate control (the caring father) and the promise of independence is a false one. Although most publications in the West are not particularly secretive about Western corporate desires to control Eastern European science and technology, Western control is portrayed as benevolent and desirable for Eastern Europe. The metaphor of the fledgling represents Eastern Europe as not quite grown up, as not being able to make decisions autonomously. Other writers adopt a more veiled paternalistic stance.

In an article addressing the 'immense opportunities to industry' in the former Soviet Union, for example, Rhea (1992) advises potential investors that 'the money can be kept in the US and paid out to the Russian participants for support, equipment, travel and other expenses.' This unwillingness to trust the Russians with economic responsibility is akin to the benevolent, yet controlling, father doling out an allowance to the child. In another article, Hughes (1992) outlines a meeting of the OECD where ministers from the West agreed to 'save science in Eastern Europe' by helping countries 'to make intelligent choices on big science projects'. Although these Western leaders spoke of cooperation with Eastern Europe, it is telling that they did not include as full participants in these discussions any representatives from those countries whose science they are ostensibly saving. Here we have a situation where the father figure works out the appropriate solution autocratically which will then be handed down to the child to be obeyed without question. In contrast to the passive role ascribed to Eastern Europe, the West takes the active, authoritative role of 'aiding', 'helping' or 'saving' Eastern Europe (Aldous, 1990; Dickman, 1990, 1992; Palca, 1990; Richardson, 1990, 1992; Gaynor, 1992; Holden, 1992; Hughes, 1992; Kublin and Shepherd, 1993; Layman, 1992; Williamson, Tirch and Purton, 1992; Graham, 1993; Lepkowski, 1993; MacKenzie, 1992; Waxmonsky, 1993; 'Reforming...', 1990). These terms are associated with images of charity and with the benevolent, omnipotent father.

In short, many descriptions of how Eastern Europe needs Western money to keep science and technology alive use the image of the masculine hero who will save Eastern Europe from an otherwise inevitable demise. We learn that the European Community (now known as the European Union) has launched the largest effort yet to aid 'grant-starved Eastern European scientists' (Holden, 1992). Here the way in which the metaphor of the adult–child relationship is invoked bears some resemblance to how the same metaphor is used in Western descriptions of the colonized world. The accounts of missionaries often depicted natives as childlike, naïve creatures who needed to be enlightened by the colonizers. Such descriptions were used to justify an immense transfer of capital from the colonized to the colonizers. We would further argue that the images that emerge from the literature under examination imply not only a stereotypical relationship between adult and child, colonizer and colonized, but also the essentialized male–female relationship.

The West, depicted as ready to save Eastern Europe, is not just any adult figure, but a male father figure given, particularly in the Western industrialized world, the historical relationship between male authority and economic control. Even though the choice of language in these cases is not overtly repellent in the ways in which we have come to think of metaphors that evoke images of mastery, domination and control, in fact these writers are choosing to use language that appeals to notions of altruism, benevolence and caring. The effect is to reify, operationalize, express and maintain boundaries between the East and the West, between male and female, between agent and object. Changing the dominant metaphors of scientific and technological discourse, then, is not in itself any kind of meaningful remedy to inequitable relations because it is impossible to hold constant intended meanings or received meanings or meanings that variant interests infuse into words. Ultimately, language cannot be owned. Meaning moves and shifts and works in ways that cannot always be anticipated.

Our analysis of the gendered language of technology transfer between East and West, then, is not simply a discussion of literary devices, or of the political economy of trade, or of one aspect of gender studies, but is grounded in a seamless web of philosophical, economic, political and social distinctions. These distinctions are not merely restricted to the relation between East and West, or between male and female, rather they also advance representations of the larger networks that allow the possibility for particular meanings to exist at particular moments in history. Sometimes, as our analysis of the literature of technology transfer demonstrates, issues that seem to be remotely connected to more immediate feminist concerns are thoroughly infused with notions of what it means to be male or female. Although we tend to think we understand what is intended when metaphors convey familiar meanings, metaphors which may seem to be conducive to feminist ideals may be used to conceal real inequities between individuals or between groups such that our understanding may be rooted in deception. That is why it is important never to lose sight of the real, material conditions and power relations that underpin all types of social and political engagements in contemporary societies, not just those that explicitly deal with the conditions of women.

We are not aware of any explicitly feminist analyses of the relations between gender and technology transfer in Eastern Europe. As a result, it is impossible to know what the implications of the use of gendered language are in terms of access to employment, the restructuring of work and home and the power differences between men and women. These are important issues which desperately need feminist attention. We would caution those who take up these issues in the future, however, to avoid the dual traps of what Grint and Woolgar (1995) call 'technological and textual determinism', where the attempt to move away from essentialist arguments about gender and technology rely too heavily on 'the unproblematized use of linguistic conventions of representation' and which, in turn, lead to a simplistic rendering of the relation between language, technology and social relations.

Haraway (1991) suggests that 'we need the power of modern critical theories of how meanings and bodies get made, not in order to deny meaning and bodies, but in order to live in meanings and bodies that have a chance for the future'. We agree. The gendered language of technology transfer to Eastern Europe, wrapped as it is in the discourse of caring, acts as both a linguistic marker and mask of political and socioeconomic relations between East and West. Our real concern is with the relations and their implications for living in an equitable environment, both in terms of gender equity and geopolitical equity. If we are to successfully challenge these relations, then we need to recognize that deteriorating material conditions and economic oppression *vis-à-vis* the West, despite language that indicates otherwise, remain as important variables in the lives of women and men in Eastern Europe.

References

ALDOUS, P. (1990) 'Helping Eastern Europe', *Nature*, **344**, April, p. 803.

ANON. (1992) 'Doing business with the bear', *Management Today*, July, pp. 40–5.

ANON. (1990) 'Reforming Stalin's academies', *Nature*, **343**, January, p. 101.

ANON. (1990) 'The great European experiment', *Nature*, **344**, April, pp. 599–600.

ANON. (1992) 'United States and Russia announce cooperation on wide range of trade and economic issues', *Business America*, June, pp. 14–16.

ANON. (1992) 'The true cost of stability', *New Scientist*, February, p. 11.

CHARLES, D. (1992) 'Western funds for Russia may miss their target', *New Scientist*, March, p. 13.

COLLARD, A. with CONTRUCCI, J. (1989) '*Rape of the Wild: Man's Violence against Animals and the Earth*', Bloomington, IN, Indiana University Press.

DICKMAN, S. (1990) 'Eastern Europe comes on-line', *Nature*, **348**, November, p. 29.

DICKMAN, S. (1992) 'Science aprés le déluge: struggling to stay afloat', *Science*, **256**, April, pp. 474–5.

FELLER, G. (1990) 'Tapping Soviet/East European scientific and technical prowess', *Research-Technology Management*, **33**, 5, September/October, pp. 16–22.

GAYNOR, G. H. (1992) 'Learning to manage in a free economy', *Research-Technology Management*, **35**, 2, March/April, pp. 5–7.

GRAHAM, L. R. (1993) 'Downsized yet still potent Russian science seen emerging from current political crisis', *Research-Technology Management*, **36**, 4, July/August, pp. 2–3.

GRIFFIN, S. (1978) *Woman and Nature: The Roaring Inside Her*, New York, Harper & Row.

GRINT, K. and WOOLGAR, S. (1995) 'On some failures of nerve in constructivist and feminist analyses of technology', in GRINT, K. and GILL, R. (Eds) *The Gender-Technology Relation: Contemporary Theory and Research*, London, Taylor & Francis, pp. 48–75.

HARAWAY, D. J. (1991) 'Situated knowledges: the science question in feminism and the privilege of partial perspectives', in HARAWAY, D. J. (Ed.) *Simians, Cyborgs and Women*, New York, Routledge, pp. 183–201.

HASTE, H. (1993) *The Sexual Metaphor*, Cambridge, MA., Harvard University Press.

HOLDEN, C. (1992) 'Eastern scientists flood grants programme', *Science*, **258**, November, p. 894.

HUGHES, S. (1992) 'Boost for big science in Eastern Europe', *New Scientist*, March, p. 13.

JOHNSON, R. (1991) 'Privatisation in Hungary is creating investment opportunities for US firms', *Business America*, January, pp. 17–18.

KUBLIN, M. and SHEPHERD, J. (1993) 'Technology transfer from the commonwealth of independent states to the United States', *Industrial Management*, **35**, 2, March/April, pp. 26–9.

LAYMAN, P. (1992) 'Meeting targets: Eastern Europe investment fears', *Chemical and Engineering News*, **70**, 11, March, pp. 11–12.

LEPKOWSKI, W. (1992) 'Poland struggles to forge new policy for science', *Chemical and Engineering News*, **70**, 21, June, pp. 7–9.

LEPKOWSKI, W. (1993) 'More science, technology support urged for Eastern Europe', *Chemical and Engineering News*, **71**, 1, January, pp. 26–7.

MACKENZIE, D. (1992) 'Can Europe save its eastern promise?', *New Scientist*, February, pp. 20–1.

MERCHANT, C. (1980) *The Death of Nature: Women, Ecology and the Scientific Revolution*, San Francisco, Harper & Row.

MITCHELL, J. K. (1993) 'Split of Czechoslovakia means changes for chemical industry', *Chemical and Engineering News*, **71**, 1, January, pp. 9–18.

PALCA, J. (1990) 'Eastern Europe: missing an opportunity', *Science*, **248**, April, pp. 20–2.

RHEA, J. (1992) 'Prospecting for science in the former Soviet Union', *Research-Technology Management*, **35**, 6, November/December, pp. 13–17.

RICH, V. (1989) 'Soviet bloc research criticised', *Nature*, **337**, January, p. 296.

RICHARDSON, J. G. (1990) 'Western execs welcome, Czech minister says', *Research-Technology Management*, **33**, 5, September/October, pp. 2–3.

RICHARDSON, J. G. (1992) 'OECD research ministers confront emergency of R&D unemployment in former Soviet Union', *Research-Technology Management*, **35**, 3, May/June, pp. 2–3.

SELTZER, R. (1992a) 'Boost in US–Russia cooperation in chemical research urged', *Chemical and Engineering News*, December, pp. 21–2.

SELTZER, R. (1992b) 'US buys Russian technology', *Chemical and Engineering News*, **70**, 14, April, pp. 24–5.

SIETMANN, R. (1990) 'East German scientists wary about unification', *Science*, April, p. 23.

STEELE, L. W. (1991) 'Letter from Budapest', *Research-Technology Management*, **34**, 6, November/December, pp. 4–5.

STEVENS, C. (1990) 'The 1992 technology challenge: enter East Europe', *Research-Technology Management*, **33**, 5, September/October, pp. 12–15.

WAXMONSKY, G. R. (1993) 'The survival of science in Russia', *Chemical and Engineering News*, July, pp. 34–6.

WEIMER, W. O. (1992) 'East Europe technology needs examined', *Research-Technology Management*, **35**, 1, January/February, pp. 5–6.

WILLIAMSON, J., TITCH, S. and PURTON, P. (1992) 'The curtain rises on telecommunications in Eastern Europe', *Telephony*, **222**, 1, July, pp. 27–33.

Chapter 15

Disciplinary Practices?
Older Women and Exercise

Marilyn Poole, Dallas Isaacs and Judy Ann Jones

Body image and body maintenance are widely discussed in both the popular press and in academic literature. Both seem inextricably intertwined and a plethora of work has arisen to explain the materiality of the body and the regulatory norms which constrain and regulate that materiality within particular cultural contexts. This small empirical study explores what some of these concepts mean to a group of older women who are exercise instructors teaching exercise-to-music classes to older people (50 years and more). All these women not only taught others but had a high commitment to exercise themselves. This study seeks to explain some of the reasons for this commitment.

Writers such as Wolf (1990, p. 17) believe that interest in our bodies and appearance is a result of an influential and pervasive market manipulation which has resulted in a new form of control or discipline, particularly over women. 'The obligatory beauty myth dosage,' says Wolf (1990, p. 70) provided by women's magazines 'elicits in their readers a raving, itching parching product lust, an abiding fantasy.' The fantasy is that of transformation, that appearance can be controlled, improved and changed provided the right products are purchased and the prescribed regimen followed. However, these messages appear aimed at the younger woman, so that she might prevent deterioration and defy ageing. Turner (1991, p. 168), however, speculates on a new form of control emerging in that 'The changing structure of populations in late capitalism suggests a new discourse of demography centred on a regimen of diet, jogging and cosmetics to control the alienated and disaffected citizens of retirement compounds.' This control, which according to Featherstone (1991, p. 170) is exerted through 'The vast range of dietary, slimming, exercise and cosmetic body-maintenance products which are currently produced, marketed and sold point to the significance of appearance and bodily preservation within late capitalist society.' It is within a consumer culture, through the media and advertisements, that the benefits of body-maintenance are emphasized – benefits which are largely to be achieved through diet and exercise, benefits which can be obtained by older people as well as younger.

The discourses of diet and exercise promulgated through the media are authenticated by 'experts' in a plethora of scientific or pseudo-scientific articles in newspapers, magazines and on the television. Women are being told that to be overweight is a serious health risk. 'Female fat', according to Wolf (1990, p. 187), 'is the subject of public passion, and women feel guilty about female fat, because we implicitly recognize that under the myth, women's bodies are not our own but society's' . These discourses are not necessarily recent. What is interesting is that terms such as 'stout' , 'chunky' , 'obese' and 'average' still remain tantalizingly undefined. In a review of risk factors associated with women's health including weight recommendations, O'Dea (1991) claims that the rate of obesity in Australia (as indicated by National Heart Foundation evidence) is similar for both men and women. The risks for people in this group include heart disease, high blood cholesterol, gall stones, diabetes and some cancers. She concluded that the overweight are at a slightly but not a greatly increased risk compared to those who have normal body fat. What emerges from her review is that the notion of a 'medical standard' of weight is very vague. This has enabled researchers, health workers, nutritionists and others working in the field to 'medicalize' the whole issue of weight. The result has been the legitimizing of the discourses of diet and exercise (through which weight control is achieved) by health authorities and the promotion of these by women's magazines and the media generally. The commodification of weight control has spawned satellite industries which have developed around exercise such as sports clothing, fitness videos, gyms and fitness centres and personal trainers (Finkelstein, 1994, p. 97). The growth of industries concerned with diet are evidenced by the proliferation of diet foods and drinks in supermarkets and the popularity of weight reduction clinics, such as Jenny Craig and Gloria Marshall.

Featherstone (1991, p. 177) notes 'Within consumer culture the body is proclaimed as a vehicle of pleasure: it's desirable and desiring and the closer the actual body approximates the idealised images of youth, health, fitness and beauty the higher its exchange-value.' Older women, however, do not fit this ideal body-subject. Rather, they are often subjected to negative stereotypes and considered physically unattractive, asexual and dependent both physically and socially (Wieneke, Power, Bevington and Rankins-Smith, 1994, p. 179). There are of course exceptions. The images of stars from the entertainment industry such as Joan Collins, Tina Turner or more recently Sophia Loren starring in Altman's film *Pret-à-Porter* confound these stereotypes and demonstrate that the bodies and appearance of these women still have high exchange-value and can be 'sold' to a mass audience. These stars have triumphed over age and the bodily deterioration of the ageing process.

Within a consumer culture the health benefits of diet and exercise are marketed not only as a means of defying the deterioration of ageing and battling the onset of disease but also of 'looking good' which is part of today's acceptability. Chapkis (1988, p. 14) notes that 'the relationship between Beauty and the body is . . . extremely problematic, all the more so for women for whom both qualities are central to identity.' Approximating beauty can be essential to a woman's chances for power, respect and attention. Our appearance does matter and has always mattered. 'But in late capitalist society it has become our peculiar form of pathology which expresses in exaggerated form its underlying character structure' (Lasch, 1979, p. 88). Evidence of this can be seen in the individual time and effort that are put into the regulation of physical appearance and in the industries which have developed supporting these efforts. Again and again, it is women who are found wanting. While the burden on young women is immense, we can ask what of the older woman for whom youth is now long past and for whom the pursuit of an idealized body-image as presented in the media is an unachievable goal? If the body-beautiful is an essential measure of women's worth, we can conclude that for the older woman, loss of youth and beauty might be equated with a general lack of respect, a lack of worth accorded to her and indeed the invisibility of older woman in our society (Hepworth and Featherstone, 1982, pp. 114–36).

Foucault provides us with some useful insights in explorations of inscription of the body through his interests in the regulation of the body and the surveillance of populations. In *Discipline and Punish*, Foucault (1977, p. 137) says that power is exerted on the body by means of discipline. Discipline in this case being 'methods, which made possible the meticulous control of the operation of the body, which assured the constant subjection of its forces and imposed upon them a relation of docility-utility, might be called "disciplines"'. He goes on to say:

> What was then being formed was a policy of coercions that act upon the body, a calculated manipulation of its elements, its gestures, its behaviour. The human body was entering a machinery of power that explores it, breaks it down and rearranges it . . . Thus discipline produces subjected and practised bodies, 'docile bodies'. (p. 138)

Bartky (1988) argues that Foucault does not differentiate between the bodies or the bodily experiences of females and males. The disciplinary practices, according to Bartky, which are exerted on women's bodies are different than those of men. She cites the dieting disciplines and the very specific exercise programmes for women where it is difficult 'to distinguish what is done for the sake of physical fitness from what is done in obedience to the requirements of femininity' (p. 65). The very language used in the fitness industry in aerobics classes (mostly attended by women) is an indication of this. Terms such as 'body blitz', 'new body', 'body sculpt' all indicate that if 'body work' is performed then bodies can be changed or transformed. The ageing body can be viewed therefore as one where insufficient maintenance has taken place. This leads to further implications of low value because it does not fit with the socially validated ideals of youth, fitness and beauty.

Grosz (1994, pp. 141–2) argues that bodies are inscribed by both involuntary and voluntary means. Involuntary inscription may occur, for example, in prison where the body is confined and supervised through a variety of corporeal measures such as being handcuffed. Ageing might be considered an involuntary inscription in that with increasing age bodies tend to become heavier, flabbier and weaker. Voluntary inscription in this study might be considered the regimen of exercise which the women use to maintain their bodies. Within the discourses of the health and fitness industries, responsibility is given to the individual to maintain health and prevent disease. For example, the Heart Foundation poster proclaims 'Anybody can get heart disease, everybody can prevent it', the prevention being achieved through exercise, diet and health checks. Individuals assume agency when they exercise. Not only are they maintaining the body to conform to cultural norms as to what is attractive, but they are also taking responsibility for maintenance of their own health and prevention of disease.

What of older women? There are '1.3 million women 60 and over, that is, 17 per cent of all Australian women, but the lives of women over 60 are largely invisible, untold and unspoken, even in feminist circles' (Anike, 1991, p. 7). Older women are under-researched except perhaps when they become a problem to their families and the community when they are classified as the 'frail aged'. There are many older women who are not in that category, who lead independent lives and therefore cannot be accessed by community or welfare services. In this research project we were interested in older women who had a commitment to exercise and we speculated as to why this should be so. We wanted to investigate whether this commitment to exercise was a result of the normalizing discourses of the health and fitness industries or whether, seeing their bodies as commodities which carry a certain value, exercise was one of the disciplinary practices they exerted upon them. We were interested in finding out from a group which are generally under-researched, what benefits they perceived would accrue from regular exercise.

Method

The research sample consisted of seventeen women aged between 52 and 73 years living in the eastern suburbs of metropolitan Melbourne. They were all qualified instructors of exercise programmes for older adults, which range from the fit and active 'over fifties' to armchair exercise programmes for the frail aged. The sample were self-selected members of an association of instructors who had all undertaken a training course (VICFIT) sponsored by the Victorian Department of Sport and Recreation. The association provided a means for the women to attend workshops to upgrade their skills and provided general information on health and fitness. This course of instruction did not require any formal academic qualifications as prerequisites nor certification of any kind in sport or recreation.

We wanted to interview women over 50 who had a commitment to exercise, which we defined as a minimum of 2–3 hours per week over the last two years. We excluded activities such as gardening, vigorous housework or a short walk to the shops from our definition, assuming that these activities are done by most able-bodied women in reasonable health. All the women in our sample were white and able bodied (although a number had recovered from serious illness and some suffered potentially disabling conditions such as arthritis). Although we had defined commitment to exercise as 2–3 hours per week this was surpassed by all the women in the sample except one who had severe arthritis. Conducting two exercise classes per week plus one or two activities such as playing 18 holes of golf, swimming, tennis or taking long walks on a weekly basis was more usual. One woman aged 60 was taking ten classes per week; a 68-year-old commented that four years ago she taught eight classes per week and now only taught four; another 61-year-old taught three aerobics classes per week, was a participant in another two, taught three water aerobics classes per week and still found time to swim on Fridays and go to country line dancing (Boot scooting), two evenings a week.

All the volunteers were contacted and interviewed in a semi-structured interview format for approximately one hour in a location of their choice. For some, this was in their own homes; for others in the community centres or church halls where they conducted their exercise-to-music classes. All the interviews were taped and later transcribed. In the course of the interviews, which were conducted in an informal conversational style so that a rapport between researcher and interviewee might be established, we also talked with the women about their lives, their education, their jobs, children and partners. We tried to gain insights into their lived experiences and personal circumstances so that through their own comments and our interpretations we might explore what commitment to exercise meant to them and what meanings they attributed to the discourses of health and fitness.

Discussion

We realize that this is a very limited sample and not representative of women in this particular age group. Australia is a multicultural society of people from many different backgrounds. Our sample, however, was predominantly Anglo–Celtic. The sample was limited to the eastern suburbs of Melbourne which is, generally speaking, middle-class though not necessarily affluent. Most of the women had retired from the paid work force and a number of the women said that the income they derived from the classes (usually $4 per class per person) was a useful and sometimes necessary addition to their family income. In fact they had to calculate carefully that they did not invoke higher taxes or reduce their pension benefits through these earnings. All said the income was important: it made them feel professional, that this was a job not a hobby. One also commented that she had noticed that many women of her age (62) who were not in paid work had aged more rapidly than those who were still in the work force in some way.

All considered the payment, which for some left them at break-even point, to be worthwhile. Only one woman did the work on a volunteer basis and this was because she gave classes at the local YMCA where she was a Board member.

We found it interesting that the commitment to exercise was so high and that the women participated with such zest. In our analysis of responses we found that all the women in this study had, without exception, been involved from their youth with activities ranging from organized team sports such as netball or athletics to callisthenics. They had all taken breaks in their exercise programmes. For the majority, this was when their children were very young or when they had been involved in the paid work force and also had family responsibilities. For many, the children growing older was a time when they again began to be involved in regular exercise programmes although not necessarily of the same kind as when they were in their teens or early twenties. For most of these women the impetus for a high commitment to exercise had returned after they left the paid work force and for some after a period of ill health. When asked how much support they received from their families there was a mixed response. Some found that their husbands and children were most supportive. Some husbands who had retired helped carry their gear to classes and put on the urn for tea and coffee after class. Other husbands clearly resented the time spent away from them: they 'grizzled', which was placing a strain on their wives. One said 'he probably doesn't like me going out of a night time. But that's just bad luck.' She went on to say 'it won't do him any good because I'll still go.'

Many said that now they had retired, their husbands wanted to take time off for holidays in off-peak times and this was not possible as their classes followed the school terms. Most of the women said they intended to exercise 'until they dropped' but some planned to give up as instructors because of family commitments (mostly retired husbands). The 73-year-old anxiously asked after the interview was concluded how old the other women were and whether I considered it unreasonable that she was taking so many classes and intended to continue to do so 'for ever'. Some of the women reported lack of interest or indifference by their children but others said that their children were active participants in sports and their own involvement was a point of mutual interest and source of conversation with their children. Many reported how it helped them relate to grandchildren who came to see them put on displays in local shopping centres (such as in senior citizens week) and that the need to choose the music for their exercise tapes kept them in touch with the young. They felt that it gave an image to their grandchildren of someone who was active, interested and in touch with the world. Responses from the women interviewed indicated that participation in exercise programmes made them 'feel good' and 'in touch'. This could mean that they had internalized the regulatory norms of our society: that women of whatever age should fight the ageing process and feel good about doing so.

Marilyn Poole, Dallas Isaacs and Judy Ann Jones

Discourses on the Body

I'm flabby, I've gotta lose weight

In response to the question 'How do you feel about your body shape nowadays?' a number of different comments were elicited. All except one of the women were not particularly happy with their body shape.

> It could do with a bit of improvement (laughter). Somehow or other I have got a middle-aged spread. (age 59)

> Everything drops. I feel I'd like to be a little bit less podgy. But that's me, and I don't think I ever will be slim. Menopause yes, even if it's just a thickening of the abdomen – you know how you get that tummy. And that's what I don't like. But I don't think that we can change that. (age 55)

> My body shape (groan) is awful, the exercises keep me fit and useful. Obesity is a problem in my family so I have to watch it. Fitness can't be stored, fatness can . . . If you stop you lose muscle tone, when you exercise you might not lose weight but the distribution changes, I am very conscious of this. All ages, figures, body shapes change. (age 69)

There was general acceptance that the older you became the less of an issue body shape was. All agreed that mid-life brought with it weight problems, that most older women developed a heavy abdomen, gained weight and lost muscle tone. This bothered them. They exercised because it restored muscle tone, prevented stiffness and assisted in the distribution of weight so that they looked 'trim'. Trimness rather than slimness had become a desirable and achievable goal. None believed that exercise could reduce weight. However, they all seemed to agree that exercise might change its distribution. This change in distribution was appreciated by the women themselves and others. One woman commented on the women who came to her classes 'They say their husbands comment on their changing shape – don't lose weight but the distribution is better.' The following comments sum up the general feeling that exercise does not make you lose weight.

> You know the old saying once a pear, always a pear. I just think that you've got to watch what you eat but I don't believe that exercise – and I could be wrong here – but I don't believe exercise on its own is going to help you. (age 60)

> Oh, I'd like to lose a stone. I think I'm like everybody else . . . I think healthy would come first, trim is definitely a motivator. It keeps people supple. I mean, I can do things with my limbs that, you know, 50, 40-year-olds can't do. (age 62)

For all the exercise I've been doing over the years I'm not slim and I think that's my genes and it is not anything to do with how much I am doing. (age 59)

A lot of people do get recommended to come to class because they are overweight. But I do say to them I can't guarantee that I will lose your weight but I will guarantee that I will change your shape if you come long enough. (age 61)

All the women were keenly aware of the changes in body shape that had occurred with ageing. They accepted it but were not really happy about it. They had internalized the normalizing discourses of what it is to be attractive – that is, to possess a slim, well-toned body. Despite their own considerable commitment to exercise, flabbiness, the heavy abdomen and excess weight were clearly identified as aspects of ageing which they disliked and were not able to control. The discourses of the women also revealed they did believe some kind of transformation of self was possible. If they worked hard enough at exercise, an attractive distribution of their weight or 'trimness' was achievable, some toning of muscle was possible, even if slimness was not. The women's commitment to exercise could be interpreted as one of a number of disciplinary practices exerted on their bodies in order to achieve what was, for them, an ideal body-subject, a body which was trim and supple. To a limited extent the women subscribed to the view expressed by Finkelstein (1991, p. 103):

The body has become an object to be shaped at will, in accord with prevailing fashions and values. As we imagine we need new appliances, new possessions, new adventures and experiences to realise our social ambitions – and we are prepared to pay the price of them – so, our desires for a new physical image, a better appearance, a stronger sense of sex appeal, a more youthful appearance and so on, can be met by treating the human body as we would other consumer and fashionable items.

Discourses on health

To keep me fit and healthy

In response to questions as to why they themselves exercised and why they thought the people in their classes exercised, many responses indicated that health was a major factor:

Health, social and body shape – all are important but health is probably the most important. (age 69)

Often the response to the question as to why they exercised was straight to the point and simple:

> To keep me healthy, more than anything. (age 62)

One woman said her class told her:

> Tuesdays, and Thursdays and Fridays are wonderful days because we sleep so well after we come to your exercise and we eat so much better.

A number of women commented that doing exercise regularly helped their endurance for other things in life and prevented tiredness:

> Yes, number one we exercise, we must be firming and then along with that comes that little extra bit of energy. (age 62)

Another said:

> One very important thing that I have noticed, is that if I am reasonably well exercised and reasonably fit I don't feel tiredness. (age 52)

Another perceived the benefit of exercise was independence:

> When I see women my age, I really think, oh my god. One woman in particular I know she shuffles doesn't walk, I don't want to become like that, because my children worry. They live such a long way away and I am on my own. (age 61)

Another said:

> People are becoming more health conscious, older people included. They want to remain mobile and independent, at least that's what they say. They are not fussed about their bodies. (age 64)

The discourses on health were well represented by the women in this sample. They cited many instances of women coming to their classes and improving walking skills, of joints becoming less stiff, of people recovering much quicker than expected after surgery, the extra energy and endurance that followed the exercise regimen. Basically the view was if you feel fit you feel good. Extra energy meant these older women need not feel passive or dependent.

Featherstone (1991, p. 183) comments that preventative medicine and its offshoot health education has persuaded individuals to be responsible for their own 'body maintenance' through the assertion that those who do maintain their body best through exercise and healthy diet (abstaining from unhealthy practices such as smoking, overeating and lack of exercise) not only conserve their bodies but will also live longer and enjoy better health. However, no matter how worthy this image of health may be, no matter what the rewards, the only way this message is sold by health educators is through 'looking good and feeling good': that is, through the cosmetic rewards of fitness and the images of people who have more energy and thus can get more out of life. Featherstone notes that, 'The popular media and commercial interests have found the "looking good and feeling great" health education is a saleable commodity. The media "endorse body mainte-nance as a part of the consumer lifestyle" and "pass on the message to a wider audience with frequent articles on slimming, exercise, health foods and appearance"' (1991, p. 183). Bordo (1988, p. 89) questions why our culture is so obsessed with 'keeping our bodies slim, tight and young' and Wolf (1990, p. 187) notes the compulsive attention which is given to weight in the media, attention which quite outweighs the health risks associated with obesity. For older women, positioning themselves within this discourse, exercise can be seen as not only an activity to be enjoyed but one which is done for one's own good. The women in this sample accepted the normalizing discourse that to be fit was to be healthy and that each individual takes responsibility of their own health maintenance.

Social Networks

A motto of one of the organizations which sponsored the exercise classes where the women were instructors was 'fun, fitness and friendship'. While the evidence is compelling that women, including older women, have internalized the normalizing discourses of body image and health and fitness, these do not provide the only reasons they have for attending classes and being so involved in various activities. The importance to the women of the friendships they made in class and their connectedness to social networks cannot be overesti-mated. While the women in our sample had some pithy and insightful com-ments to make about body image and the benefits of 'feeling fit and looking good', the data from their stories was overwhelming in terms of lively anec-dotes, the depth of feeling and the pleasure that the women derived from the friendship and fun they found in their classes. Story after story emerged of women who were isolated and who had gradually found friends in their classes, of the women who lived alone or were vulnerable because of ill health and of the support networks which were formed around them. Women benefited from the support networks formed and fostered in the classes. The women we interviewed, the instructors, not only understood the importance of such social networks but were active in their formation.

One of the women discussed a social group which had formed as a result of meeting at exercise classes:

> Oh, yes, there's been some very staunch friendships made – I am thinking of one group away walking this weekend and every year for the past nine years . . . a social weekend. About 22 of us would go down and have a lovely time together. And many of those were widowed. And many of those would come, you know, a year or so after they were widowed and needing to be able to get away, something different, people to talk to.

Another said these networks were forged 'through getting together for coffee afterwards and just generally supporting each other during the class . . . and the coffee times afterward, plus some of the outings the teacher arranges from time to time – those things forge bonds'.

The instructors all provided tea and coffee after class unless it was held in a community centre such as the YMCA where a small cafeteria already existed. Most of the instructors also organized end-of-term or end-of-year gatherings such as a Christmas lunch for class participants. Others did this more regularly, for example, the class going out for lunch on a monthly basis. These support networks not only have social benefits for fun and recreation but enable people to talk about their troubles. One of the instructors commented:

> And some people, you know, if they've got an ache or pain, they just seem to give up, whereas if they mix with other people, they realise they are not the only people who've got this little ache or pain and they can talk about it. The group I've got here, it's just like a social gathering.

The following statement from one of the instructors sums up the general picture:

> I think they get a feeling of sharing, particularly a lot of my people and I'm sure there are the same cases in lots of classes. There are single women living on their own, widows or spinsters and I think they are fairly lonely, a lot of them, and they find a great social interaction and I think they benefit that way. Also we have sort of caring and sharing sessions and people know if they want to say something to me they can come up afterward. I can tell if someone is hanging back a bit so when everyone is gone we have a little chat. I find they tell me all sorts of things and I do tell them medically I am not equipped to answer their questions but really they just want to talk something out . . . if a new lady comes in I always introduce her to the whole class but specifically to one person and she might work with her until they have found someone else. So social interaction, friendships, they go out for lunch sometimes now. Lots of these ladies go out and see films.

What is emerging from the data is that older women who attend exercise classes do so for a number of reasons. While the discourses of health, fitness and body image may be important, there are other more powerful reasons. The discourses on health, which include social and emotional health and wellbeing, stress the importance of social support and connectedness. A stereotype is often presented that as people grow older they become more socially isolated and that this isolation has a negative impact on their health. Cusick and Quinsey (1990, p. 7) found that, 'Social isolation has a strong association with health status in older people.' By forming and facilitating the social bonds between class members, the women in this sample not only improve their own health status but also assist other women. The women's stories indicated how much they felt that the exercise classes they ran benefited women who were alone, lonely and those who were ill or disabled in some way. A number commented that the women in their classes who suffered Alzheimer's disease or were recovering from major illness or who were somewhat frail or disabled not only showed signs of improvement in terms of strength, flexibility and mobility as their involvement in exercise continued (evidence supported in other studies: Doress and Siegal, 1987, p. 62; Linder-Pelz, 1991, pp. 137–8) but also became more active and sociable within the group. For many older people, 'feeling well' often means having social contacts, activities and interests rather than being free of disability or chronic illness (Saltman, Webster and Therin, 1989).

Conclusion

This chapter explores the reasons for older women's commitment to regular exercise. Given their comments and their very high commitment to exercise, there seems little doubt that exercise forms part of the disciplinary practices associated with the discourses of health, fitness and beauty. There is a sense of agency here. It would seem from their conversations that the women are providing evidence which disproves notions of the decline associated with ageing. They were breaking the conventional images associated with getting older. They were resistant to any construction of themselves as 'old'. They knew that chronologically they were in mid-life or older but they consistently denied responses associated with ageing or decline, such as taking things quietly or taking a back seat. Instead they provide us with an interesting glimpse of individuals who may have positioned themselves within the discourses of our consumer culture in terms of body image and body maintenance but are not victims or dupes of that positioning.

The poststructuralist discourses of Turner, Featherstone and others are not adequate in explaining the commitment to exercise of the women in this study. Such discourses do not take into account the lived experiences of a group such as this. The normalizing discourses of the health and fitness industries and the disciplinary practices they produce do not exert total control over the individual. Even within these discourses, individuals exert personal power. The women in this study went beyond this: they exerted power through their social connectedness, networking and empathy with others, attributes discussed in the more conventional feminist and sociological literature and often ignored in poststructuralist theorizing.

What has emerged from the narratives that these women may represent a new kind of selfhood for older women: one which contests, opposes and resists the discourses on ageing. What we see here is a multipositioning of the women in a number of contesting, even oppositional, discourses. The value of sociability to these women was of paramount importance. It gave meaning to their lives and the lives of others. Through their social networks, their connectedness with other women, they were achieving feelings of self-worth, respect and social power so often denied older women.

References

ANIKE, L. (1991) 'Women over 60 growing old: who are their allies and where is their equality?' *Refractory Girl*, **39**, June, pp. 7–9.

BARTKY, S. L. (1988) 'Foucault, femininity and patriarchal power', in DIAMOND, I. and QUINBY, L. (Eds) *Feminism and Foucault: Reflections on Resistance*, Boston, MA, Northeastern University Press.

BORDO, S. (1988) 'Anorexia nervosa: psychopathology as the crystallization of culture', in DIAMOND, I. and QUINBY, L. (Eds) *Feminism and Foucault: Reflections on Resistance*, Boston, MA, Northeastern University Press.

CHAPKIS, W. (1988) *Beauty Secrets: Women and the Politics of Appearance*, London, The Women's Press.

CUSICK, A. and QUINSEY, K. (1990) *Social Isolation and the Health Status of Senior Adults: Key Issues and Strategies for Action* (a literature review and recommendations for health promotion and community development action), Sydney, St George Health Promotion Unit.

DORESS, P. D. and SIEGAL, D. L. (1987) *Ourselves, Growing Older*, New York, Simon & Schuster.

FEATHERSTONE, M. (1991) 'The body in consumer culture', in FEATHERSTONE, M., HEPWORTH, M. and TURNER, B. S. (Eds) *The Body: Social Process and Cultural Theory*, London, Sage, pp. 170–96.

FINKELSTEIN, J. (1991) *The Fashioned Self*, Cambridge, Polity Press.

FINKELSTEIN, J. (1994) *Slaves of Chic: An A–Z of Consumer Pleasures*, Port Melbourne, Minerva.

FOUCAULT, M. (1977) *Discipline and Punish: The Birth of the Prison*, New York, Vintage Books.

GROSZ, E. (1994) *Volatile Bodies*, St Leonards, Allen & Unwin.

HEPWORTH, M. and FEATHERSTONE, M. (1982) *Surviving Middle Age*, Oxford, Blackwell.

LASCH, C. (1979) *The Culture of Narcissism*, New York, Warner Books.

LINDER-PELZ, S. (1991) *Well Over Fifty*, Sydney, Allen & Unwin.

O'DEA, J. (1991) 'Trends in the nutrition and health status of Australians: are we creating adverse effects?', *Journal of the Home Economics Association of Australia*, **XXIII**, 2, June.

SALTMAN, D., WEBSTER, I. and THERIN, G. (1989) 'Older persons' definitions of good health: implications for general practitioners', *The Medical Journal of Australia*, **150**, 17, April.

TURNER, B. S. (1991) 'The discourse of diet', in FEATHERSTONE, M., HEPWORTH, M. and TURNER, B. S. (Eds) *The Body: Social Process and Cultural Theory*, London, Sage, pp. 157–69.

WIENEKE, C., POWER, A., BEVINGTON, L. and RANKINS-SMITH, D. (1994) 'Women and the social construction of ageing', in GERMOV, J. (Ed.) *Health Papers: Presented at the 'Social Theory in Practice' TASA Conference*, University of Newcastle, New South Wales, Department of Sociology and Anthropology.

WOLF, N. (1990) *The Beauty Myth*, London, Vintage Books.

Chapter 16

Women's Studies and Working-class Women

Christine Zmroczek and Pat Mahony

We began talking with each other about social class more than ten years ago. We are both from working-class backgrounds on any common sense or socio-logical definition of this term and we have both benefited from a number of years in higher education. Between us we have several degrees and both of us now have full-time salaried positions as teachers and researchers in higher education. We each have a car, a mortgage and many of the other trappings of a middle-class lifestyle, yet we retain the sense of being long-term guests in someone else's house where, however well one knows the rules, it is still not home. It is as though we have learned another language and are conscious of its grammatical structures in a way that native speakers are not. What are we then? What do the terms 'working-class' and 'middle-class' mean for women in our position? These are just two of the questions with which we started when we first began to think about the role of social class in our lives.

A lack of suitable language to describe ourselves is one of the frustrations felt by many working-class women who have been through higher education. As we have explained elsewhere (Zmroczek and Mahony, 1996), we started to use the term 'educated working-class women' at one point, since this would at least signal our discomfort about ignoring the differences in the opportunities and privileges available to us, compared with our sisters or cousins. However, we have subsequently become uncomfortable with this on the grounds that it could merely reinforce the kinds of stereotypes which we were trying to challenge of 'them' and 'us': them (the 'rough', 'salt of the earth', 'uneducated' women) on the one hand and us (the 'educated', 'more refined' and 'nearly-middle-class' women) on the other.

In the early days of our discussions, we found that the more we talked about class the more we had to say. It was good to let off steam together when we were offended by colleagues', friends' and other middle-class feminists' ignorance or indifference about class issues, or at a conference, when we heard yet again that radical feminism in which we had both been active for very many years 'is middle-class'. We began to ponder the effects of this criticism which, in rendering us invisible, also stole our contributions. The more we talked, the more urgent it became to find out how to place ourselves as two white women[1] distanced from our undoubtedly working-class back-grounds but certainly not always comfortable in – and at times positively

192

enraged by the oppressive behaviour of – the largely middle-class world we now inhabited.

We knew two more women who were also concerned about these issues. In the mid-1980s the four of us formed a group and we met regularly together for two years of intense discussion. We consisted of three ex-Catholics (an African–Asian Scot, an English Pole and an English–Irish woman) and an Asian–Muslim woman. One of us had children, two identified as heterosexual, one as (sort of) heterosexual and one as lesbian. Our ages ranged from late-forties to early-twenties. All of us had working-class backgrounds and all of us had been to university and were in middle-class occupations. When we met to talk about the ways in which the constant drip of negative and oppressive experience operates at a personal level to recreate gendered class and race divisions in Britain, we became convinced that there was a great deal to be explored. We all agreed that we learned a lot about our similarities (rooted partly in social class) as well as the very real differences for us as women who identified as Black, white, lesbian and heterosexual living in a racist and heterosexist society.

We tried to clarify the contexts and situations in which we felt 'other' and to analyse whether issues of social class were dominant or whether racism, heterosexism or other factors combined to give our experiences different meanings. Throughout all of it we shared our strategies for coping with and overcoming the obstacles which had faced us at school, in higher education, at home and in our workplaces. Another important theme of our meeting was the rediscovery and revaluing of some of the strengths which accrued to us by virtue of our working-class backgrounds. There were times when we rocked with laughter as we told our stories of 'beating the system' rather than being beaten by it. After two years of intense discussion we had only just begun to scratch the surface when new jobs, relocation, increased pressure of work and various family crises made it impossible for all four of us to be in the same place at the same time.

However, two of us (the authors of this chapter) worked together in another context and we continued to discuss the issues. We talked with other working-class women, Black and white, from a range of backgrounds and sometimes with middle-class friends about class. We came to the conclusion that for many women, it is a difficult issue to address for many different reasons. For working-class women, for example, it can be painful thinking again about the hurt encountered in the process of obtaining an education, or recalling alienation from family and former friends as well as empowering when considering the gains, resourcefulness and strength shown in overcoming those problems. Middle-class women with whom we spoke also often seemed to find it a difficult subject. It is not that they were unpleasant about it, just that they tended to acknowledge class as important in principle but in practice the conversation would hurriedly move on. When asked, some have said they simply did not know what to say, not having thought about it much before. Others felt guilty. Some women seem to be afraid of discussions of class differences. One woman (a lecturer in higher education) reported, for instance, that when she suggested running a session on class in a Women's Studies programme, her Head of Department said: 'Class? Oh no. I wouldn't do anything about that, the students don't like it.' She also informed us that she had ignored this advice, had enjoyed the ensuing discussions with the students and been pleased with their positive feedback. She concluded that exploring issues around women and social class can be instructive, relevant and exciting for a majority of women and that she was proposing to include more of it in her teaching in future.

And so it was that our own growing awareness, the resistance we experienced from some women and the interest expressed by others, combined to spur us on to explore further and in a more systematic way the issues for working-class women in education. To date we have given a number of papers and workshops at conferences, facilitated and participated in a variety of groups and discussions, invited women to write to us and begun work on a number of edited collections, all with different themes and intended for different audiences. We have begun to test the relevance of our work within an international context (Mahony and Zmroczek, 1994) and have found that women from a range of countries, cultures and regions can relate to our findings. In what follows, we draw on our discussions about class with Black and white women from a range of backgrounds and geographical locations in Britain.

Our Findings about Women and Class in Britain[2]

The Literature

We have found that despite an extensive general literature on social class and the burgeoning of feminist texts in the last 20 years, there are still relatively few feminist analyses of class grounded in the experiences of working-class women. There are some notable exceptions, such as books by Carolyn Steedman (1986), Valerie Walkerdine (1990), the Taking Liberties Collective (1989), and in the USA, bell hooks (1981, 1989), Michele Tokarczyck and Elizabeth Fay (1993) and a recent collection by Julia Penelope about lesbian perspectives on class which includes writing by working-class lesbians (1994). Nonetheless, women report that this relative dearth of thorough, on-going and easily accessible feminist debate and analysis on class leaves a legacy which is unhelpful in our striving to become strong women in control of our own lives.

To be precise, working-class women who have been through higher education report time and again how it leaves us in confusion and uncertainty about who we are and where we fit, if indeed we do fit at all. It leaves us with an inability to identify, name and locate the feelings of shame, humiliation, invisibility and under-confidence which are the felt effects of the oppressive experiences described repeatedly by the women who have spoken with us. While these experiences remain unnamed and unidentified, working-class women are powerless to challenge them in an articulate and effective way when they recur. It takes practice to recognize and explain what is wrong and why, as feminists have learned to do in relation to, for example, sexual oppression and sexual harassment. Finally, our invisibility as working-class women in education, including women's studies, creates a disjuncture with our pasts and makes it difficult to acknowledge the source of some of what we know by virtue of being working-class. It leaves us feeling bereft rather than enriched by knowing how to operate in two different worlds. In our view, the advantages of this dual cultural knowledge are many and we will return to this point later. Predictably, however, our 'difference' and 'middle-class ways' are often highly visible within our working-class families, so that we often become 'outsiders' here too. In sharing these confusions, a number of recurrent themes have emerged from our work as ways in which women report experiencing oppression through social class.

Material Resources

Poverty has been a common experience for many women, at least in childhood and is a significantly different experience from not having much money to spare. The struggles of our mothers to put food on the table have left vivid memories for some:

> I was astonished the first time I went to a middle-class boyfriend's house for a meal. First we had tea and cakes from a trolley (that really wiped me out) and then later we had a huge meal with the food in bowls on the table and you helped yourself. I was used to the food being dished up and spread over the plate to make it look more. I took too much and couldn't eat it all – unheard of and embarrassing.

Economic hardship was often expressed in painful memories about clothes:

> I remember feeling dreadful about winning a scholarship when I was eleven. I knew my parents couldn't afford the school uniform for me. When I went into the VI form I invented some political garbage about continuing to wear school uniform because I simply didn't have any of my own clothes to wear. I think I rather hoped to set a new trend but it didn't work.

The lack of clothes also structured our social lives:

> I couldn't go out much with friends because I had nothing to wear. I had one yellow blouse and a skirt with yellow balloons on it which my

aunt had bought for me. Lurex was the 'in' thing so I would have been well out of place, imagine.

Others remember that lack of money for school equipment, sports gear, musical instruments and school trips led them to pretend not to be interested in school, in an attempt to keep a sense of dignity. Our school reports portray us consequently as 'sullen', 'diffident' and 'unwilling to participate'. To get some extra money, some of us took Saturday jobs which branded us as 'not seriously academic' or to be more precise 'common', all the more so if these jobs were in Woolworths (Boots the chemist was considered slightly more up-market according to one woman). All these experiences played a part in structuring our choice of jobs or career. Some of us left school as soon as we could, either because we were so alienated by the whole experience or because of the pressures we felt for a variety of reasons, often financial:

I knew my parents couldn't afford for me to stay on when my sister got a scholarship, they needed another wage coming in so I left and got a job.

Similarly, another woman told us:

It wasn't that my parents made me leave school, but other relatives and neighbours began to make remarks like 'What's a big girl like you doing still at school when your mother needs your wages?'

Another common experience is illustrated by the woman who told us how she insisted on leaving school 'because I wanted to have some money to buy clothes and do things, but also because I wanted to become grown up like other girls of my age in our street who were out to work already'. Others said that they chose to go to college near home so that they could avoid the financial pressures of a residential life as a student, a trend which is increasing in the 1990s in direct proportion to the rise in student poverty. All these experiences live on in the present. As one woman put it:

I haven't been able to accumulate much in the way of savings or for that matter material goods. I was a mature student starting my degree at thirty. I also started late in the mortgage game after two divorces and still owe tens of thousands of pounds. Now that I have got a well-paid academic job after years of part-time and casual teaching, it seems cruel, and very frightening, that cutbacks and redundancy are the future I have to anticipate.

Other women have told us of their anger at the assumption that 'everyone' these days will inherit property or savings from their parents. For many the reality is similar to that articulated by this woman:

A well-off friend recently said she couldn't understand why I was always so concerned about money, as I would inherit my mother's house when she dies. My mother lives in a council house, and I help her pay the rent and her council tax. Not much hope of inheritance there.

Many working-class women have parents who have not managed to save much money at all, despite lives filled with hard work and economy:

My mother is a pensioner who prides herself on saving something every week from her part-time job. She has always scrimped and saved, even on real essentials like heating, and yet the total of her savings wouldn't be enough to take a family of four to Disney World for a week.

The memory of the hardships experienced by our parents are hard to put aside. Several women told us of finding it difficult not to calculate the cost of a meal out with friends in terms of what their parents live on each week. It is true that not all working-class people are grindingly poor: some are quite comfortable, some are even rich. Lack of economic resources are not always or only what working-class women have to face.

Cultural Resources

Middle-class worlds have in common particular cultural assumptions and particular rules. Because these are taken for granted as the norm, the knowledge which is needed to negotiate them is rarely made explicit. Middle-class women usually do not realize what they know in this respect and because it is not explicit, it is difficult for working-class women to learn (and learn it we must if we want to survive in middle-class occupations). We are not talking here about the useful connections which open doors to jobs and other opportunities, for these are well known. What we are referring to is the 'know how' which is needed to feel at home or to retain our dignity. For some of us, learning it has been perplexing. Often, issues around food have been significant:

It always used to amaze me how people knew what was a good wine and before they'd even tasted it. It's a real muddle, to this day I can't stand the palaver of it all but neither would I buy Liebfraumilch. Is it really awful or have I just learned to think that?

When I first went to university I felt as though I was constantly trying to crack the codes. I used to watch to see how to eat things I'd never come across before. I remember being invited round to dinner and I turned up six hours early at one o'clock.

Again, what to wear or dressing appropriately for the occasion has been a constant preoccupation and for some of us continues to be a source of disquiet, even when we have attained positions sufficiently high in the academic hierarchy to receive social invitations from the Vice Chancellor:

> What do you wear to the Vice Chancellor's house when you've been invited to lunch and it's 'Dress Informal'? Thank God I asked around and didn't wear my track suit.

We also know there is an enormous range of other 'cultural' resources which have to be learned about if working-class women are not to miss out. We are referring here to enjoyable experiences such as theatre, music and art which have not necessarily been accessible through prior knowledge in our own homes:

> I get really cheesed off when people are surprised that I'm keen on classical music. Why shouldn't I be? It's even worse when they find out that I like some things and not others, as though it's odd that I know enough about it to have likes and dislikes.

These stereotypes sometimes operate in reverse ways in relation to some Black women who have told us that it is frequently presumed that they are working-class (often wrongly) and that all kinds of assumptions follow from this. For example, an African woman working in an English university described having become aware of class in a different way. She talked about coming from an upper-middle-class family which owns land and a cattle station and of her father who is head of a big international oil company. In discussing the 'unjust relationship between the professional woman and the woman domestic worker' in her country of origin, she said:

> Here I get the feeling that people outside the university think I'm a domestic worker. It's difficult to explain and it's subtle.

It also needs to be recognized that having high expectations and knowing how to go about fulfilling them is another cultural resource from which working-class women often seem to be excluded. One woman described it thus:

> My family's highest ambition for me was that I should get a 'good' job, the best of all would be in a bank. Well, I got a job in a bank as soon as I left school and I didn't like it much either. Later on, I was the first in my extended family to go to university and in terms of guidance about what is the best career path to follow, how to assess opportunities, how to make opportunities it has all been down to me and a bit hit and miss really.

One of the intriguing things about having to learn another culture is that the workings of that culture are often clearer to an outsider. Almost as anthropologists, working-class women in education are in a position to accumulate knowledge about what goes on in middle-class cultures. This allows us to analyse what has previously been hidden from view in the same ways as feminists have analysed the previously invisible workings of patriarchy and male institutions in society. It is by undertaking such analyses that many women have identified themselves as working-class now, not just that they used to be.

Language

The issue of language figures largely in our experience as one of the major ways in which we were put down. Many middle-class people retain a hint of a regional accent and this can be quite acceptable and even fashionable in some circles. But the systematic attack on strong regional accents and vocabularies which instantly reveal a working-class background left many of us unable or unwilling to speak in public. We were then caught in a vicious circle of lacking the confidence to explore our ideas and thus missing the opportunity to gain the practice we needed to become articulate. Women have their own particular versions of this all-too-familiar story:

> At my selective school not a year went by but my school report criticised me for not being able to express myself. No one ever suggested how I might learn and it never occurred to me to challenge how this and the criticism that I was too talkative, could both be true.

Elocution lessons have particular painful memories for some of us:

> At college we were sent to elocution lessons to learn not to flatten our vowels. While a Welsh or a Northern accent was tolerable (though there weren't many of those either), a London accent was perceived as 'not speaking properly'. And so we sat week after week with a tape recorder and mirror trying to change how we spoke. My aunt phoned one evening after one of these sessions. 'Oh,' she said, 'Haven't we gone posh.' And I felt ashamed. The effect of all this trying to learn to 'speak properly' was disastrous. I became so self-conscious that I was unable to speak at all in class and after a term the Principal told me I was an uncooperative student. It wasn't until years later that I learned that Received Pronunciation was invented by the boy's public schools to exclude 'new money'.

The significance of these accounts cannot be underestimated for we know there is an intimate connection between language and thought, confidence and 'ability'. Learners simply do not flourish unless their ideas are treated seriously and we do not share our ideas or rehearse and practise them unless it is safe to do so. Written language has proved equally problematic for some women. The failure to distinguish between 'proper English' and 'standard English' caused many of us unnecessary difficulty. Not all of us were born into a world where the evil of the split infinitive was at the forefront of our minds. Working-class women are not stupid because we do not know the rules of standard English when we have had little or no opportunity to learn them. If it is important to learn the language of power (which we believe it is), then these rules need to be made explicit for what they are: that is, as mechanisms which distinguish the relatively powerful from the relatively powerless. Many working-class women entering higher education will need continued support if they are to develop their written and spoken skills in this language of power in ways which do not deny their own creativity, knowledge and expressive abilities. The sensitivity with which this is approached is crucial to their intellectual development.

As well as being a source of distress, though, a number of women have also cited higher education as a place of achievement, for example, as the place where they finally learned how to learn:

> It was always a mystery to me how the other girls knew how to get the meaning of a poem or a picture. How did they know who wrote this or that piece of music or where bits of the world were? We had no reference books at home and the idea of going to the library didn't occur to me. Anyway, what would I have looked up? As far as I was concerned what you knew was what you'd learned in school and how anyone knew what we hadn't been taught could only be explained by invoking their cleverness. Not until I was 23 did anyone show me how to use a library and not until 21 after that did I learn about Bourdieu's theory of 'cultural capital'.

Other women have stories to tell about the confidence they gained from teachers who valued their potential and encouraged their self-expression even if it was unorthodox:

> I will never forget the woman who taught my first ever feminist course. She gave me such a boost of confidence when she encouraged me to write a feminist analysis of menstruation, at that time a very under-researched area. She actually thought I could do it. I can still feel the thrill, the challenge and the power her confidence gave me. It has probably propelled me through the last 20 years of struggle as a working-class radical feminist. I didn't realise that it was possible to write what I thought; that it was valid, was a revelation, that it was necessary and part of the feminist struggle was a gift from my feminist tutor.

Gaining Confidence, Anger and Advantage

The issue of confidence emerges consistently in what women have said. Many of the experiences outlined above have conspired to undermine us and have sometimes left us feeling stupid, socially inept and ignorant. It is also true that working-class women who have gone through higher education emerge, if nothing else, more confident and perhaps also more angry. As we learn more about how to 'play the game' we become more aware that there is a game being played: it is one of exclusion.

However, as we have already explained, working-class women in education inhabit a number of worlds and although this has its price, there are also tremendous advantages. We are familiar with the middle-class world from the perspective of the spectator as well as the participant. We suggest that this can enable us not only to identify but to expose what has hitherto been so intangible as to appear 'natural'. This is knowledge which can be developed in the same ways as feminists have developed understandings of the ways in which other forms of oppression operate: starting with our own experiences.

For the future we propose that working-class women and in particular working-class women in Women's Studies insist on developing our knowledge and making our contributions to the future of feminism; that we refuse to be silent, refuse to be written out, refuse to be invisible any longer.

In writing this piece our aim has been to begin a debate which our discussions with working-class women have led us to believe is important. The absence of analysis which we have identified in respect of working-class women, we would argue, also applies to middle-and upper-class women who also have inadequate knowledge about their collective experiences of social class. Thus women of all classes could be encouraged to investigate these issues for themselves. We hope that our analyses and suggestions about the issues for working-class women will prove to be useful, enlightening, thought- and theory-provoking.

Class in Women's Studies

The obvious place in which to develop feminist analyses of class, grounded in women's own experience, is in Women's Studies. Yet judging by what women have told us, it would seem that on many courses, current debates about class in feminist politics are entirely absent. Why? Working-class students repeatedly speak of their disappointment and frustration with those women's studies programmes which ignore class and with teachers who marginalize it or 'treat it as a diversion'. This is not just because their life experience is rendered invisible but also because space is not created for exploring whether more varied styles of teaching need to be developed in order to maximize students' opportunities for learning. In a discipline which, more than most, has taken seriously the potential contradictions between content and methods, theory and practice, political beliefs and personal practice, this represents a surprising and very worrying omission.

In class-divided societies such as Britain, class is a formative experience for all of us and one which goes on being reformulated in the experiences of our adult lives. There is no reason, therefore, why it should not feature as a prominent part of the women's studies agenda. Just as Black women and lesbians have insisted that feminism and women's studies address differences and power relations between women, so working-class women's experiences need to become visible. Perhaps in this we have the potential for a dynamic and much-needed breakthrough in feminist theory and action.

Notes

1 Here and throughout this chapter, we use the terms Black and white as political categories. There are huge debates about the use of these terms and their meanings which cannot be explored in this chapter where we are focusing on women's reported experiences of being working-class.

2 This section develops some ideas published in an earlier discussion of our findings (Zmroczek and Mahony (1996) forthcoming).

References

HOOKS, B. (1981) *Ain't I a Woman?* Boston, MA, Southend Press.

HOOKS, B. (1989) *Talking Back: Thinking Feminist, Thinking Black*, London, Sheba Press; Boston, MA, Southend Press.

MAHONY, P. and ZMROCZEK, C. (1994) 'Invisible boundaries', presentation at the 6th International Feminist Book Fair, Melbourne, July.

PENELOPE, J. (Ed.) (1994) *Out of the Class Closet: Lesbians Speak*, Freedom, CA, The Crossing Press.

STEEDMAN, C. (1986) *Landscape for a Good Woman*, London, Virago.

TAKING LIBERTIES COLLECTIVE (1989) *Learning the Hard Way*, London, Macmillan.

TOKARCZYK, M. and FAY, E. (Eds) (1993) *Working-class Women in the Academy: Labourers in the Knowledge Factory*, Amherst, MA, University of Massachusetts Press.

WALKERDINE, V. (1990) *Schoolgirl Fictions*, London, Verso.

ZMROCZEK, C. and MAHONY, P. (1996) 'Working-class radical feminism: lives beyond the text', in BELL, D. and KLEIN, R. (Eds) *Radically Speaking: Feminism Reclaimed*, Melbourne, Spinifex Press, forthcoming.

Chapter 17

My Skin Still Bleeds When Cut:
A Performance Piece

Quibilah Montsho

At seven years old, a cut knee bled without request
At seventeen, the bleeding came by pure self discipline and control
At twenty seven, it came by crafted force
At thirty seven, perhaps the flow will have been stemmed

My teacher Mrs Crocodile[1] defied all sense, with the proclamation,
See!
Your blood is red, too.
She expected me to express the surprise she experienced herself
My red blood has always been red, except when I inhabit the body of the
    royalty from which I am descended.

There is a book whose title goes 'Labelled a Black Villain'[2]
I regularly feel like that villain
By force rather than choice
And what has this life been but a series of coercive actions imposed by
others for others?
In distress, too easily dragged off to the local bin
In danger, discarded
In trouble, so quickly rejected
In a difficult place, completely ignored
It is this thing that has so far been my life
My Skin Still Bleeds When Cut
Twenty years of cutting
Slicing up the shame
There's NO attention-seeking
It's 'just' my private pain

It was when I was fifteen years old
That I discovered the art of self harm
I hadn't the words, music or tools of the trade
But I did have a blade
My school biology lab unknowingly provided it

Free of charge
My right hand cut my left arm
And my left hand cut my right arm
And with the rise of the fashion of punk
Rose my self harming behaviour to respected fame

A disturbed adolescent
Survivor of life's farce
Seeing all that is transparent
The world speaking through its arse . . .

They forced me into a prison they called a hospital
I was surrounded by white people
With masks for faces
And chemicals for medicine
They called themselves doctors and nurses
This was not my family
I could recognize none of my sisters here
Their betrayal
Their absence
My pain

You're young enough, there's time to change
They nonchalantly state
Then whisper doctor whispers
Against my zombied stare of hate . . .

Then they brought their weapons of torture
Their books, theories, hypotheses
'Justifying' their actions
They pumped me with liquids
I slept for two weeks
I didn't eat for three weeks
I didn't speak for five months

They kept me in isolation
They tried to force feed me
They never asked me how I felt
They never asked me what I wanted
They never told me I was valuable
They never told me I was good
They never told me I was intelligent
They convinced me I was sick
They were right
I was sick of their lies

I was sick of their abuse
I was sick of their ugly white faces
I was sick of their power over me
I was sick of their prison
Alone,
I stayed alone

I could still think
And I did think
I could still feel
And I did feel
I never stopped being human
I still heard their racist remarks
I still cried silently
I still felt the pain of separation

The second time
I stood on the cliff top pointing to myself
was the moment in which I found a reason to live
And that reason was simply me
I had the right to be alive
I had been born
That was enough
And so I dared to sleep that night
And when rest became my friend
My enemies were upon me
My head ached and my body screamed
I was the only person in the world
There were only questions
There was only me
The world had exploded and I had survived
What could I do?
The answers that came told me to embrace the loneliness
Simply be alone
And survive

For my hide they came in the dread of night
For this body beaten by their pulping chemicals
For these sinews prompted by cattle prod strokes
When the hollow of invisible owls conversing
Closed my ears to caution
And tired eyelids dared to descend towards sleep
The sirens of others' emergencies died in my mind
And the flow of crafty commuter cars had long since ceased
My skull hid between blankets of dew and fear

The hands of men in white masks
Held down these black bodies throughout the city
Children ran with fear and 'common sense'
(They had seen this happen before)
When the pale stained steel punctured the skin of this proud Ghanaian
    queen
She stood stiller than the water of the eternal lake
Where even the concrete crocodiles dared not enter
And she waited for the earth to fall
Again
And the walls crashed around our tumbling worlds
An a dis praffeshan dem caal sackiatree

She had again been 'Sectioned'
Her reality composed of her own isolation
Disgusting, dirty, smelly
Time ceased to move
Freedom ceased to be an option
Movement ceased to be possible
Family ceased to come
In a place such as this, even fire would refuse to burn
She was filed under 'Actively Psychotic'
'Humph'
'Is waar kine af tchupidness dis?'
'Sectioned'
Again
Even the echo of her own words could not change that reality

Dem can taalk bout alternative terapee and tings
But a waar kine of treatment di people dem reelly can get?
Seckshan dis drug dat is all wi can si fah all a wi
Di system a disgustin

Where can I seek consolation
In this world of disconsolation
Which avenue can I tread again
When others' footsteps litter my conscience?

Give thanks to they who brought me life
Give thanks to they who prolonged it.
Give thanks to all who fight the good fight
Give thanks to the breath
I breathe every day
Quibilah Montsho, pronounced Kwu-bee-la Moan-show,
Is an Afrikan name

as I am an Afrikan woman born of the sons and daughters of slaves,
All of them survivors
Like them,
I am also a survivor
With my tongue twisted by the incongruities of the English language
I had to learn to pronounce my own name properly
There are those who also learn with me, and those who do not care to learn
One day they will have no choice
And still the struggle goes on . . .

Notes

1 A thick-skinned emotionless creature. Skin sometimes binds and draws us together; sometimes it drives us apart.
2 *Labelled a Black Villain*, Trevor Hercules, Fourth Estate, 1989.

Notes on Contributors

Magdalene Ang-Lygate is currently completing her PhD in Sociology at the University of Strathclyde, where she is part-time lecturer in Women's Studies. Her work is about the application of feminist postcolonial theory to empirical sociological research. She is an Executive Member of the Women's Studies Network (UK) Association and recent publications include 'Women who move: Experiences of Diaspora', in Maynard, M. and Purvis, J. (Eds) *New Frontiers in Women's Studies: Knowledge, Identity and Nationalism*, Taylor & Francis, 1996; 'Waking from a Dream of Chinese Shadows', in *Feminism and Psychology*, 6(1) March 1996; 'Shades of Meaning', in *Trouble and Strife*, 31, 1995. She is a Director of Engender, a research and campaigning organization for women in Scotland, and a founder Director of Meridian, the first information and resource centre for 'Balck' and ethnic minority women in Scotland.

Yvon Appleby is at the Division of Education at Sheffield University where she is completing her PhD about the experiences of lesbian women and education.

Usha Brown lives and works in Glasgow. She has been involved with campaigns around 'race', gender and poverty.

Clara Connolly lives in London and works at the Commission for Racial Equality. She is an Irish member of Women Against Fundamentalism.

Chris Corrin is Senior Lecturer in Politics and Convenor of the Women's Studies Centre at Glasgow University. Her publications include *Superwomen and the Double Burden: Women's Experience of Change in Central and Eastern Europe and the former Soviet Union*, Scarlet Press, 1992; *Magyar Women: Hungarian Women's Lives 1960s to 1990s*, Macmillan, 1994; and *Women in a Violent World: Feminist analyses and responses across Europe*, Edinburgh University Press, 1996. Chris has been actively involved with women's groups and networks throughout Europe for the past 15 years.

Pamela Cotterill is a Senior Lecturer in Women's Studies and Sociology at Staffordshire University. Her teaching and research interests include women and social policy, feminist auto/biography and epistemology, gender and ageing. With Gayle Letherby, she has published articles in the area of feminist auto/biography, epistemology and methodology.

Anne Gatensby is a doctoral candidate in the Programme in Social and Political Thought at York University in Toronto. Her areas of interest include social aspects of science and technology, feminist critiques of science and technology, sociology of knowledge and the political economy of science and technology policies in Canada. She is currently working on her dissertation on knowledge production in the biomedical sciences.

Susan Hart is one of the original contributors to the development of the Zero Tolerance Campaign and currently works for Edinburgh District Council Women's Unit developing Zero Tolerance Initiatives. She has previously worked for a variety of national and local voluntary organizations focusing on issues such as homelessness, substance abuse and employment as they relate to women. She trained as a community worker and has carried out development work on a paid and voluntary basis for many women's groups and organizations. She is particularly known in Edinburgh for her campaigning work on the defence of abortion rights and is an active trade unionist.

Susan Hawthorne is Lecturer in the Department of Communication Studies at Victoria University in Melbourne. She is the author of three books, *The Falling Women* (a novel), *The Language in My Tongue* (poetry) and *The Spinifex Quiz Book* (non-fiction). She has contributed to many journals and magazines internationally and also works as Publisher at Spinifex Press. She is currently working on a collection of poetry and a work of non-fiction and is doing research on the impact of new technologies on the publishing industry.

Millsom Henry graduated from the Universities of Durham and Stirling as a social scientist with specific teaching and research interests in the sociology of ethnicity and gender, especially in relation to culture/media and the social implications of new technologies. She is currently employed as Deputy Director of SocInfo based at the University of Stirling. She has presented many papers at international conferences and her publications include *Portraits of Black Women in Popular Culture*, Centre for Women's Studies Seminar Series, University of Glasgow, 1993; 'Ivory Towers: Ebony Women: The Experiences of Black Women in Higher Education' in Davies, C., Lubelska, C. and Quinn, J. (Eds) *Changing the Subject*, Taylor & Francis, 1994; 'Equality and CAL in Higher Education', in *Journal of Computer-Assisted-Learning*, **11**(May) Blackwell Publishers, 1995. Currently completing a part-time PhD, entitled *Uncomfortable Viewing: Exploring the Images and Identities of British Women of Caribbean Decent in Popular Culture*, at the University of Stirling, she is also actively involved with a number of related professional and community-based organizations.

Dallas Isaacs is employed as a sociologist at the Telstra Research Laboratories, Australia. Her role there is to explore the relationship between telecommunication technology and people's need to communicate. She came to this position after holding academic positions at Australian universities where her field was the sociology of education.

Celia Jenkins teaches Sociology and Women's Studies at the University of Westminster, specializing in the field of education. She is an Executive Member of The Women's Studies Network (UK) Association. As a result of doing research with Ruth Swirsky on the advertising of sexual services by prostitutes, she is now involved politically in this area. She is hoping to edit a book with Maggie O'Neill and Ruth Swirsky on prostitution. She is also continuing to research the new education movement in the early twentieth century and its implications for mothers.

Judy Ann Jones is Senior Lecturer at the School of Human Movement, Deakin University. Her major area of research is on the promotion of health for older women through regular physical activity, with a major focus on social and emotional wellbeing. She is also a team member researching and evaluating Commonwealth-funded physical activity strategy development initiatives in communities, workplaces and tertiary education campuses.

Nora Jung left her native country, Hungary, in 1982 for Canada where she now lives. As a graduate student in the Department of Sociology at York University she is completing her dissertation which focuses on newly emerged women's groups in Hungary. She is a guest editor of the *Canadian Woman Studies/ les cahiers de la femme*. She has been involved with immigrant women's organizations and with shelters for abused women.

Annette Kilcooley works part-time in a local comprehensive. She is also a part-time lecturer at the Centre for Extra-Mural Studies, London University on the Certificate and Diploma in Psychoanalytic Psychology. Her work is a mixture of Freudian theory and deconstruction and her research interests include feminist intellectuality and its repression in Lacan and Freud.

Renate Klein works as Senior Lecturer and Deputy Director of the Australian Women's Research Centre at Deakin University and is the (co-)author/ (co)editor of four books on feminist theory and five books on reproductive medicine. She is co-founder of FINRRAGE (Feminist International Network of Resistance to Reproductive and Genetic Engineering) and has been working closely with women's groups in Asia on the impact of contraceptives as well as new reproductive technologies on women's human rights.

Gayle Letherby is a Lecturer in Sociology at Coventry University. She is currently completing a PhD on experiences (predominantly women's of 'infertility' and 'involuntary childlessness'. Her interests include women and health, the sociology of crime and deviance, the sociology of the family and feminist research methods. With Pamela Cotterill she has published articles in the area of feminist auto/biography, epistemology and methodology.

Cathy Lubelska is Principal Lecturer in Social History and Women's Studies and subject leader for Women's Studies at the University of Central Lancashire. Her current research and reaching interests include the development of feminist methodologies within women's history, gender and professionalization and the history of women's health. She has published studies and chapters on feminist pedagogy and curricula issues and is coeditor (with Mary Kennedy and Val Walsh) of *Making Connections: Women's Studies, Women's Movements, Women's Lives* (1993) and (with Sue Davies and Jocey Quinn) *Changing the Subject: Women in Higher Education* (1994).

Pat Mahony worked for many years in Initial Teacher Education before becoming the Head of the Department of Educational Studies at Goldsmiths College. She has recently moved to a senior research post at Roehampton Institute London where she is enjoying the luxury of researching government policy rather than trying to manage the effects of it. She has published in the areas of 'equal opportunities' in school and teacher education and is joint Irish and British editor of *Women's Studies International Forum*.

Julie Matthews is a research student at the University of Central Lancashire. The title of her work is 'Working-class women as users, providers and mediators of health care between 1948 and 1979' which is the subject of her PhD thesis. She also has an interest in disability issues.

Quibilah Montsho is a political Black lesbian (of African descent), a poet, writer, performer and trainer currently based in Manchester, England. Her areas of interest and specialism include 'race', mental health, sexuality, gender and sexual violence. In her spare time she enjoys bodybuilding (seriously), riding a motorcycle, cinema (strictly thrillers) and music. Her future aspirations include riding a big motorcycle, living in a big house and travelling further in Africa and Asia.

Maggie O'Neill is Senior Lecturer in Sociology and Women's Studies, Staffordshire University. She has conducted feminist research with female prostitutes and also young people involved in prostitution. She is committed to feminist thought, research and practice through action research, teaching and writing.

Pragna Patel lives in London and is an active member of Southall Black Sisters and Women Against Fundamentalism. Her current work focuses on policing of Black communities.

Marilyn Poole is Senior Lecturer in Sociology at Deakin University. She was born in the UK, spent many years in the USA and now lives and works in Australia. Her research interests include gender and education, homeless youth and how body image is related to concepts of self.

Diane Richardson is Senior Lecturer in the Department of Sociological Studies at the University of Sheffield. Her publications include *Women and the AIDS Crisis* (Pandora, 1989), *Safer Sex* (Pandora, 1990), *Women, Motherhood and Childrearing* (Macmillan, 1993), *Theorising Heterosexuality* (Open University Press, 1996) and, as co-editor, *Introducing Women's Studies: Feminist Theory and Practice* (Macmillan, 1993). She is currently working on a revised and enlarged second edition of the latter.

Robyn Rowland is Director of the Australian Women's Research Centre at Deakin University. She has taught Women's Studies for twenty years and written on women's human rights, women's identity, sexuality, mothering sons, feminism and the generations, and feminist ethics. For fifteen years she has been a leading radical feminist voice in debates on reproductive technology and genetic engineering. Her books include *Living Laboratories Women and Reproductive Technology* (Cedar Press, 1993), *Woman Herself: A Transdisciplinary Perspective on Women's Identity*, and two books of poetry. She is Australian, Asian and Pacific editor of *Women's Studies International Forum*.

Felly Nkweto Simmonds teaches Sociology at the University of Northumbria, Newcastle upon Tyne. She writes on issues of gender, 'race' and identity in both her academic and creative writing. She has also written on her experience of breast cancer.

Ailbhe Smyth is a feminist writer, critic and activist. She is Director of the Women's Education, Research and Resource Centre at University College Dublin, Ireland, and a co-editor of *Women's Studies International Forum*. She has been active in the Women's Liberation Movement since the 1970s, including work on campaigns around the issues of abortion/reproductive rights, citizenship and women's education. Her research and writing focus on feminist politics and culture.

Ruth Swirsky teaches Sociology and Women's Studies at the University of Westminster. As a result of doing research on the advertising of sexual services by prostitutes with Celia Jenkins, she is now working politically in this area and hopes to edit a book with Maggie O'Neill and Celia on prostitution. She is also continuing to research the impact of migration on Jewish women's lives.

Sharon Tabberer is a full-time PhD student based in the Science and Technologies Studies at Anglia Polytechnic University. She is working on a thesis entitled 'Gender and the dissemination of technology: a case study of RU 486', examining what happens when a new reproductive technology enters the mainstream Health Service and the factors that may influence this development. The research is fully funded by the University through a studentship and is under the supervision of Professor Michelle Stanworth and Dr Andrew Webster.

Christine Zmroczek is Senior Lecturer in the Department of Women's Studies at the Roehampton Institute, London, and Managing Editor of *Women's Studies International Forum*. She is a member of the Executive Committee of the Women's Studies Network (UK) Association and served as Chair 1995–1996. Together with Pat Mahony she is editing three forthcoming volumes about women and social class. She lives in the country, wishes she had more time for her garden or at least for sitting in it, and is passionate about Goralska Muzyka, the music of the Tatra mountains in Poland.

Index